Gimme the Money

Gimme the Money

Iva Pekárková

Translated by
Raymond Johnston and
Iva Pekárková

The translation has been subsidized by the Ministry of
Culture of the Czech Republic

Library of Congress Catalog Card Number: 00–100222

A complete catalogue record for this book can be
obtained from the British Library on request

First published in 2000 by Serpent's Tail,
4 Blackstock Mews, London N4 2BT
website: www.serpentstail.com

Typeset by Intype London Ltd
Printed in Italy by Chromo Litho Ltd

10 9 8 7 6 5 4 3 2 1

ACKNOWLEDGEMENTS

I learned about what it's like to drive a taxi in New York from my colleagues, the taxidrivers and the dispatchers in several garages in Brooklyn, Queens and Hell's Kitchen (now known as Clinton); they're too numerous to be mentioned here by name. I'm indebted to Fidel F. del Valle, the former chairman of the Taxi and Limousine Commission, for interesting information. I should thank my friend the taxi-driver/screenwriter Donald Schwarz and also an allegedly connected member of the Russian mafia of Brooklyn, Roman "Left Eye" L., for both theoretical and practical information about guns and shooting. Dr George Braun, MD, was indispensable for his truly valuable medical information.

I should like to thank several of my acquaintances from West Africa for their patience with my slow-to-understand white brain. I had better not thank them by name, though, as it would become obvious that I've shamelessly borrowed their (American) names for this book with which they have nothing to do plot-wise.

Anna Balev deserves to be thanked for innumerable glasses of white wine, an open-air pool and hospitality. The writer Katherine Arnoldi and screenwriter Raymond Johnston helped me tremendously by urging me to write.

This book is a novel. Any similarity to any person, living or dead, or any taxicab, running or junked, is coincidental.

The horse could not do without Manhattan. It drew him like a magnet, like a vacuum, like oats, or a mare, or an open, neverending, tree-lined road.

– Mark Helprin, *Winter's Tale*

Chapter 1

Gravity

Big cities emit gravity, just like big planets. A person seldom decides to arrive in one. Into a big city, you have to fall, usually head first. Some of the immigrants are lucky enough to be allowed to slowly, stealthily orbit this or that metropolis; they can feel it from a distance first (just like it's possible to touch New York from Philadelphia, or Paris from Zurich or Amsterdam). They are allowed to learn its skyline by heart and very slowly descend into it. They can descend safely and painlessly thanks to the safety nets provided by their relatives, friends and acquaintances, by films, books or even a language. These happy travelers are dressed in a space suit sewn together out of everything they've heard about a city, and the space suit makes it easier on them when landing in the city's atmosphere.

But some of us have none of these. The gravity of big cities captures us from the other side of oceans, across nine mountains and nine rivers. Big cities reach out their tentacles like huge octopuses. And when people let themselves be lured and attach themselves to these tentacles, as if they were umbilical cords, very soon they find themselves flying upwards and far away on a silverish spiral, at such a speed that their inevitable butt-falls can be made gentler only by their love for the City; for the unique and thorny planet.

Whenever, before the break of dawn, Gin was driving back to Manhattan from her last trip to Brooklyn, she had a feeling that she was rapidly climbing up to Manhattan Island on the metallic lace of the Brooklyn Bridge. She felt the bridge twitching and vibrating under her wheels just like the muscles on a horse's back. And at the same time she felt like she was falling toward Manhattan from a terrible height on a steep toboggan (whose vibrations penetrated her whole person, filling her with sweet sadness). Other times, she felt the magnetic powers of Manhattan Island draw her near, as if she was a steel bullet, ready to jump to its surface with a clunk. And when the bridge ended, and all of a sudden she already WAS on the island, she was always surprised that the impact didn't shatter her. Instead, she landed soundlessly at the foot of the bridge; the asphalt quietly hissed under her tires like a tide. In front of her there was a whole maze of streets crossing each other at right angles, well known to her, made penetrable and available to her as if it was a map of her own head. Late at night, toward morning, Gin's thoughts were spread like a map on the gray asphalt and concrete, her thoughts, adventures, memories and hopes included. Memories and adventures became those beer caps, flattened aluminum cans or glass shards forced deep into the asphalt by numerous tires.

Hopes had the shape of reverse arrows left in the wet concrete by pigeons' toes.

Chapter 2

Morning

"Vibrator!" articulated Gloria with an authoritative voice, raising the plastic limb up with an almost prophet-like gesture. "Make sure you soon get something like that. Otherwise, all those lovers of yours will drive me nuts."

Gin, who had just entered the room, noticed, from the corner of her eye, the unrealistically blue color of the contraption. Perhaps, if it was a little deeper, it would remind one of a Shiva reincarnation. "What's up with that?" she asked with a yawn.

"All those assholes you're involved with will drain you out of every penny." Gloria accusingly pointed the vibrator at the answering machine. On its display a bright green 13 flickered under "number of messages." "That HUSBAND of yours kept calling again." Gloria tried so hard to show her contempt for the word husband that a Yorkshire terrier with the very same name jumped out of his plaid-padded basket and scurried to his mistress's feet. "Down, Hubby!" Gloria yelled at the dog. "I mean, that – MAN – of yours has been calling you all night long."

It was half-past five in the morning. Outside, the dawn had

broken. Gloria sat here, dressed in a long sky-colored robe, nervously shifting the vibrator from her right hand into the left. Her face was swollen with sleep and uneven tufts of hair stuck haphazardly out of her skull. She had had it shaved some time ago.

"It's the beginning of the month," Gloria added, scratching her scalp noisily. "And therefore I know very well what that – man – of yours is after."

Gin threw her knapsack into the corner. She didn't answer. Instead, she untied her sneakers and lined them up by the wall. The left sneaker was all right, the right one had a slight limp. Its sole was worn out unevenly from stepping on the pedals. Gin took off her socks and – holding them by the toes – shook them. She watched as a few sweaty bills of a promising greenish tint fell to the floor.

Gloria fell silent to make counting easier. "Well, how much did you make today, Gin?"

Gin cursed and gave her a number. "What do you expect? It's Monday night."

"Monday night! Monday night! You make next to zip Monday night, because it's Monday—"

"Well, what do you expect—"

"—Tuesday you make zilch, because it's Tuesday—"

"Well, what can you—"

"And Wednesday you come home with a big fat zero, because it's Wed—"

"As if you didn't know," Gin sighed, "that the only decent nights now are Fridays and Saturdays. Every other day—"

"But you drive a cab to make MONEY, don't you? Don't you? Maybe you'll have to learn to drive FASTER, or you have to keep going to the airport and . . ."

"OK, why don't you quit painting and drive a cab yourself? D'you think that I want to hear—"

"You are telling me to qu—"

"Can't we discuss this after I have some sleep? PLEASE?" Gin cast a loving glance at her mattress under the corner window.

"It's me who lives in this apartment," Gloria reassured her with a rising tone of voice. "If it wasn't for me, you'd have to live in some dirty hole and pay three – no, five times – as much as you pay here. And you—"

Hubby half lifted himself from his padded lair and yipped.

"Don't yell so much," Gin chastised Gloria, or the dog, or both. "You'll wake up Josito."

José Manuel Constitucion Ramirez slept like a cherub in his little bed. Both girls were – for a second – flushed with a feeling of giving gentleness. That gentleness, they knew, wouldn't last much longer than José's sweet dream: In an hour or so, he'll wake up and start crying "Mommy, mommy, mommy," – but his mother was serving four years in the New York state pen. Josito wound up in Gloria's house, and she immediately fell in love with him: he was so beautiful when he was asleep, and anyway, Gloria thought, overwhelmed with her own big heart, we Cubans help one another. She was watching an orange shaft of light penetrate her first floor, or, rather, basement apartment. She recorded it on her retina as a part of the City. Gloria had long ago finished her New York studies: she had touched it and walked it through and through, she had mastered its colors and shapes, and she knew that there was never enough of this festive morning color in the City. Sometimes she felt dejected because of the fact that this yellowish orange hue was the only tropical thing she remembered of her childhood. And that was only because of her aunt's stories (about the orange mornings in Cuba), and thanks to the color of the papayas that were sold in a deli on 10th Street and Avenue B for $2.99 each, while they were still green, so they had to be left to ripen before the orange could claim them. The sunray made dust specks light up, and so Gloria stored it all, the color, the feeling, the texture, somewhere behind her eyes.

"In fact, I wanted to ask you for a favor," she said cautiously.

Gin's eyes were now hopelessly squinting. She plopped onto the mattress, beneath both the window and the sunray, and pulled off her sweater. Then she unhooked her bra on her back, yawned, and began digging it out through the sleeve of her T-shirt.

"I've got an offer for an exhibition!" Gloria shrieked.

"Oh yes? Really?" Despite the deadening exhaustion she tried to sound pleased.

"But, you know . . ." (José's light snoring could be heard from the next room and filled Gin with terror) " . . . I need to explain to you, you know . . ." (Husband rose in his padded lair again and wriggled his rat's tail a couple of times) " . . . to tell you the truth, you understand, the exhibition isn't for free."

"That's good."

"I mean, they want some cash up front so that—"

"YOU are supposed to pay THEM?"

"—so that they can rent the space. It's right down here on Essex Street."

"But it's THEM who's supposed to give YOU a percentage, isn't it?" Gin was painstakingly trying to use her meager knowledge of the art world. "It's not that you are supposed to pay them on top of everything, is it?"

"They'll pay me as soon as something gets sold. You must understand: this is not some stupid pseudo-artsy exhibition in some tycoon's stupid gallery. This is a HAPPENING, an art event, right down here on Essex Street. The Rivington School is in charge!"

Gin stretched out on the mattress, covered herself with a blanket and sealed her lids. Gloria grabbed her shoulder, shaking her: "Don't you fall asleep on me! It's not even expensive! They ask—"

"And how much are they gonna sell the paintings for?"

"Well . . . so far they don't say. But now . . . now they want me to pay fifteen cents per square inch. That's not too much, is it? I just measured the canvases—"

"How about sculptures? How do they charge for them? By the cubic inch?"

"Gin . . ."

"So . . . so BIG artists will pay much more than small ones?"

But this kind of sarcasm never registered on Gloria.

"You'll help me, Gin, won't you?" she whispered hoarsely. And bored into Gin with her deep black eyes.

At that moment the light on the answering machine started blinking. Gloria's facial muscles tightened. She pointed her vibrator at the green signal. Obeying her command, Gin reached for the phone.

"I love you!" she heard from the receiver, "IloveyouIloveyou-IloveyouIloveyou!"

"OK. How much do you need?" Gin sighed into the phone.

Chapter 3

Surviving

It was almost three in the afternoon when Gin left her home with several empty plastic milk containers and went south on Avenue C. The denizens of the East Village had built their own recycling center there, right next to an abandoned lot that was presently – before someone starts building on it – completely occupied by humongous sculptures created (by Gloria's account) during the happenings organized by the Rivington School. Plates of rusted iron, pipes and rods, canisters, consoles, broken wheels, the bowels of washing machines, TVs and refrigerators, bizarrely twisted mufflers – all that metallic junk was indiscriminately welded into cyclopic monstrosities that menaced the nearby car skeletons, the ruins of brick walls and splotchy fresh green vegetation. The monsters were spray-painted with silver-gray graffiti. The paint, in conjunction with sheets of rust, peeled off them like fish scales and drizzled slowly on the brick debris and vegetation. On windy days the whole sculpture garden rustled and rattled in a ghastly manner. At night it cast motionless, bizarre shadows on 4th Street, like the petrified shadows of enormous prehistoric plants.

Gin lifted up the cover of a large recycling bin marked

PLASTIC MILK CONTAINERS. She was just about to throw the aforementioned empty vessels into it, when a grayish hand shot out of the bin. A face with a matted grayish-white beard shone in a sunray. "Spare a dime, miss?" the face said.

Gin backed up half a step but didn't get too scared. She happily realized that she's beginning to get used to this continent. Only a year ago she would undoubtedly have reacted to a similar surprise with a less than distinguished sound, not dissimilar to a hen's cackle.

"Is it you, Randy?" she said today, dropped whatever she had in her hand, and began rummaging through her pockets.

Randy profusely thanked her for the fifty cents. He rose, shook off several squashed plastic containers and made his way out of the recycling bin, squinting in the sunlight. "All the time people throw something inside. All the time. Right on my head!"

"Oh, I'm sorry. But, you know, this box is sort of MEANT to be used—"

"But if I could latch it from the inside, I could sleep in peace."

"Isn't it too tiny for you?"

"Well, I do feel a bit like a pretzel, Gin," Randy admitted, "but, on the other hand, it doesn't rain inside and – and, when I'm inside it feels a little . . . like my own brain, you know? When you pop up some coke. Total darkness with just a snow-white lash of light like a magic spiral. Imagine sleeping rolled up like a fox in your own screwed-up brain! Did you ever try to paint the contents of your own brain, Gin? I mean – the space?" Randy asked pensively, gawking at the darkness in the receptacle. "I am a painter, you know, and these are my creations!"

He squatted next to a rusty old sheet of metal and caressed a wild spray-painted pattern with his palm. "This is my brain, Gin, the universal brain, this City's brain, the essence of the brains of all those who ever lived and croaked in this City; this is my rusty, abused brain, Gin, and this . . ." he patted a twisted muffler of a truck, welded by some Rivington man to the sheet metal, "this is the celestial spiral! Can you paint things like these?" he bellowed, jumping up. From his grisly gray palm silverish specks of rust were snowing.

Gin looked up the twisted muffler. It shot high into the sky and only all the way up it was connected to the nearby sculpture, to prevent it from falling. Even so, it rocked dangerously under the weight of two prancing pigeons. One of the birds lifted his ass and dropped something. Gin watched the excrement's fall and her eyes watered from too much light.

"I'm not an artist," she said.

In the first few days and weeks after her arrival she lived in an apartment that belonged to a certain photographer. It was a dinky hole on the top floor of a tall apartment building in Chinatown, right under the tar roof two local whores stomped on with their high heels night after night, making the photographer nuts, and throwing used rubbers on a heap behind the chimney where they dry-rotted in the sunlight. The photographer couldn't help imagining how every little rain washes billions and billions of dead sperm cells out of them, which then seep through the tar paper deeper and deeper into his ceiling, so that one day not so far away those brownish yellow microscopic cadavers will start raining on his head or on his photos or on his camel hair bedcover. Gin used to gawk out of the window, across the rooftops to the east – back, so to speak. For some hard-to-understand reason, most of the apartments she lived in at that time, and there were quite a few, had windows facing east or south, and this is what helped her get oriented, get used to the new space and time. In New York, nobody says "to the right" or "to the left," they all say "west" or "east" or "north" or "south." From all the apartments she ever lived in during the sweet-and-sour times of surviving and getting used to things and sadness and emptiness filled with humongous boxes organized at right angles (whose shapes found their way into her dreams), from all those apartments she begged and paid and promised and fucked her way into there were only two she couldn't see the east from. In one of them, on 64th Street (where she shared one cubicle with seven cats and their owner – the cats climbed over her while she was sleeping, the owner, thank God, didn't, although she had to cook and clean and pay the phone bill and listen, without any visible signs of boredom, to endless ranting and raving), the little window looked at the airshaft that was tiled in fresh green, to remind the tenants Nature existed. The other one was her eleventh apartment in Greenpoint, Brooklyn, where she felt a little thrown away because it wasn't in Manhattan and everyone spoke Polish to her in the stores. On the plus side, through the window, overlooking the west, she could see the whole of Midtown. She could see the midriff of the island of her desire, the tapering spire of the Empire State Building sticking out of it, and she could see the Queensborough Bridge and the Williamsburgh Bridge twinkling at night, connecting her with Manhattan Island. And so she just sat there, happy and slightly thrown away. The City sparkled in front of her eyes like a fluorescent postcard. It was rosily foggy in the morning, work-like and strict in the afternoon, and in the evening, sometimes, endowed with a sharp skyline that pierced the reddened western sky like a copper cut-out.

Gin spent hours and hours sitting by the window because even here, in Brooklyn, New York was still unreachable. It seemed reserved and far-away as if it was too good to come off the postcard for her. She didn't even have enough cash to buy a subway token, but at least she could watch its skyline vibrating with the heat of the autumn air that condensed into clouds above it and flew away. Gin sat by the window, drinking in the City with her eyes – the City into which she had arrived and still hasn't arrived. She tortured her head, wondering how to make a living. She had found, to her great surprise, that she didn't have any real skills. She sat there swollen with pride for getting as far as New York. She sat there, feeling sorry for herself. The skyline of Manhattan lured her into itself with an enormous colorful Unknown. And so Gin cursed, chose the least shameful ensemble from her threadbare wardrobe, and let the hypnotizing strings of desire lead her to the Williamsburgh

Bridge, with its colorful lights perched atop its suspension cables like will-of-the-wisps. She walked over that bridge all the way to Delancey Street and strolled around in Soho where, sprawled on the hood of his Yellow Taxi, she met Talibe who would become her husband.

Chapter 4

Talibe

"You my wife, *mais* . . ."

"Well, that's what I am—"

"You my wife *mais* you no want live with me. I miss. You. At night. *Mais* . . ."

"Talibe, don't you understand—"

"This what I want? You think? I marry you? For this?"

With great contempt (rather theatrical), Talibe lifted up a wad of twenties. They had been ironed so neatly with Gin's palm that only an expert would know that each and every one of them had been once hidden in her sock. Then Talibe let the notes fly slowly from his fingers onto the table, one by one, snorting contemptuously. Seventeen times in all.

"I your husband. I. I want live with you. *Mais* you—"

Gin sighed. During their year together she began to understand that there was no point in arguing with Talibe about anything. A year ago, she believed that thanks to some unforeseeable miracle – and while she was at the bottom of her misery – she'd found a nice, quiet, pleasant guy she could talk to. Such guys are usually described as "agreeable." Problem was, Talibe was agreeable as long as she agreed with him on everything. And Gin had really wanted to speed her marriage up. She managed to squeeze the getting-to-know-each-other-and-cooing-into-each-other's-ear period into less than two weeks. Less than two weeks of the mating dance were enough for them to make it all the way to the Justice of Peace across the black-and-white marble pavement in front of City Hall, and legalize that connection which, after all, somewhat resembled the black-and-white pattern of the tiles. At least that's how Gin felt about it. She didn't talk about it with Talibe very much. He didn't have any grudges against Gin's whiteness, not at all – he came from a country black enough to not know about colors and not want to know about colors. He didn't think in black and white; she used to like that. Even though, on the evening they met, he grabbed her hand in a bar where she was having a screwdriver and he orange juice with ice. (From his drink only one straw was sticking, Gin's screwdriver had two, that was for Talibe, just to make sure, he wanted her to think that he was drinking with her but he had to be careful: in his religion he wasn't supposed to touch alcohol, or tobacco, or a woman, although with women, well . . .) Talibe had grabbed Gin's paw, interlacing his fingers with hers, and said: "Beautiful, *non*?" – and at that moment Gin felt such an urgent twitch of desire that her insides all constricted with the anticipation of . . . something; Talibe penetrated her being, over two yellow glasses, so dazzlingly and fully and sweetly that everything darkened in front of Gin's eyes and the chessboard of their interlaced fingers mingled into a warm, brownish gray, into the color which, maybe, their children will have one day. And thanks to that most beautiful (because only imaginary) connection with him Gin sprouted completely new, black-and-white eyes; all of a sudden she started recognizing that black-and-white chessboard in everything. In the pavement in front of City Hall. In piano keys. In the frolicking of the shadows of trees on the sun-lit sidewalks. In the fresh snow falling on dark tree branches. That winter, Gin knitted two wool shawls: a snowy white one for Talibe and a black one for herself. And then she felt a little hurt when Talibe, instead of wearing it, used it for a pillow.

"I your husband," pronounced Talibe painstakingly in his pretty broken English that, after five years in the States, was still permeated with French grammar, French pronunciation, French idioms and West African thinking.

"Wife. Should live with husband. Wife. Husband, he no have to live with wife. He can with other wife live. *Mais* wife—"

"And how many goddamn wives have you got?"

"*Mais chérie*! Don't you know you—"

As a matter of fact, counting of husbands and wives wasn't Gin's favorite pastime. Sometimes it seemed to her that Talibe showed her the pictures of his beautiful sister's four children with a father's, rather than an uncle's, pride. It also seemed to her that too many bucks disappeared to his relatives across the Atlantic month after month. But all Talibe's countrymen verified that yes, this is the situation, that Talibe is a loving son and brother to his family. (Only they, while saying this, often gave a suspicious wink.)

The dialogue between Talibe and his wife has been notoriously lagging for months. Perhaps it never existed, only they didn't notice it before. Gin moved out of Talibe's apartment on 116th Street and Powell Boulevard when she found out about her duties as a wife. They consisted of sitting at home, not going anywhere (but, of course, making as much money as possible, it wasn't entirely clear how), changing the bedsheets every day for the benefit of some tribal spirit who didn't like to live in soiled beds, clean, cook, take care of Talibe's well-being, spread her legs whenever he felt like it, and shut up if she dared to not be happy with something.

The truth is that she never cooked very much, she bungled something all the time. More than once, Talibe rightfully reproached her for not even knowing how to fry okra. All she knew was how to open a can of tuna. Their respective culinary opinions were 180 degrees apart. And while Talibe kept saying that a single unopened can of tuna is enough to attack all his food and spoil it, Gin's stomach permanently turned at all the food Talibe was cooking, which she called his African inedibles. While they were trying to live together, Talibe, with a frown on his face, concocted his African inedibles in his stinky kitchen, while Gin devoured her tuna, her salads and raw vegetables, washing them down with grapefruit juice and sinking her teeth into wholewheat bread. She did her eating, exiled to the fire escape, wrapped in her winter coat, hat, and gloves. It was a tough winter. All this drove Talibe to despair.

"I not interested in here money at all, *chérie* . . ."

(Where were the times when she was willing to fall in love with Talibe just because of his French; when every word like *chérie*, mixed into English, turned her on and reeked with the fragrance of far-away horizons! Now she was only pissed off because Talibe never called her by name. Her real name, Jindřiška, couldn't ever make it across his lips, and calling her Gin like everybody else – well, that would remind him too much of a certain hateful devil's beverage.)

They had to wait another year. Then the bureaucrats will invite them to the immigration department and interrogate them separately. They'll want to know where's the place they live together, what the apartment looks like, how many times a week they make it and what brand of toothpaste their spouse uses. Gin was almost looking forward to it: to telling them what kind of shit Talibe stuffs his face with, calling it food. And when it came to toothpaste – ha! Talibe wouldn't even dream of touching the devil's invention, made in the USA. He cleaned his teeth by chewing, for hours on end, the aromatic roots of some insufferable tropical plant.

And when all this is over, then – then, HOPEFULLY! – there will be a permanent green card for Gin, a permanent work permit, no more living together, no $350 dollars a month for her share of the rent in an apartment she doesn't even live in. And all the husbands of the world, including Talibe, can ceremoniously kiss her ass.

"You must with me live," her husband sounded like a broken record. "*Mais* you—"

"But here in Harlem, it's kind of hard on me."

It was true. While Talibe was, thanks to his blackness, pleasantly blended into West 116th Street, Gin wasn't. And even Talibe began to mind.

"I tell you. Many times. *Mais* you not want to hear."

"Talibe, please, don't start."

"When you drive with taxi. You need amulet. You not safe. Drive with taxi! Who hear of this! Woman with taxi! I not recommend this charm. For real woman. They stop . . . every month . . . have blood. *Mais* you not real woman. It is not dangerous to you."

"Talibe . . ."

"And charm work. Really! I hear many stories . . ."

"Perhaps only in Mali?"

"In Mali? You think? In Mali people have not guns like here. In Mali policemen have not guns, how can people! In Mali—"

"So what's the charm good for there?"

"In Mali you have charm for everything. For children! For love! For money! New tree. You shift it and hold the branches by rope—"

"OK, Talibe, so why do you work your ass off in the US like a jerk when all you have to do in Mali is—"

"Not enough trees! That why people poor. And then you have to break rope. Charm bring you to the ground. Destroy. *Mais* what I offer you, against bullets—"

"That one doesn't destroy you?"

"*Mais non*! You only wear amulet. Wear all the time. When you go out, wear. At home, wear. Because you hear stories: they shoot woman through her door. Accident. Accident bullet. If she wear amulet—"

"The bullet would jump off her, make its way through the door the second time and hit the shooter right in his heart."

"Yes! So powerful! I worry for you, *chérie*, *mais* for me I don't have to."

"But you take it off before you go to bed, don't you?"

"Before I MAKE LOVE. When you wear it and you touch woman, the charm—"

"So you can't touch me now, can you? That's how it is?"

Talibe, with panic in his eyes, backed up against the wall. "Only touch, give hand, OK. *Mais embrasser, faire l'amour, non, non, non*! It lose all power." Talibe pushed Gin away from him with his left hand and tried to tear the good-luck charm off his neck with his right. He placed it reverently on the top of a chest of drawers – the good-luck charm was a worn leather strap with three tiny leather pouches. They contained quotations from the Koran as well as secret animist inscriptions, known only to the tribal shaman. Talibe made sure the good-luck charm wasn't touching anything made of metal, or any text. Then he threw himself on Gin.

On his bed, the white shawl she had made for him served as a pillow. In the wool Talibe's fallen hairs got caught, decorating it with minuscule black rings.

It isn't worth shit, Gin concluded (she was already in a horizontal position), I shouldn't have come here. Next time I'll make a date with him on one corner or another, just so I can give him the money. After all, you gotta pay for a fake marriage, so what? . . . Oh shit, this is almost painful, he's well equipped but it's damn too LONG! Doesn't HE get blisters on it, too? Ouch! Can't he be more careful, for god's sake? Gin was crawling sulkily away from the powerful thrusts of her husband's, but he followed her bit by bit without breaking his rhythm until he pushed her all the way into the corner and kept crawling closer and closer. It's really screwed up, she thought for herself when her head was already squeezed next to the wall at a weird angle, when she had no other place to crawl to and all the nicks and crannies of the wall got plastered to the back of her head. HE FUCKS LIKE A STUPID BROKEN DILDO, she thought, and on top of everything he'd like me to live with him, well, fat chance, I'd have to stuff my face on the fire escape again and every night I'd have to suffer through THIS, and not just once, maybe as many as FIVE times, don't I know him. If it didn't make me so INCREDIBLY mad, she reasoned, it would actually be quite GOOD, maybe this is exactly the rhythm some girls appreciate . . . At least he lasts quite a while, them Africans aren't so terrible in the sack, after all, she thought, and she looked at him, at the perfect smooth monolith of his body that imprisoned her into the corner behind the bed so powerfully, fragrantly and rhythmically that she couldn't even move; Talibe's lovemaking resembled a bout with a silkily naked black tiger; white merged with black, colors merged with colors, like the spinning of a big colorful wheel. Talibe's color penetrated her own white and pink; shit, this isn't bad at all; Gin sank her fingers into her husband's kinky hair, with her suddenly sensitized fingertips she touched every little hair, every tough black lock of it, every ebony-colored magical spiral . . . Oh fuck, he knows what I need, he's ABSOLUTELY GREAT, he's unbelievably fantastic, I've never had a lover like this ever in my life, I swear! And this knowledge shot through her brain like a bolt of purple lightning, the world got musical, pulsating in her like a mysterious planet, and Gin grabbed her husband by the butt and brought him even closer to her core and sucked him in. "Talibe, that's wonderful! Jee-zus Christ, that's wonderful! Talibe, PLEASE, do it like that for a while longer, I wanna come at least once more and JUST like that!"

At the moments when they got detached from one another, as long as nobody bothered her (and Talibe was great because he fell asleep immediately, resting his brushlike head under her left breast) little antennae grew all over Gin's body, and with them she could draw the whole street, the whole Harlem, the whole New York and the whole world into her. All over the surface of her body visual sensors sprouted like she was a rainworm. Tentacles emerged from her belly like she was an octopus, and their gentle suction cups stroked the whole world. The world stroked her back.

During moments like that she felt she belonged . . . to something, to the secret brotherhood of blue distances perhaps, to the brotherhood of those who DARED. New York was chock-full of those who dared, but the more of them were here, the more people in the same situation Gin met in the streets, the stronger, better and more real this feeling of belonging was. Because the souls of all the immigrants merged together into one huge mega-soul that protected the whole City with its invisible netting: just like the tiny down feathers on a pigeon's wings.

Talibe's head, resting under her left tit, felt like a shoe brush, and the magical spirals of her husband's hair transported Gin away far and wide, into the sky-blue THERE that the homeless Randy liked to talk about, and they cast her, bit by bit, all over the City, along its streets and avenues, so in the end in every traffic light that swung in the wind there sat a few brain cells of hers, sending red, green and yellow flashes toward her. Scraps of her thoughts rambled around in the form of flown-away broadsheets, printed with stock prices, news, disasters, murders, horrors, pictures of whores and politicians, personals and advertisements, and eyewitness' testimonies, flying in little circles right on the corner of 7th Avenue and 34th Street, pretty close to Penn Station. They swayed in the wind, performed somersaults, and whenever they were about to land on the sidewalk gracefully, just like stingrays resting on the bottom of the sea, they flew up again like Chinese kites, dancing on the aerial whirlwinds and getting torn to shreds by them. And that's how they, never ceasing to move about, got old and died, the information in them wasn't current anymore and was falling into the precipice of history. But the newspapers themselves still circled around, carried by the wind and their own mangy, yellowish, balding angels' wings. In moments like those Gin's soul took advice from the Indians and got reincarnated into the souls of the trees in Central Park, which, as she heard, some garden architect had planted in such a way that in the spring they started to blossom like a symphony: one swing of the baton – yellow, one swing of the baton – pink; then, accompanied by strings, the buds burst, the leaves are spreading out, the hues of greenery and tone are deeper and deeper as the spring goes on, one instrument after another joins in, until, some time in June, the symphony peaks with a victorious staccato – and then everything starts dying off again, the musicians are packing up their instruments, they pour saliva out of mouthpieces, rest their violins in their cases in which they'll sleep till next spring, and hundreds of New York-based tourists flood the Sheep Meadow which got its name from the fact that herds of sheep were supposed to graze on it, their fluffy wool adding a new quality to the whole pastorale . . . But right now it was fall and Gin's tactile cells invaded the stems of leaves that were turning all colors and were about to fall off, the cells of her skin got yellow like the leaves of the ginkgo trees on Manhattan Avenue, her skin rocked softly on the waves of the Hudson and the East River, it bounced off the banks with splashing noises and got lit with the lights of all the bridges Gin had ever crossed. The bridges connected her to reality, convincing her that she lived on an island. Her antennae that suddenly got wet brought her the news that a shower had begun, and Gin was so excited by all the water around her, under her and above her that a white-and-blue striped sailor's shirt got knitted on her body. Then it occurred to her that there should be customers outside. She pushed her husband's head to the side. "I gotta go." She got up out of bed.

Talibe came to, grabbed her by the leg and pulled her back. "*Mais* . . . more . . . at least one!" And he made for her crotch.

"I got my car in front of the building."

"*Mais* . . ."

"Wait, let go! Leave me alone!"

"*Mais* . . ."

"I got my taxi in front of the building!"

"*Mais* . . . *je t'aime, je t'aime*!"

Her husband opened her legs with his left hand and the ceaseless stream of his dubious proclamations merged with the raindrops.

"Maaah, maaah, maaah," she bleated uncooperatively but there was no way out. And so she even unpacked for him one of the condoms he kept in a brown bag right next to his bed, just in case.

Chapter 5

Gloria

Gloria stood with her legs firmly planted in the middle of the living room and with a concentrated expression on her face she kept throwing, one after another, 365 dead cockroaches, each of them dipped in clear acrylic, on a canvas that stood on an easel right under the window. She was creating a painting named A YEAR OF POVERTY, UN AÑO MISERABLE.

To get together 365 fully developed, healthy, fresh, well-preserved and unstepped-on roaches without their legs torn-off or their shellcovers falling apart was, as she found out, a surprisingly tough job. Before she started this particular painting it seemed to her that in her apartment there must be many more roaches running around than 365 (all of them healthy, fresh, well-preserved, fully developed and overfed). Their little antennae wriggled in every corner, in every nook and cranny, in the sink in between the unwashed dishes; the most daring ones would go on food-searching expeditions even when the lights were on – to the great delight of Husband who lay in wait for them and hunted for them; he'd learned to wait until they were far enough away from all possible hiding places, and then squash them with his paw. Husband's hunting, in fact, resembled fratricide: the dog was so tiny that even with his deckled, hairy profile he reminded her of a humongous, happy cockroach.

Gloria, however, had to learn to hunt for roaches with much more care: she had to lay in wait for them, then grab them gently between her thumb and forefinger and toss them into a jar with a few drops of thinner. That killed them pretty much without fail which made Gloria, sometimes, wonder whether – since the roaches croak so quickly when surrounded by the fragrance of the thinner – whether it doesn't, after all, kill herself, and José, and all the other people who ever set foot in her apartment. . . . The whole place was flooded with drying acrylic paintings: canvases in various stages of being worked on were drying on easels and then, when almost dry, stored in huge vertical drifts, half-forgotten and turned toward the wall; all the chests and shelves and the refrigerator and every possible or impossible surface was covered in them, even on the bed a couple of them lay in the daytime, and Gloria always had to lift them up with both hands and put them down on the floor before she could stretch on her mattress (and this action, obviously, just begged for comments from the girls and women with whom Gloria stretched on her mattress; perhaps most of her lovers imagined that they themselves became, for a while, a piece of art, a canvas Gloria was working on right now). Gloria's painting clothes, T-shirts, sweaters, blouses and shirts, everything was soaked in acrylic, and most of all those old torn jeans which hardly fit her anymore but that she still liked to wear in the street because they made her belong. Those were the jeans she used to clean her fingers and her brush on, when she was swept away by creating and sometimes also on purpose; she turned her painter's jeans into a painting, too, the painting of herself the way she wanted to be seen by the passers-by. Thanks to those torn jeans she belonged to the East Village brotherhood, along with the aging Puerto Rican who nobody called anything but Hoo-hoo and who'd parade himself around the East Village in a black leather jacket, bedizened all around: in the front, in the back, on the lapels, on the sleeves, on the pockets, on the collar – with colorful lightbulbs and reflection mirrors (on his back they formed a cat's face with green cholesterol eyes) – and he would wander around the streets night after night decked out like that and flash far and wide; he'd shimmer under the lights of cars like a highway sign; he'd blink and change colors like a traffic light gone berserk; he'd glisten like cocaine crystals, and, in that leather jacket of his (which, with all those circuits and switches and lights and wires must have weighed at least thirty pounds), he had to change the batteries daily.

Those jeans – too tight, overwashed and paint-encrusted – gave Gloria the right to fit in here just like any other artist, like Mario who, at the age of sixteen, had gone through two detox clinics – once for booze and once for coke – and in front of whom (now when he was clean again) a whole new life opened up like an unbearably long, straight, gray highway – and so he tried to counter all those feelings by painting every street corner, every wall, every closed shutter with the grandest colors he knew; he painted spacescapes or seascapes with striped fish (that, after all, could just as well have been spaceships) and with sea anemones, full of tentacles in neon-pink and purple – and he fought with at least another street artist for the northeast corner of 10th and B, right next to Tompkins Square Park, so that when Mario painted a clown with blue-and-white striped cheeks, yellow eyes and a starry nose, the clown got rolled over within a couple of days with a paint roller and on the grayish-green scar that was left after him there was spray-painted CRACK KILLS. Which Mario, of course, couldn't just let be and so he begged his money for paints and did a psychedelic version of the US flag on the wall: its stripes were greenish-yellow worms or snakes whose gaping mouths hissed angrily at passers-by, and instead of the stars there were sea anemones and poisonous sea stars. Then, of course, the flag disappeared under the new coat of paint and that other artist who, after all, was most likely a woman, and pretty radical at that, spent a lot of time and effort on a painting that stressed the similarity between a syringe and a male sexual organ, warmly recommending both if you intend to croak of AIDS. Mario must have known a thing or two about that, his sister apparently died of it . . . and that's why that menacing, naivistic painting stayed there for a long time.

Even the homeless guy Randy with his celestial symbolics was a member of the club, and also another dusty white man who decided to decorate all of 8th Street, St Mark's Place, beginning at Tompkins Square Park and Avenue A, with white-and-blue china shards, and day after day he walked his way west, while covering the bases of building and streetlamps and everything else with blue-and-white latticework.

The punks that made their nest in an obscure bar on 10th Street were, after all, members of the same club. That's because their whole personae were magnificent paintings – temporary paintings, true, because hair spikes flatten out in a few hours and makeup crumbles – but, on the other hand, more complicated and harder to make than many of Gloria's own. The punks wore heavy chains and rings with secret symbolism, and many more earrings than they had ears – and the huge metal rings that pierced the cheeks of some of them represented surprisingly strong symbols of the transience of the world. People usually don't wonder whether the canvas feels pain when it's soaked in paint, when it's folded, when it gets cut into pieces – but every permanent and unnecessary hole in a human face makes them ponder the transience of that face, its aging; human mortality is much better visible on the background of the agelessness of iron rings – and everyone who paints right on the body, who makes a painting or a sculpture out of himself, who uses his skin like canvas, his meat like clay, his tendons like connecting cables – installs feelings in other people, feelings that a regular, non-living painting can't ever install in them.

Gloria hasn't learned to paint with her own flesh yet.

Gloria was Cuban. True, she was born in New York City, in Washington Heights, but several years ago she escaped here, to the East Village, to the hub of all New York artists, that is those REAL ones, to the artistic hub of the world – because New York may not be the capital of the United States, not even the capital of New York State, but it's indubitably the capital of the WORLD, it's the artistic gravity point of the whole UNIVERSE – at least that's how Gloria was feeling while wandering, decked out in her filthy painter's jeans, along East single-cipher streets; the fact that she managed to move here was the proof of Gloria's upward movement through life because in New York, as it is, upward movement through life means the descent down the rope ladder of streets, the higher your social status, the lower the number of the street you gotta live on (with the exception, perhaps, of those dumb rich people who for the last fifty years haven't really ever left their fancy apartments somewhere around the Sixties or Seventies and Park Avenue, who sit there, frozen in their gilded shells, at the most prestigious and dullest zip code of 10021). However she, Gloria, managed to perform this magnificent social transformation in one huge leap: from 174th Street and Amsterdam Avenue (from a huge apartment building in whose bowels her aunt's apartment seemed to be swallowed once and for all, it wasn't all the way up nor all the way down, it wasn't all the way to the left nor all the way to the right; it was imprisoned in a huge apartment building like that building was the belly of a whale, and submerged in the oily stench of fried platanos and boiled yams, in that sticky substance as thick as salsa music) – from that place Gloria, with only one stretch of her rather attractive calves managed to leap all the way down Harlem and Central Park, soaring on her wings spread wide over Midtown, and she landed right here, on a street whose name contained only one cipher; on a street where everyone DIDN'T start talking to her in Spanish the minute she flashed her face somewhere (although she did look Latino and she had no reason to be humbled by her looks: pure white skin and shiny eyes and cheeks with dimples and raven's hair, which she'd shaven off recently during one of her political binges, when she wrote all kinds of messages all over her body using various measures; however, under the bluish-black fuzz she had a beautiful, round, regularly shaped skull with no scars, zits or other marks) – and Gloria preferred to speak English, her Spanish was a bit creaky (not talking about the fact that in that language everybody who talked to her immediately assumed familiar airs), but still she retained a faint Hispanic accent, it was basically just a sharp "ess," and that sharp "ess" took her apart from all the whities, from all those who were white to the core, to the bone marrow, from all those inside whom that dull whiteness grew all the way, like cancer – and who refused to realize that Gloria's cream-colored complexion doesn't make her one of them at all – and that's why those sharp "esses" took her apart, they saved her from getting drowned in that cold pail of milk; Gloria knew that her complexion might be white, yes, but inside she's COLORED, she's warmly brown like an Indian, like LATINOS, like the two or three black women she'd managed to date and whose skin resembled well-baked bread crust, and smelled just like that. Gloria kept her sharp "esses" deliberately, but she still almost envied her roommate Gin's thick, unmistakable and ungotten-riddable-of Slavic accent that took Gin out, too (by the ears of everybody in front of whom she ever opened her mouth), out of that dull pail of white into which on the other hand – and unlike Gloria – Gin BELONGED, and even though Gin's English was simply funny to listen to, Gloria couldn't help herself: she had to envy her her lack of knowledge of the New York world. Gin's naivety (so great that only a person thrown into the melting pot of the City from a planet that had no clue whatsoever about hues of skin, about black, yellow or red, about creamy white that, however, hides warm brown hues underneath it) made it possible for her to regard the whole colorful palette THE WAY IT WAS, without any prejudice, without filtering all those colors through the sluice of certain private politics that most native New Yorkers had managed to make for themselves; Gin dived into white, yellow, smokey-colored, even bone-marrow-deep black societies with an ease that Gloria could only dream about.

*

Gloria stood in front of a painting and with a weary hand she kept throwing the last few dozen roaches onto the canvas. In her head, numbers were dancing. Not only those 365 fully developed, healthy, well-preserved cockroaches with their shellcovers in all hues of brown.

If "Year of Poverty" is forty-nine inches long, well, let's say forty-eight, I can get away with that, and seventy inches tall, then when I pay fifteen cents per square inch . . .

And then I could put there, she thought, perhaps "Trail of Tears," I gotta get at least two paintings in that exhibition, at least two . . . and I've already measured "Trail of Tears": fifty-two over sixty-three – man, these canvases aren't THAT big – and then Little José, he cried and cried . . . I let him trample the canvas with his little feet covered in paint, well, he liked that and zigzagged on it happily but then I had to wash his soles with thinner –

Gloria dispatched the 365th roach onto the canvas with a great arc, wiped her fingers on her painter's jeans (so that the acrylic glued a bunch of cockroach limbs to them) and fell on the sofa with a scrap of paper and a pen.

She multiplied for a while and then jerked back in horror. But even on the second and third try the sum was the same.

Chapter 6

The Street

A weather-worn, wet Yellow Cab fluttered around glistening streets like an insomniac butterfly, and on the wide hood in front of Gin, the City got reflected: upside down and all yellow. The traffic lights stretched their colors like stems toward her on the wet asphalt. It was a bit after 3 a.m. but Manhattan had already completely emptied out, and Gin's yellow butterfly now flew all the way down Columbus Avenue, accompanied by a green, inviting meadow of street lights in which once in a while a red blossomed up – so she had to stop underneath that flower. Empty Yellow Cabs flew together and sat down with a screech under that one flower, just like a fleet of butterflies, intoxicated by its scent.

Once in a while, a window of one of the Yellows got rolled down, and a face of that color or another emerged, yelling: "Hi, Gin! So how's it going?" Gin's lovemaking antennae haven't had time to break off yet and the whole City entered her like a low, rhythmic song. The tops of houses on both sides of Columbus made way for her on the hood of her car – there was a whole wide, drive-through tunnel that kept collapsing onto her eyes from four sides. From her position behind the wheel she couldn't see much farther up than the second floor, but on nights like tonight the whole tall verticality got reflected, just for herself, in an uneven yellow mirror. Huge, tall buildings lay down on the yellow color in front of Gin, moving along it with supersonic speed, vibrating with the roar of the engine and rocked by the rhythm of potholes on the road.

After an unsuccessful attempt to pick up a passenger (who got snatched from her by some Yellow asshole who, as he made his way rudely into her lane just inches in front of her, had the audacity to blow his horn, that jerk!) she decided to quit for today. She gassed up at Hess and then she drove her Yellow nag with medallion number 4P68 into the garage on 47th Street.

Today's night must have been lousy because all the remaining seven taxis that belonged to that garage were already parked by the curbs. The shutter of the Busy Bee wasn't down; from inside the garage warmth and the smell of gasoline wafted out. Today, nobody was left in the garage but Ramon, an illegal immigrant from Honduras who served here as a mechanic for forty dollars a week and the permission to live on the floor. Ramon spoke a strange mixture of Spanish and some Latin American mountain Indian tongue. Nobody understood how the boss and other mechanics in the garage could communicate with him, but they managed. Ever since Gin had known him, Ramon looked like they'd dragged him through a waste main-line: filthy overalls became one mass with his skin, melted together into the shape of something that lay on the sidewalk all winter long, covered in slush and dogshit. Ramon was sleeping on the day before yesterday's issue of *The New York Post* that he had spread on the mud, oil and sawdust that covered the garage floor. The oil from the floor and Ramon's rags had already saturated the paper, making it brown, and Ramon breathed like a baby on that tabloid, his head embedded in news about murders, shoot-outs, fires, hurricanes and a boy from Brooklyn who got cut into pieces by his own daddy who was sorry for him. Between his thighs, using his thumb for a cork, Ramon petted a half-finished bottle of Corona beer, and his body on the paper looked like another New York disaster, one which they forgot to write about in *The Post*.

Gin climbed the iron staircase into the office where she put the taximeter and car keys on the desk. Laila, a gasoline-soaked bitch who lived in the garage just like the guy from Honduras, watching it just like him, got up from a fetal position in the corner under vertically stashed, menacing-looking Chevy mufflers and circled Gin's legs, leaving greasy spots on her jeans. Both green parrots who, now, when they were quiet, she couldn't recognize one from the other, slumbered happily next to each other on the bar, their heads under their wings, both beautiful and well-groomed, just with ruffled tail feathers and a few downy tufts on their necks. Gin could never quite understand how is it possible that those birds don't get choked on gas fumes in the garage and how can they stay so beautifully grass-green while everything around them, alive or dead, is soaked and stunk through with gasoline and dust that forms a floury-brown-gray finishing paint. She'd like to wake up both parrots and listen to what they have to say to that but she decided not to be so cruel. She carefully descended the stairs, stepped over Ramon with one long careful stride (while Laila tripped over him), and then walked to the corner to get a taxi home.

Laila, the gasoline-soaked bitch, followed her with a long sad look, wiggling the remnants of her tail, and with one ear up, one down.

Chapter 7

Give Me the Money

On Gin's bed there lay a message, written in careful longhand on the back side of a Carolina rice bag:

Dear Gin,

I need $1000 for that exhibition. But that's not expensive, really! Do you know how much paintings like that go for? I need it right now. Otherwise it's no use and I'll miss that exhibition! I'm counting on you, Gin! Pretty, pretty, pretty please, give me the money!

She was almost falling asleep when she heard child's blabber in the next room. Little feet ran across the parquet floor – and Little José fell on Gin's belly with his whole weight. Gin huffed. Tears were overflowing from Little José's eyes. He hugged Gin with both his arms and dug his chin into her breasts. He was heavy and all puffed up from weeping but kind of sweet and nice and warm. Gin felt kindness wash over her like the Pacific Ocean. She wiped his nose on her handkerchief.

"*Malo*!" Little José sobbed, "*sueño malo*!" A bad, bad dream!

Gin held José in her arms, enjoying his warmth. While she

was falling asleep she wondered if this could be child abuse: that warmth she's sharing with him, that warmth she's stealing from him, even though it's him, Little José, who's cuddling next to her with all his might while Gin only put her arm around him because she had no other place to rest it; she wondered whether her head that's so close to José's scalp on the pillow couldn't generate some adult vibes . . . whether her thoughts (not at all evil, just adultlike) couldn't destroy something deep in the creases of Little José's brain, whether they couldn't deepen them too soon and DIFFERENTLY, whether they couldn't install different grooves into them like he was an LP . . . a little scratch – and here we go: from that moment on, the needle will always slip in a certain groove and the sound will go khrrr . . . until his death the whole melody of José's life will be altered and changed. And it will all happen just because right now, at this moment, Gin has put her arm over his body, and because their heads are lying on the pillow too close to one another.

The interference of thoughts, opinions, ideas and heads, however, penetrated through the entire City.

ALL the heads here left their signatures on one another; all the opinions, loves, hates, happy and unhappy thoughts, ideas, emotions, inspirations – absolutely everything that ever took place in human heads got reflected in the heads of all the others, whether they liked it or not, like rainbow-color interference stripes —

People in this City wore bubbles of their beliefs around their heads like life circles – just like everywhere else, for that matter, only here there was no room for those protective bubbles, even the tiniest ones barely fit among the balloons that the others wore —

(Gin thought as she was falling asleep, surrounded by her bubble and that of José's; José's bubble was still fresh, nothing was written on its surface)

– New York was a City of astronauts in space suits —

– the bubbles scratched and hurt one another, they

penetrated one another and sometimes, for a spell, they merged together in a scream of empathy and passion; they destroyed one another and burst in spasms of pain; they didn't fit into this City, there were too many of them —

— as an individual you simply couldn't exist, live or create here because the interference from all those other heads took your concentration away from you, and some people wore porcupine's quills on their bubbles, one had no time and no space to listen to yourself —

But when you submerged yourself in the City (like it was a whirling foam), then every cell of your body got permeated with its rhythm, its plasma circled in your veins, and therefore you became, just like everybody else, a building block, a cell, a molecule in that humongous, colorful, crazy mosaic; in the same vibrating, breathing, ever-changing mosaic that you yourself watched daily from all over – and which had dragged you to the City in the first place.

A thousand dollars, Gin thought, a thousand dollars to be spent only so Gloria the painter can, for a few days or perhaps weeks, buy her own bubble, her space, her own couple square yards of wall in an obscure gallery on Essex Street, and I'd like to make it possible for her but WHERE DO I GET THE MONEY? Maybe if instead of taking Sundays off I worked for thirty-six hours straight a couple of times – but if I do that I'll collapse and I've no money to see a doctor, she thought, wondering whether she really took every possibility into account. If Gloria and I lived on tea and spaghetti for a few weeks . . . actually, I've lived through that already, that was when me and that guy (but I don't wanna remember him!), when we squatted in a certain shrink's Upper East Side apartment, and none of us two had a job, but that guy (that alcoholic!) sold mice in the street without a license, I mean wooden mice with a tail that moved, and every night at eleven, when they were closing that Italian restaurant a few blocks away from us on Madison Ave, I'd sneak out – I mustn't forget, otherwise we'd go hungry – because they always threw the remnants of uncooked spaghetti right on Madison Avenue so that the next day they can open a new bag. I had to be there before the local dogs lifted up their legs to the spaghetti; what a piece of luck that the homeless weren't so keen on them, they wouldn't have a place to cook them anyway, but I and that guy (that guy I don't wanna remember at all!) stuffed our faces day after day with pasta. I made spaghetti, long and short, thick and thin, I cooked linguini and angel hair, hollow macaroni of all kinds, crinkled slabs of dough intended for lasagna, three-colored pasta – yellow, green from spinach and red from carrots (what a traffic light that was!) – fettuccine, spaghetti rice, tortellini, tortelloni and cheese ravioli and all – this was the diet we lived on then and my butt grew really big just because we had no money for food! Well, back then I was still illegal, that was my first year here, I lived in my seventh, perhaps eighth place – and that guy (that alcoholic! that dopehead!), well, he —

But all that didn't matter anymore, memories only a couple of years or months old got all mixed together in Gin's head, they were being pushed out of her brain by a never-ceasing humongous NOW that punched her from every side and angle daily. Little José was slumbering happily under her arm (while the grooves in his brain were being altered), from Gloria's bedroom she could hear two voices and a soft hum of the vibrator – and spaghetti, whole forests of the spaghetti that they devoured together with that guy (that alcoholic! that dopehead! that jerk!) were projected in front of Gin as she was falling asleep, they stood upright in a menacing position like medieval rapiers, they snugged up into spirals, the same spirals that took the homeless guy Randy into the blue skies, and then (as if the huge rolling pin of destiny flattened them out) they got wider and wider, round spaghetti became fettuccine, then got dyed green with spinach – until, at the beginning of a horrendous nightmare, a whole primeval forest grew out of them in front of Gin, a thorny, impenetrable, greenish primeval forest of one housand dollars American.

Chapter 8

The Garage on 47th Street

"And what you think?" Gin's boss Alex yelled. "D'you think I make money, yeah? I tell you, Gin, every month, EVERY MONTH at least ten thousand I lose on this garage. At least!"

Alex stood with his legs wide apart on an oil slick in front of his garage and under his loafers a rainbow-colored interference layer was slowly floating. He made hand gestures in all directions. He spoke English but – as she was Slavic, too – he'd switch to Russian in moments of greatest excitement: "*Chto ty doomayesh? Kazhdyi mesiats!*" The wind kept blowing and reblowing a lock of his rather thinning hair from the right to the left, changing Alex's profile from a pigeon's to a roadrunner's in the process. From a certain angle, and when he kept his mouth shut, he almost resembled an eagle, in a certain light he looked like an owl, but under any circumstances there was a bit of a raven in his looks, including those few gray hairs at the root of his beak. His mother could have sued almost any bird for child support.

Alex drew closer to Gin's behind and squeezed her big butt with both hands. Gin (who was just trying to play the game by the rules) gave out a tiny scream and moved to the side.

"Jee-zuz Christ, you are so beautiful!" her boss commenced his mating dance. "So when I can come to you?"

For over half a year and in vain Gin was trying to think up an answer that would fit. Sometimes it occurred to her that, perhaps, it might be easier to spread them for him once and therefore get rid of him. However she had no intention to get in trouble just because of Alex's amorous advances (after all, the faithful Gana, his wife of twenty-two years, sat just upstairs in the "office," smiling at cabdrivers and taking money from them). I mean, you never know. In the previous garage, on 21st Street, she started up something with the dispatcher – well, she did it partly out of curiosity, partly out of a good heart. But he understood her act completely differently – that means he apparently concluded that Gin is trying to screw her way into his heart and in return for that she expects a nice car every day, and along with him all the drivers of both day and night shifts concluded the same, ABSOLUTELY all of them, and as it was a big garage there were at least seventy-five of them on each shift. So in the end, the truly pleasant getting acquainted with that guy resulted in a major trouble – and Gin had no choice but to leave that garage. Even so, for a long time afterwards, various Yellow drivers would bellow at her in the street, not necessarily in a nasty manner, just with a wide, knowing smile that made the blood curl in her veins. "Hi, Gin, how are you to-daaay?" – so Gin had no choice but to lean out of those wrecks in which she was driving her ass around these days for a change, and with a grin on her face (so she could pretend that she thought they didn't know what she knew they knew), she yelled back at them: "Fiii-ne! And you?", and the cheekiest of them had the audacity to answer: "And what is the thing you're driving today, Gin? You gotta get a real caaar!" Therefore getting stuck, let's say, at Kennedy Airport, at the holding lot for taxicabs in front of the International Arrivals Building, wasn't short of a purgatory and Gin could have fallen through the crust of the Earth with shame – until, finally, this gossip about her got thinned out a bit and she could breathe freely again.

Getting acquainted with Kenny was a pretty pleasant affair, actually. It took place on a roomy (and surprisingly clean) bed of the hourly hotel Liberty Inn on 14th Street and West Side Highway that inspired Gin: the receptionist was a muscle with a frown behind a thick pane of plexiglass, and all around the hotel whores of both sexes were standing, and their legs, clad in high heels, were buckling under them with fatigue. When she and Kenny were leaving after two hours paid for in advance, they walked out through a separate door equipped with a box right next to the door, and the box had a hole cut through the top so that you could throw the room keys into it. You crawled out of the place into the fucked-out reality of the street and the darkness and the night and the exhausted whores of both sexes whose knees were buckling under them, as they were wearing high heels. You snuck out of the hotel through a one-way door as if you had drawn a semicircle in that hotel, there was always some unfinished business hiding in the corners and in the pillow and in the toilet bowl along with used protection; the chambermaids never managed to quite get rid of it.

You sneaked out so you didn't have to look into the eyes of that muscle behind the reception desk, and then you went —

Well, in their case they went for coffee a couple of blocks east down 14th Street, and life was OK. It was only during that coffee in a 24-hour joint, that she really, REALLY looked at him, because never before . . . never before THAT did she touch him, there'd been no way for her to touch him although Kenny tried to chat her up for at least two weeks – so now, finally, the visual part got merged with the tactile part: she could see those coarse tufts of hair above his temples completely differently; they were cropped really close, sticking like tufts of moira grass from the dark sand on the seaside; and she could see them differently for one reason only: that is because she was touching them a few minutes before, a few minutes before they were hurting her fingertips when —

Never before did she see his lips LIKE THAT: the upper one was brown-black, the lower one with scattered islands of a surprisingly pink color – and it was only because never before did they embrace her, never before did they embrace her lips, the artery on her neck, her clavicle, her nipples, her navel, her clit – all the seven marked points on her body remembered, during that moment over coffee, their touch, the pattern of creases on them . . .

Kenny moved his coffee cup close to hers, hugged it with his palms and touched the tips of his little fingers to the tips of hers.

"Was I your first, h-hm, nigger?"

Gin shuddered.

It was caused partly by the electricity that got activated by this connection and finally closed that circle, that circle they'd opened up two hours ago in the hotel room. And mostly by that hated word she herself couldn't ever get through her lips.

The electric circuit tickled her body, strolling up and down her spine and thickening at the seven marked points. She remembered the little fat-creases on his belly; tough and rolling, they reminded her of her grandma's washboard.

She looked down at her coffee.

And Kenny, as it seemed, didn't quite get the fact that Talibe who'd worked at his garage six days a week not so long ago (before he decided to become his own boss and lease a cab by the week) was, after all, Gin's husband. He looked under her eyelashes inquiringly, pressing his little fingers to hers.

"The first? Really?"

The next day, the minute she appeared at the garage door, a shiny 6M57 was waiting for her. It was the brand-newest new car that the whole garage owned: canary-yellow and without a single scratch on it. Kenny waved its keys at her, grinned and threw them backhanded across the whole length of the garage. Maybe he was afraid that the electric circuit between them might get connected again.

The way the situation developed next wasn't that wonderful, however. At first they fucked occasionally on the desk in his dispatcher's booth – and only late at night when the likelihood that someone would appear in the garage was really low – but then Kenny's tastes grew more and more audacious. At the end he tended to forget to buy rubbers, so toward morning, when all the delis nearby were hopelessly shuttered, she had to go down to 16th Street to purchase one or two or three of them from the hookers which, of course, brought with it all kinds of special attention.

But Kenny wasn't just a dispatcher, he was also a mechanic, and an inspired one at that. Not only did he call each of the Yellows by its first name and knew by heart and in detail all the scratches and nicks on them, every dented fender, banged bumper, damaged door (and he treated his Yellows like children or, perhaps, yellow chicks that return every morning and every night under the wing of their mother hen), but he also knew how to heal them. All Kenny had to do was open the hood of any ailing car ("Open wide, baby!"), and TOUCH SOMETHING SOMEWHERE INSIDE – and the stalled-out engine started purring, the pistons pumped, the belts rotated, the carburetor carbureted, the transmission transmissed. Kenny smiled while he was at it, talking to the cars, patting them with his huge paw and leaving black grease spots on them. Everybody agreed that he fixed cars thanks to some magic he'd brought with him from the Islands because he was unable to explain to anybody what exactly it was he did to them, and not even the other mechanics in the garage, who watched his work daily, could duplicate it.

It occurred to Gin that even her insides must somewhat resemble the guts of a Yellow Chevy.

All Kenny had to do was open her knees just like the hood of one of the Yellows – and she began purring, she started up, she functioned to the full measure, and she drove away with him along an open highway with infinity for a speed limit toward breathtakingly beautiful imaginary landscapes.

Well, that could, on the other hand, explain why it ended badly. The electric circuit worked better and better for them; now he didn't even need to touch her with the last digits of his little fingers: the circuit got closed with the help of keys to the best car in the whole garage – the keys swooshed toward her along the ballistic curve pretty much every day, the minute she appeared in the doorway, and the other drivers started complaining, naturally, and for a good reason: she was the only one who could drive whenever she wanted, any night at all, Fridays and Saturdays included, and the brand-newest 6M57 was waiting for her in the garage because, after all, even a telephone cord could be a part of that electric circuit. Gin, however, had absolutely no intention to get ahead of others, pissing them off. So she kept telling Kenny: "Once in a while you gotta let me wait for some old wreck!" but he just refused to hear it. "We'll get gossiped about one another!" But that was what Kenny, as it seemed, actually wanted, she was the only woman in the whole garage and every other guy kept hitting on her. And so he became almost exhibitionistic in his desires, until one day that electric circuit between them peaked and shorted out at the same time; that happened at 4:37 p.m. one day when Kenny, despite her protests, decided to climb into a taxicab with her. It was one of the junkiest ones, 5H72 that had broken down on the night before in Queens all the way on Parsons Boulevard, stalled out in a cloud of smog, and its transmission was just being changed by two of the garage mechanics. So Kenny demanded to be taken up in that car with her on the lift, all the way up, right under the ceiling, above the hands of those two Mexicans, above their upturned heads, above curses, above all the other drivers, both the night-shift ones who'd been loitering about for a long time, trying to figure out what the hell's going on, and the day-shift ones who'd started to return to the garage after their shift's end, forming a mob, keys in hand, around the dispatcher's booth. But the dispatcher wasn't there, the dispatcher was —

Gin stood in her white-and-blue sneakers (the left one of the pair as good as new and the right one worn out unevenly) on the oil slick in front of Alex's garage and a rainbow floated slowly between her feet toward the curb. It dripped on the road surface one drop after another, joining the rainbow on a local perpetual puddle. Is it possible that this terrible piece of gossip about her DIDN'T make it from 21st Street to 47th? She moved her ass away from Alex's palm.

"Well, when you don't make anything, why do you have this garage?"

Alex rolled up his eyes, tilting his head back like a drinking seagull.

"I must this garage have. I have for you, for you all! Who would of you take care if I throw shit on this business? I no ask you for deposit, no deposit at all. Other garages, before you start driving, you must pay hundred-fifty dollars, two hundred dollars, FIVE HUNDRED dollars – in my garage, nothing. Because I trust you!" (Again he moved his hand closer to her butt, stealthily this time.) "And you know how much money I pay when you break my cars, when you have accidents, when you hit somebody – you know what happen at Kafka's garage? A driver brings car in, something rattles in the engine, he says, I don't think it's the transmission, maybe it's axle, or maybe do I have loose muffler? – And I tell you, Gin, what it was: It was a woman!"

"Yes, I know . . ."

"It's a old street lady. She jump right—"

"I know . . ."

"—and he, like he was turning corner somewhere on West Side, he just took her by the bumper and he knows nothing about it! Then he said he feels some bump but he thinks he hit the curb on the right side."

"I know . . ."

"So THIS IS what drivers you are, Gin. The old woman, she never sued nobody, she dead, and she doesn't have any relatives, she lives in the street many years but you just imagine—"

"I don't have accidents, do I?" Gin said defensively. The anecdote of the old lady who ended her life in a garage, taken for a defect on a car, has been told among the taxidrivers and dispatchers in numerous versions but, unfortunately, its core was apparently true.

"I don't have accidents and . . ."

"No, no, no, Gin, I know you don't. I forgive you the torn-off door, it can happen to everybody, and, after all, what for do I have guys for bodywork? Everybody hits something sometimes. If you go to the insurance company right away after every accident, nothing will happen, nothing. After all, BUMPER is on a car for BUMPING into things, right? *Nu, eto pravda*. If you don't wrap yourself around a lantern with your car and we don't take you to cemetery in five pieces like that guy who used to drive for Vinny—"

"All I'm trying to say is that the business is really bad these days. I pay at least two thirds of what I make to you, for the lease of the car. And then, just when the business is the best, I get stuck some place with that car of yours, and before they tow me away, I—"

"Come on, come on, come on, Gin, don't I tell you how much this garage to have here costs me? Don't be like everybody else, don't be LIKE THAT and don't bitch with me! You're so beautiful! Come on, go upstairs and pay Gana for the shift. I give you today the best car I have. I give you 7Y99."

7Y99 didn't resemble the shiny beauty of medallion number 6M57 of the garage on 21st Street one damn bit. Alex couldn't very well give her the best car he owned. The reason for that was simple: he didn't own such a thing. All he owned were eight rust buckets in various stages of decomposition; the word "car" didn't exactly describe them. Not talking about the fact that Alex was no match for a certain dispatcher named Kenny, not even remotely, so why the hell doesn't he take that paw of his off her butt?

Upstairs, in the "office," the green parrots were quarreling. Now Gin could tell them from one another. Their looks didn't differ, their dispositions did. Which meant that their language did, too.

The more talkative one hopped on the bar toward the shy one with his wings akimbo (in a not-exactly-birdlike manner), shrieking without cease: "Gim-me the mo-ney! Gim-me the mo-ney!" It was understandable although his pronunciation wasn't perfect. He shrieked in English with a heavy Russian accent.

The other parrot didn't look exactly scared. He seemed rather bored as he skipped backwards to avoid his roommate, he turned up his feathers, hid his neck between his arms and only when his tail feathers were badly scrummaged in the cage wires, did he say apologetically: "I don't have a-ny mo-ney!"

"Gim-me the mo-ney! Gim-me the mo-ney!" Gimme-the-Money shrieked angrily. And on the other side of the green parrots' cage, framed and crisscrossed by its wires, Alex's wife Gana sat, pronouncing exactly the same sentence right now, even though in a slightly more human voice.

"But I don't have any money!" Fakim Fakem, one of Alex's day drivers, was answering her. You could tell that if it was at all possible, he'd cover his face with a green wing. "I don't have any money, I don't book anything today, there's ABSOLUTELY no business today, unbelievable traffic, everyone going five miles an hour, I'm bringing home five bucks, there's no customers, fuck it—"

"But you must gimme the money," Gana and the parrot repeated in unison while Fakim was rummaging through himself theatrically, pulling pathetic little handfuls of singles out of unexpected holes in his clothes or body.

"How's everybody today?" Gin greeted them. Both of the actors of this theatrical play turned toward her.

"So-so. And yourself?" Gana said.

"Fuck it all, f— it," Fakim started, then checked himself in front of the ladies. He was a rather dishevelled, unshaven, wild-looking Afghan. He wasn't the offspring, however, as the less knowledgeable might think, of the noble family of the Fakems. He got his nickname thanks to his pronunciation and also an insatiable taste for the word FUCK.

"I'm driving, right," he'd relate, "and that limo driver cut me right in front. So I say FUCK 'IM! and step on it. So I had an accident, OK?" Or: "I got a letter from the Taxi and Limousine Commission, they say I have to pay a lot of tickets, I owe them maybe fifteen hundred dollars. But where can I get fifteen hundred dollars, right? So I say to myself: FUCK 'EM! FUCK 'EM! And they suspended my license!"

"So what are you bringing us, Gin?" Gana asked in a friendly manner while Fakim kept rummaging through his clothes, cursing the world. Gin felt a bit like a traitor when she pulled a neatly folded roll of bills from her knapsack and handed Gana the required ninety-five bucks. Gana reached for them with her left hand. The Bic pen in her right hand made a little questioning circle above the list of cars.

Gin said: "7Y99."

"Gim-me the mo-ney!" the parrot screamed.

Chapter 9

Penetration

The sky was tightly bound by the silhouettes of skyscrapers that got mirrored on the hood in front of her along with free stripes of blue. The color blue in connection with yellow turned a magically green hue. Across the mirror of her hood, carried by their elegant wings, white seagulls flew, their lightning-fast mirages, as well as their dark, slower shadows. The clouds ran one after another on that curvy, wide mirror in front of Gin, resembling yellowed beer foam, and the lifting of the right arm became the only code of communication. Nobody who drives just for fun, nobody who moonlights just to make a bit of extra money – nobody who drives weekends only or, perhaps, two, three, four days a week, gets to know what taxi driving really is about. You gotta work six days a week, or perhaps seven, taking just one day off every two weeks (and during that one day, after all, you have nothing to do anyway, that free day breaks your rhythm, and on top of things you feel guilty because that's the day when you're not working, you don't collect some seventy, eighty, perhaps even hundred and twenty dollars in your sock). Only then do you become a real taxidriver, a taxidriver that's worthy of that name, a taxidriver whose brain is tired to death and washed out so much it looks like puke. Then you become the real taxidriver who understands just one sign of the whole sign language – it's the one that yells I WANNA TAXI! TAXI! STOP! The seven-day-a-week cab-driver has forgotten everything else of the sign language, so – perhaps with the exception of a raised middle finger – only one letter had remained in his head but it comes in a million and one shapes and formations: written with a pencil, charcoal, in calligraphy, drawn with a bamboo stick on a sheet of rice paper, hastily scribbled on the asphalt with a stub of chalk, sprayed on the wall like graffiti, carved into tree bark in place of hearts, shot with 9mm slugs into the sheet-metal wall of a warehouse. A taxidriver like that learns to get to know one gesture only but every form of it:

The uppity-mellow lifting of the left arm of little Madison Avenue ladies whose right hand is holding a leash with a choking lap-sized dog;

The well-practiced wave of the stockbrokers and bond traders near the World Trade Center or on Wall Street;

The supplicant, soft arm of musicians, sticking from behind basses or other instruments that, as they well know, simply can't fit into a passenger car;

The windmill of arms, legs, umbrellas and heads of confused tourists who've just emerged onto 8th Avenue from a Broadway theater and found out to their dismay that it has meanwhile become a screeching, rattling, horn-blowing, stinking, slow Yellow river –

The seven-day drivers learn to know by heart that self-assured spread-armed gesture of Brooklyners who are coming home in the evening, and because they're well aware that no cabbie wants to go there at this hour, they stand right in the middle of the lane, trying to block it;

Taxidrivers know that LOOK with which, late at night, you can stop ten or more Yellows in front of a bar without moving a muscle, while all the hungry Yellows crash into one another right at your feet;

Yellow taxidrivers know that in Manhattan below 96th Street

people stop cabs just by lifting up an arm, by "hailing," but in Harlem, in Queens, in Brooklyn, in the Bronx folks lift up an arm with the palm down, while opening and closing it. And so when somebody uses that gesture on you, let's say, in front of a nightclub in Midtown, you can be pretty sure he's gonna drag you away from Manhattan and God knows where;

Taxidrivers know those desperate gestures some wheelchair bound people use to try to beg their way inside;

– and from the friendly flapping of a hooker's hand they can tell whether those girls are waving them down for business only (well, even a cabdriver needs a BJ sometimes) or whether they've called it a day and want to be driven home to Jersey.

Taxidrivers who work "full time" – five, six or seven days a week (with a single shift off every two weeks or so, on a Sunday) – know all those gestures and a hundred others. But even so, sometimes, toward morning after a long shift, it seems to them that from the edges of a streetlamp's light, outlined by the headlights of cars going in the opposite direction, the phantoms of customers are emerging; that the traffic sign post two blocks ahead will wave them down in a second, asking to be taken to Brooklyn; that the silver-and-black fire hydrant on the curb is actually a midget who's stretching the stump of his arm toward them.

And so they hit the brake really hard, the centripetal force kicking them out of their seat and banging their body against the wheel – and then the taxidrivers curse aloud, rub their eyes and get going again along the empty night street.

"Remember that guy, Gin, I mean that STATUE of a guy that used to stand on Park Avenue and 48th?" her colleague Geoffrey asked her once. "That business guy with a briefcase in his paw and a coat hangin' on his elbow, who's stretching out his other arm like he wants a taxi. They had to put that one back into the lobby, as far away from the street as they could, and you know why?"

"Because the taxis stopped for him?"

"Because there was ONE ACCIDENT AFTER

ANOTHER as the cabbies were struggling for him. And the cops were tired of that."

Night driving is immensely different from day driving: the twelve hours from 5 a.m. till 5 p.m. means twelve hours of toil, twelve hours of struggle with the traffic, which gets thicker before 8 a.m., ebbs away after ten, disappears for a while around noon and gets thicker again around three o'clock (that is as long as some big shot in a limo doesn't make his way into town, upsetting this whole order, as long as this avenue or that one isn't closed because of demonstrations, street fairs or parades, as long as Manhattan doesn't get covered in snow so that the streets become impassable and huge convoys of cars wade their way through the whitish-gray slush along the main arteries) – but at about half past four or a quarter of five, when everything's at its best and the customers begin to swarm, you gotta turn the OFF DUTY lights on and make your way to the garage as fast as you can so you are not late and fined for it by the dispatcher.

The twelve hours from 5 p.m. until 5 a.m., however, resemble a magic carpet, a time machine that cuts a few hours off this end and glues them to the other; midnight on Monday is just as dead as half past two on Wednesday, and on a Saturday night, if it's any good at all, you won't stop until dawn, and sometimes even at 3 or 4 a.m. the avenues are plugged in the most unexpected places with the visitors from the other bank of the Hudson who are trying their best to make their way back to Jersey with the help of horn-blowing, shouting and middle-finger waving, and both tunnels are too narrow for them, so if one of the whores somewhere around 29th Street and 10th Avenue waves at you, indicating she wants to go home, then – by the time you squeeze your way through one of the tunnels with her aboard and drive her along highway I5/I9 (that's horizontally striped thanks to the concrete panels you're speeding under) and through the maze of overpasses, underpasses and thoroughfares and ramps take her to the cheap little hotel she lives in – you have at least an hour for talking:

about the boyfriend who's gonna kill her dead 'cause she's bringing home less than eight hundred, about the easy-to-bite-through condoms of the Lifestyles brand as opposed to the sturdy Ramses brand, about the AIDS virus that killed her girlfriend a while ago but she don't have it, God knows she don't . . . About the fact that these days it doesn't pay to climb inside anybody's car – even if they tried to push two hundred in advance on you – and let them drive you God knows where, because them sadists / nuts / serial killers kill whores just for fun these days, or for money, as if you didn't know, they do the same to cabdrivers, don't they? – and now, you know, I should shut my mouth, it hurts like hell, it kills me, just count with me, OK? If you blow at least four or five of them an hour, or, sometimes, twelve, even, then on a Saturday night (when the Johns in their cars line up for a BJ!), then all together it makes at least . . . but I really gotta shut my mouth now, you see?

And you know that you've just driven a twenty-three-year old whore from Carolina, her name is Sunshine, she's worked in Kentucky Fried Chicken before, but I tell you, none of them Johns smell so bad as fried chickens, believe you me. In front of her hotel she gets off, she pays you, she adds a dollar, or two, or three (that's just because you had such a nice talk together) – and then, when you swoosh around (and the sun is already climbing up the skies), it doesn't seem to you that you're approaching Manhattan on a concrete highway, no, you'd swear that you're flying toward it along the deep trough of a pinkish-gray scar that the last boyfriend had carved in the face of the girl named Sunshine, from her jaw all the way to the corner of her eye, just because she'd put a couple dollars aside to buy some junk with. (But just a little bit, you know?)

When night taxidrivers make it home and fall on their bed, the film of everything they'd seen on their shift, of everything they drove past, gets projected onto their eyelids. But if they drive through the streets day by day, they witness far more things than they want to, and then they get a headache from it, a stomach ache, a liver ache – and so the drivers build barriers in themselves, barriers against perception, they put blinders on their own eyes as if they were carriage horses, and – to make sure not too much of the City enters them every night – they fortify themselves against it.

With a very strong conviction that THEY are not drivers of taxicabs. They are actors. And writers. And screenwriters. And visual artists.

With a conviction that THEY simply don't belong behind the wheel of a taxicab, that for THEM this job is just for a while, just to make some money, quick – because in Pakistan, in Punjab, in Haiti, in Nigeria they have a family to feed; because in a little village just south of Budapest their mom has been dying of cancer for a whole year now and they must have money for air tickets, in case . . .

The drivers build walls in themselves to block out the City. Day after day they snap on brass knuckles that serve just like the protective collars on the necks of attack dogs. They hide a loaded gun in their armpit or behind the cuffs of a leather jacket, from where, if you know the trick, the gun comes out with a single shake of your arm, jumping right into the palm of your hand while the trigger arranges itself under your index finger.

The drivers take great care to lock the doors of their four-wheeled homes away from home, making sure nobody can open them from the outside. Locking your doors, however, is officially not allowed, just like carrying a gun, even though the fine for locking doors is merely fifty bucks. For a revolver you'd go to jail. Under no circumstances are taxidrivers allowed to carry a weapon on them.

The drivers hide baseball bats under the seats, and also jacks and sharpened Phillips screwdrivers. These are not weapons by definition but they make their way in between your ribs and then see who has the last laugh.

The drivers distance themselves from the City, from its bustle and its moods, with music on the radio: if you tune to the right station, it'll fill up your cabin with rhythmic joyfulness, it won't let any other sound into the cabin – not the screech of brakes and the swoosh of tires, not the hollering of drunks, not the clicking of switches in the grayish green boxes that hang on every street corner, regulating the traffic lights (innervating the heart of the City, controlling its beat). The music won't allow the rumbling of trucks and the rustling of trees in the wind into the yellow protective cage; it won't let in the pleads of beggars and the curses and the shouts. Even the wailing of ambulances, fire trucks and police cars penetrates the wide, soft, comfortable wall of music only in the form of low, guttural tones that don't have anything to do with us.

Drivers who work seven days a week (just with an occasional little break, once every two weeks on a Sunday) barricade themselves from the City and from the night with the help of windows carefully rolled up (because perfectly orchestrated pairs of thieves – one of whom drives and the other one snatches – cruise through the City all the time, looking for every window that's rolled down and behind which an unsuspecting taxidriver is counting his hard-come-by cash – so quite often a car with tinted windows brakes down next to you, a hand emerges from it, grabbing YOUR MONEY INSIDE OF YOUR OWN CAR – and before you manage to lift up your gaze – ZOOM! the car is gone along with your day's bookings).

Some drivers barricade themselves from the customers by closing the plexiglass partition that cuts the car in half, into the driver's space and the customer's; that allegedly bulletproof bubble protects the driver from his passengers, and every passenger, before he gets off, has to put his money into a funny contraption that, like a swing, swings empty toward him, filled up toward the driver.

Empty Yellow cabs make their way through the City, a glowing dandelion on the roof of each. They make sure everybody sees them.

As soon as a passenger gets in, you push the button labeled HIRED on your taximeter, and the light on your roof goes off. You're taken. $1.50 appears on the display, and with every four blocks up or down avenues, another .25 flicks on. When you've reached your destination and the passenger is reaching for the doorhandle, you push the button labeled TOTAL, and the light VACANT starts shining on the display, along with that dandelion on the roof. Then for another fifteen seconds or so the information about this particular trip stays in your taximeter, and if you push the button labeled PRINT within this time frame, then all the information known to the taximeter should be printed on a piece of paper: when the trip with this passenger began, when it ended, how many miles you covered and how much it cost him. But after fifteen seconds THIS information disappears from the meter completely, it loses its individuality: it gets added to the dozens, hundreds, thousands, perhaps millions of previous "trips," so the only information retained is:

NUMBER OF TRIPS
TOTAL MILES
LIVE MILES
NUMBER OF UNITS, the taximeter's clicks each of which adds $.25 on the meter.

In other words: Your taximeter mills it all together, all the information in it gets tinier, thicker; it loses its uniqueness. That's just so its capacity won't get overfilled.

And it's the same principle that makes the days and nights, spent driving through the City, thicken in taxidrivers' heads. Their experiences are not experiences anymore, stories are not stories. Instead, just ONE BIG STORY gets saved in their heads, a long, tangled, mixed-up one. It's as if each taxidriver was unrolling on the asphalt behind him an infinitely long spool of thread.

On the spool of thread in Gin's head, a whole movie sequence was being filmed, about 200 miles a day, and every morning, as she was falling asleep, the dailies were getting projected in her head: projected, edited, rewound and fast-forwarded. Then it sank down into the past and into the indistinguished. Days and nights got fused into a single yellowish tint; the reel of film got melted together and you couldn't really see through it anymore – only in multiple exposure, and each time she went to sleep to the cooing of waking pigeons, the City reverberated in her head like a single, clear and crisp tone of a golden gong.

However, from the maze of all dreams, good ones and bad ones, intoxicating ones as well as tiresome ones, one dream emerged, a dream that got projected onto the movie screen behind her eyelids more or less every night.

She's speeding in her taxicab, for an awfully long time, across bridges and along highways and past crossroads, through forests and mountains and deserts. In her car a frog-green customer is sitting, reproaching her in an unknown tongue, poking her with a walking stick doubled up at the end like a serpent's tongue.

The taximeter, turned on, shines through the darkness like a neon light, and every so often a red light flicks on it. However, although Gin has been driving like that for at least two thousand years, the taximeter still shows no more than a dollar fifty.

Chapter 10

The Exhibition

The exhibition of paintings, sculptures and other art objects, created by the artists of the Rivington School, was opened on Stanton Street (close to the corner where it crosses Essex) in the second half of November.

There was no official opening, as the Rivington artists didn't believe in bourgeois crap.

Both girls went to see the exhibition together, around two in the afternoon, so Gin could then make it to the garage on time.

On her left side, Gloria walked Hubby on a pink leash and with a ribbon above his forehead. From a distance it most likely looked like she was walking a cheerful, somewhat oversized rat that was desperately trying to keep pace with her while, at the same time, leaving his territorial markers at close intervals on the bases of buildings and traffic sign posts, with the result that the poor beast found himself sliding down the sidewalk every now and then, being dragged by the neck on a pink leash, one leg up in the air and the remaining three clawing the concrete, attempting to stop the movement, marking with a yellow trickle different places than he intended.

The girls were holding each other through the warm little paws of Josito, who alternately ran as fast as he could, his legs scurrying almost as fast as Husband's, and then let himself be carried in suspension between the two girls, mumbling something happily to himself. It occurred to Gin that to a casual observer they must look like an established lesbian couple that managed to adopt. She resented that idea but she resented the fact that she resented it even much more. If I want to be a sophisticated Westerner, I must not mind things like that, she thought.

"Man, I'm so happy!" Gloria kept exclaiming, throwing sweet glances at Gin, "I'm so happy you helped me with this exhibit!" (She squeezed Josito's palm gratefully, as if it was the continuation of Gin's hand.) "Shit, come ON, Hubby!" she yelled at the dog that was again sliding down the sidewalk on three legs. "The first exhibit in my whole life! I mean, if I don't count those black-garbage-bag figurines we used to hang on walls to protest the war. Stop that, José! The first exhibit in my whole life. Can you imagine?"

The truth was that Gin could not imagine.

The exhibition of paintings, sculptures and objects, created by the members of the Rivington School of Art (which based its name on a Lower East Side street) was taking place in a basement.

More precisely, in a dark dungeon, in a space that the Rivingtonians won for themselves during one of their recent happenings. Somebody managed to break the lock on the metal trapdoors on the sidewalk. There was no staircase and so the exhibit had to be reached by climbing down one of the variegated welded sculptures.

Naturally, the Rivingtonians had no business opening an exhibition in a space that wasn't theirs. However, the basement seemed to have been abandoned for a long time and, in addition to that, if things didn't work out right and the police really kicked them out of there – well, then there would be just another happening, after all, an unplanned-for one, and those are the best.

Gin peeked into the dark hollow of the exhibition hall with suspicion. Behind a scratchy metal desk (divided by a belt of sunlight that penetrated all the way down there into two triangles of a different shade of green) the Korean was sitting. He was one of the founding members of the Rivington School. He was sitting there, leaning toward the light, and so the mane of his graying (checkerboard) hair was divided into two rhombuses by the falling light. Golden specks of dust were circling through the enlightened air.

When all four of them – Gloria, Gin, Josito and the dog – stopped in their tracks on the sidewalk above him, the Korean sprang up. Lifting his head backwards in a painful angle, he yelled: "Hi, everybody!", bowed his back in the oriental manner and made a motion toward the sculpture that served as the stairs. From a black mole on his chin, a thin stream of two-foot long checkerboard beard was growing. In the sunlight that fell on him from the street, the Korean looked like a prophet, luring them to visit a Himalayan cave.

Gin grabbed José, Gloria grabbed the dog, and they descended the sculpture.

Gloria's painting, "Trail of Tears," was standing on the floor in a corner, surrounded by dustballs, and already marked in many places by the imprints of numerous shoe soles that, in several spots, totally covered Josito's footprints. In its close vicinity a group of poison-green cocks was sticking out of a dripping, mildewy wall. Huge warts were stuck to the cocks and some oily, whitish substance was sprinkled on them in suspicious places. In the middle of the room a burned, rusty motorcycle was perched, its seat and handbars covered with goldleaf. This was the Korean's creation, one that reeked of oriental style. Just above Gloria's "Poverty" (that, for some reason, usurped a relatively decent part of wall) a huge colorful dragon was hanging from the ceiling on a thread, all tied artfully together from blown-up condoms. Its eyes were two new, round ones. A cardboard sign in the dragon's paws said DEATH AND LOVE IN THE '90s.

An artist who called herself (or himself?) The Dyke, created a series of paintings, consisting entirely of used and surprisingly fresh menstrual tampons. Above all those not-quite-mystical symbolic shapes she (or he) used, a sign, made of the same material, recommended: LEGALIZE ABORTION! These two pieces of art, when inspected from close quarters, turned out to be the source of the rotting, sweetish smell that permeated the whole basement.

"Don't forget to sign your name in our book!" were the Korean's parting words, as he fingered his checkerboard beard in a sagelike manner.

Gloria opened the fat notebook with a fake leather cover. It was empty. Actually, not quite: in its middle, surrounded by pages of angelic white, a weird pattern had been meticulously drawn by a heavy, dirty, shaky hand. The text explained: "That's the magical spiral. The white whip of light. Up to the sky! R."

"Jee-zus, come on, Hubby!" Gloria yelled at Husband, angrily dragging him on his three legs toward the exit. Even so, he'd already managed to leave his territorial markers on several works of art.

Chapter 11

Art

"And you know what? It IS art, it IS art, even though all the shitheads swear it isn't!

"This installation, it IS art, the SPACE they chose for it IS art, it is ART, this is what art IS, the way they put it all TOGETHER, yes, it IS art, they have a RIGHT to do it this way, 'cause that's how the world is turning!

"In today's world, we all sit on each other's heads, we climb down into the depths in order to make it all the way UP; we hang on little threads above each other on several floors in order to be INDIVIDUALISTS. This exhibition, it's an amazing SUCCESS, you see, because it depicts how LOW the real art is today, we gotta BEND DOWN toward it in DARKNESS if we want to really SEE it! You know?

"And, you see, REAL ART is ugly and disgusting and it STINKS, Gin; 'cause LIFE is just like that, and just WHAT would real art be if it didn't depict LIFE?

"This exhibition, it shows quite clearly that there is no ROOM for ART in this shitty world, Gin! I had to pay a thousand dollars, Gin, A THOUSAND DOLLARS, just to get thrown, along with the others, on this heap of junk – and

I'm PROUD, I'm proud of the fact that I've taken part in it, that I AM taking part in it, because art is the PRESENT TENSE, Gin, if you know what I'm saying!

"You gotta BREAK INTO the exhibition hall, if you want to be there, ON A HEAP. And those galleries on Madison, or even in Soho, well, I PISS on those, d'you believe me, Gin? I piss on those, really. THIS is action art, THIS, and THIS, and THIS!

"Jee-zus, Hubby, come on!

"And if you installed a camera somewhere in the street, in New York City, it doesn't matter where, it could be in Midtown, or in Harlem, or in Chinatown, or you could as well just stick the camera out of YOUR OWN WINDOW, and you just leave it there, you don't do anything, you just set everything so that every five minutes, or every minute, or every SECOND it shoots a picture all by itself, then, when you develop that film, Gin, you're gonna find the ABSOLUTE BEST pictures on it, Gin, the absolute best pictures you ever took in your whole LIFE, and that's because every photographer brings HIMSELF into his picture taking, and that's a mistake, you see, because the City doesn't NEED his personality, the City doesn't need HIS eyes, HUMAN eyes. Just set the camera on the automatic mode, and the City will document ITSELF in it, and THAT is art, because THAT is the universal. Every – and any! – moment, EVERY slice of time is ART, every crosscut through reality in this City symbolizes something!

"This City IS art and we all just struggle to express it, grab hold of it in a crosscut through time, and move that one and only shard of time some place else, a bit to the side, so we can all see it, smell it, taste it. Just like you cut a slice out of a pie and put it on a plate and place a fork right next to it. On that slice the KNIFE left its mark when you were cutting it, and THAT is art, the reflected structure of a moment!

"D'you get it, Gin?"

Chapter 12

Art, City

But then art would also be the way in which, on the Lower East Side, the spit-out chewing gums – pink, white, blue and light green – get trampled into the asphalt of the streets.

Art would be the windows of abandoned buildings on 117th Street, right off Manhattan Avenue, in Harlem; windows sealed with cinderblocks that made those beautiful, dying buildings look like beggars blinded by a vicious emperor.

Or art would be three sleepy-eyed seagulls standing on one leg each in a puddle at Kennedy Airport; the darkening blue skies and clouds with a silver lining are reflected in the puddle, as well as the exquisitely grayish tips of the seagulls' wings.

The bark on a thin trunk of a ginkgo tree that, on the corner of 57th Street and 5th Avenue, obediently grows out of a hole in concrete that was assigned to it. Next to a bus stop, the bark got all soft and smooth, thanks to the touch of millions of hands.

The tires of cars and trucks driving through the City serve as brushes, putty knives, scrapers and hammers as they push deeper and deeper into the asphalt the flattened-out beer cans, lost shoe strings and buttons and bags, and thrown-away business cards, and whole handfuls of pennies that the homeless guys on Houston Street and 2nd Avenue had tossed away from their begging cups, angry that they got nothing but copper – and every street, every corner, every square yard of the City becomes an ever-changing mosaic, an impermanent painting on the asphalt, that hungry black canvas.

Art is the skyline of Manhattan as well as the way the weather changes it: the way it sometimes pierces the skies like a proud cornfield and sometimes it bashfully hides inside the clouds that cover the tips of the World Trade Center so perfectly that you can't help yourself, you gotta start thinking that the Twins don't end inside the clouds, that they've broken into the cupola of the skies instead, and only after the clouds disappear, you can start believing again that no gods live on the tips of New York skyscrapers.

Art would be that half-rotten rag that has been lying below the curb on 10th Avenue and 46th Street for as long as anyone remembers, every downpour working it deeper and deeper in between the sewer grating, and every day that rag is a bit more earth-colored, and every day it grows into the earth a little better, into the dirt, into the street, into the City – just like the hair and faces of homeless guys: These, too, as the days go by, look more and more like the sidewalks they sleep on, and like their wet rags, and like their rain-damaged cardboard boxes . . .

Art would be the mangy wayward dogs who, down on Columbia Street, next to the Brooklyn shipyard, stick their muzzles into huge black garbage bags and eat; dogs that run through the streets like desperate hungry hyenas, their tails hanging deep between their legs with tips pointing downwards . . . just like that magical spiral of Randy's that this time, however, points under the ground . . .

And art would be the whores who on East Myrtle Avenue, deep in the guts of Brooklyn, stand on the sidewalk completely naked, the moonlight falling on their hanging washboard bellies . . .

and . . .

And all that meant that even Gin's daily travels across the asphalt somewhat resembled the painting process – just like on a night photograph the back lights of cars trace spectral red lines.

Gin, too, was an artist who was working day after day on a humongous canvas – the Manhattan Island – creating yellow pictures on it with jerky motions of her brush. Her tires stroked the surface of it, leaving their imprint, and Gin, day after day, was choosing again and again how to make her opening brush stroke.

Sometimes she had power over the motion of her brush across the canvas, the motion of her tires across the asphalt, and sometimes she didn't. At one time it was hard for her to choose – at every street corner – whether to go right, left or straight, and at other times she was just like a pingpong ball, constantly sent from one end of the City to another.

The wanderings of each and every one of Gin's nights were tied together by random events as well as minor decisions, forming a Gordian knot of possibilities: chances she didn't make use of, mistakes that screwed up her whole shift, streets she did or did not drive through, customers who she did or didn't have.

Chances were chained one after the other – and Gin was painfully aware that with every YES she loses a NO, with every RIGHT TURN she loses a LEFT TURN or KEEP GOING STRAIGHT, that behind every chance there is a whole mob of other chances hiding, chances that had escaped Gin forever.

It simply wasn't possible to drive along all the streets in all directions at the same time, picking up, in her inflatable Yellow Cab, all the customers and all the adventures AT THE SAME TIME – and the skyscrapers and the lives and the whole City. Every chance cut down on the other chances of the night, and in the end, nothing was left of that variegated tree of possibilities with which she was leaving the garage every day at 5 p.m., but a single, long, entangled line.

Every day Gin with EVERY action of hers was choosing a single one of the possibilities of a certain moment, branching her day into the Tree of Decision.

Along its branches (of which every single twig was hurting her, especially those that didn't exist) Gin was climbing day after day into fragile and entangled chances and serendipities that broke off under her wheels with shattering sounds.

Chapter 13

The Tree

That day,

1. Gin got 2H72 with only a five-minute delay. Alex crammed her butt into the car, sighing amorously. Her nose was attacked by the clouds of exhaust fumes that penetrated the cabin of 2H72 from God knows where and although the drivers complained about it every other day, bringing the car back to the garage for a checkup, none of the mechanics, not even Ramon, was able to locate and plug that microscopic hole in the muffler somewhere. The stench of smog almost overpowered the other stench, that one left on the blue fake leather by Fakim's sweaty T-shirt.

2. "The exhaust fumes smell like hell in here," Gin says, making her way back out, but Alex's palm rests lightly on her tit, the touch gaining in momentum as Alex pushes her back into the cab.

"It will drift away, Gin, Jee-zus Christ. You know what I breathe and all the mechanics here in my garage? And you only open window and . . ."

3. Gin, already made dumb by the stench, does not protest anymore.

4. She doesn't back up, like so many others, in the wrong direction through the one-way 47th Street back onto 11th Avenue. She takes the roundabout route instead, taking West Side Highway to 50th Street.

5. Straight across 11th Avenue.

6. Straight across 10th.

9. It's 5:16 p.m. On the southwest corner of 50th and Broadway, a jerk in a light-colored jacket is standing, urgently lifting his right arm.

"78th and York," he greets Gin as he sits down.

10. "Wanna go through the Park?" Gin suggests.

"What?"

"Up 6th Av and through the Park to 72nd? There won't be so much traffic there."

"Go straight."

"You mean to go crosstown on 50th? Are you sure? But 1st Avenue—"

"Go straight."

11. Gin does what the jerk tells her to do. On 1st Avenue she makes a left – and just like she'd expected, she runs into the metal colossus of all the others who, too, had decided to go Uptown on 1st Avenue at 5:23 p.m. The jerk lifts up his eyes from the paper he's been reading and clicks his tongue testily. It sounds like a hungry swamp, sucking you in by your boot. "How long have you been driving?" he asks angrily. "Couldn't you've chosen a better route?" – "Oh my God, what's taking you so long?" he lets himself be heard on 53rd Street. "You're not AGGRESSIVE at all! God, just take that lane on the left!"

12. Gin takes that lane on the left.

13. A limo driver leans on his horn but the fenders don't bump into one another. Above the waning screech of brakes curses are reaching Gin's ears: "Asshole! Prick! Idiot! Shithead!" Gin gets so sweaty with fright that her back gets glued to the front seat.

"God, was that close," the jerk on the back seat comments and he decides to be nice for a change. He folds his *Wall Street Journal*. "Where are you from? How long have you been here? You speak English pretty well, where did you learn it? How long have you been driving a taxi? How late do you have to work tonight? Aren't you afraid, driving through the night all alone? Where do you live? Is your family here, too? Are you married? Do you have children? How do you like the United States? Oh, yeah, I see, oh, yeah, no, really?"

19. On the northeast corner of 78th and 1st Avenue she gets rid of that businessman. He'd decided to walk that last block.

20. From there, she jumps like a kamikaze toward the left, across six lanes of heavy traffic, because on the southwest corner of 79th Street a lady with an orange hairdo and a cow-spotted coat is standing. Gin hits the brake and stops next to her pumps.

"Oh, a woman!" the lady says delightedly as soon as she slams the door shut. "Boy, it's so nice to see a woman behind the wheel of a cab for a change! Why don't you turn around so I can look at you! Where are you from? How long have you been here? Where do you live – Brooklyn? Is this your own taxi or do you rent it? How do you like the United States?"

In the meantime, the light has changed. Gin starts slowly and timidly moving forward as the cacophony of horn-blowers is pushing her with the force field of their sounds.

"Where do you wanna go?"

"Oh! Oh! Oh my God, I've forgotten to tell you, can you

believe that? But that's only because I was so surprised. Seeing a young woman behind the wheel . . ."

21. A taxicab with a medallion number 7B67, a private one, at least judged by the letter B, touches to Gin's back bumper and begins to push her forward. An angry Haitian inside it is leaning on his horn with his left hand while pounding his forehead with his right, trying to inform Gin that she's missing most of her marbles.

22. "WHERE do you wanna go?"

Gin has about two seconds to think about it. She decides to go straight. She has to go SOMEWHERE or else they're gonna murder her.

"Jee-zus Christ!" the lady screams half a second later. "You should have turned LEFT, I'm going DOWNTOWN! This way we'll lose two blocks. Really, I expected a better service from a WOMAN than I'm getting from all those male bastards . . ."

27. 6:08 p.m. On the corner of Park Avenue, a couple is standing but Gin is stuck on a red light. The man is almost ready to cross the street and jump into her taxi, but the woman lifts up her right arm and Gin has no choice but to watch dejectedly how a sparkling Yellow butterfly with some Egyptian guy in it lands right at their feet.

33. Between 56th and 55th Streets there's a closed lane on Park Avenue. Gin gets stuck. Other taxicabs fly past.

34. One of them picks up a girl on 55th. If it wasn't for him, she would be Gin's.

42. She gets stuck at the traffic lights on 49th Street, which brings her a customer. A young guy in a minimalist-style leather jacket bangs on the hood, gets in, makes himself

comfortable and articulates in a challenging manner: "Astoria. Are you going there or aren't you?"

43. "But of course," Gin replies with the most velvety voice a cabbie can muster. She has to take "ANYBODY ANYWHERE ANY TIME," that's how rule 213 specifies it. Rule 213 deals with "refusals." ($500 fine and you have to show up in taxi-driver's court.)

With her mental eye, however, she already watches a scene in which –

50. – an empty Yellow Cab with a medallion number 2H72 is making its way back toward Manhattan at a snail's speed, across a jammed up, stinky, screaming, horn-blowing, seriously frustrated 59th Street Bridge that (or is it just Gin's imagination?) wiggles on its pylons alarmingly under that huge load of metal. In Gin's pocket, there's $9.50. She could have made $25 or more had she stayed in the City.

51. Down, definitely down 2nd Avenue.

54. 7:38 p.m. On 57th Street a female customer is standing, luring Gin to make a right. Gin is sitting in the rightmost lane. She puts on the signal light, she waves back but –

55. – out of the lane to the left of her, the nasty snout of a Yellow rival is easing out, inch by inch. The cross-direction didn't even get the yellow light yet, and an obdurate African, irritatingly reminiscent of Talibe, blocks Gin's way, almost touching her headlight – and that customer is already opening his door . . .

56. As she's in the right lane, she decides to turn, and some thirty yards later she spots two businessmen standing on the curb. They're not lifting their arms or anything but their whole demeanor somehow shows that they would like a lift.

58. Gin steps on it (to the left of her, competition has appeared) and then lands at their loafers with a jerk. The businessmen get scared, they jump back but – thank God – they're making their way inside. Under their coats both of them have a dark gray jacket, a white dress shirt and a red tie, the classic "power look." Except they're both Sikhs with their heads wrapped up in huge turbans, the same shade of red as their ties.

"How's business today?" they chant in unison. "Sorry, but we only want to go to Lex and 62nd . . ."

The night is rolling forward, the number of chances steadily increasing. This night's Tree of Decisions is branching farther and farther, wider and wider.

Perhaps, had Alex given her, instead of her today's vehicle, the fancy 6B23, in which, believe it or not, the radio was working but, on the other hand, it didn't pick up at all, that Pakistani guy who fought for a fare with her on chance number 316 would have jumped her, after all, and she wouldn't have driven those two drummers, their instruments included, to Park Slope, Brooklyn.

Perhaps, if she was driving 3H74 – in which the transmission acted up – then her car would break down some place in between chances 243 and 244, right in the middle lane on Broadway and 137th, on one of the least pleasant corners of West Harlem she knew, and as soon as she would make it, in a cloud of smog and noise, to the curb, a Dominican driver of a gypsy cab would helpfully lean out of his window and yell at her while leaning on the horn: "*Que pasa*? Problem? Need push, no? Es-pick es-pannis?" – and then Gin would have to call the garage from a payphone on the corner, its receiver all greasy with the pomade used by Dominican drug dealers. Only on the tenth ring or so Ramon would wake up from his sleep all curled up on the floor on a yellowed issue of *The New York Post*, and then he'd – his thumb still stuck in the mouth of an unfinished bottle of Corona Beer – make it up the stairs to

Alex's "office" to answer the phone: "Sarr-vees." And then she'd spend the rest of her shift waiting for them to come and fetch her . . .

And, perhaps, had Alex given her, instead of the stinky 2H72 in which she was getting suffocated, just any other Yellow car he had, then the Park Avenue lady she met on chance number 93 wouldn't wrinkle up her nose – "Oh, it SMELLS in here!" – and turn toward the doorman, "Get me a TAXI, will you?" before slamming the door shut.

And, naturally, in any other car than 2H72 Gin wouldn't have breathed so much of the exhaust fumes that had gotten her high, on a completely different level of experience. That would mean that reality, as it existed just before dawn, would correspond with totally different cells of her brain – and nothing unusual would then take place. But as it happened, this time, when she dragged herself through the yellowish fog all the way to one of the last bifurcations in the chances and opportunities of today's night, she saw it.

At chance number 613, on the corner of 68th and Columbus, the Tree was standing. Tree of Decisions. The long coat he's wearing mingles with the blackness of the night; under one arm he's squeezing a guitar and stretching the other one toward the Universe, like half of a cross. Gin is stuck at a red light there, her heart beating like crazy, because –

614. – a taxi from the cross-direction is getting close to the Tree. It slows down a bit but then passes him, frightened by his looks.

And that's why Gin can land, with that wayward Yellow barge of hers, under the left arm of a wounded cross – and the Tree is making his way inside her car. On his head ALL the chances of tonight's night are gently swaying, in the form of long, thick, entangled dreadlocks. But what do you mean, tonight's night: The entangled and crisscrossy chances of ALL of Gin's nights are growing out of his head like tropical vines, like the branches of breadfruit trees, like sea grass. And the Tree jiggles all those chances to the right and to the left, back and forth and sideways, just like they were a black halo, he sucks up into himself the traffic lights and street lamps – and Gin isn't sure whether she heard well when Clyde leans over to the hole in the partition, a few branches of his hair cascading onto the front seat (where they smell like oceans) and asks politely: "I don't want to be impertinent, I mean, I don't, but have you ever made love in the back seat of this here taxicab?"

Chapter 14

Three Tigers

She had on a long-sleeved T-shirt on which three striped tigers sat. When she arranged the front of it on her body the right way then the noses of the two smaller ones fit exactly over her nipples, the big one was sitting on her belly.

She knew that it turns men on – the way the tigers' noses are sticking out of the fabric, the way the T-shirt is stretched – and when they dare they start stroking the smaller tigers on the face. But Clyde didn't. Clyde just smiled, reached for the biggest tiger and placed his palm on him. He just placed his palm on him. He didn't stroke the tiger; he didn't try to force his hand through the T-shirt closer to Gin's body; he just allowed the heat of his palm to penetrate and permeate her navel, the center of her being – and he smiled – and then, when they were already doing it, he kept his hand on her belly; his musician's hand with long fingers, their last digits calloused from the guitar strings, the guitar, in its black case, was resting idly in the corner; and Gin could feel the thin wall of her belly between his palm and himself; she felt it like it was a fresh, moist clay plaque into which Clyde was engraving some ancient inscription in an ancient tongue.

It was a living, feeling plaque, blood was running through it, and Gin was melting into the dreads . . . into all those choices, chances and possibilities of her taxi-driving nights; she was climbing up every tiny hair on Clyde's head, inside him, into the focal point of decisions as if it was the focal point of distance.

Chapter 15

The First Snow

Josito.
Husband.
Roaches.
Gloria.
Gloria. That traitor whore.

Gin staggered unsteadily into the bathroom and wrapped her head up in a wet rag. Look up, then close your eyelids. Meditation. And as soon as you reach a semi-hypnotic state, keep repeating like a fucking nut:

I DON'T GIVE A SHIT.
I DON'T GIVE A SHIT.
I DON'T GIVE A SHIT.

Like a fucking nut.
Otherwise, it won't work.

Then comes the first snow that falls inaudibly on single-digit streets in the East Village, slowly and imperceptibly turning them into a dream, into a lithograph on which the traces of pedestrians and tires expose the blackness that then turns grayish with more snow.

Gin, in her thoughts, lies down on the black rectangle left after a parked car, letting the snowflakes moisten her soul. Just like when Granny used to whiten the linen on a meadow in front of her cottage in the highlands.

On the hoods of Yellow Cabs the snow is melting a little, thanks to the engine's heat, and then it freezes back in the form of translucent crystals that chop the yellow color up into fragments, like the faucet eyes of dragonflies. On the perpetual puddle in front of Alex's garage the car wheels keep breaking and rebreaking the ice. Down its fragments a rainbow is crawling. It's chopped up, too.

"It's Christmas, you know," Gloria explained to her with an apologetic shrug. "And at Christmas . . . at Christmas every dyke is supposed to spread them for a man." Gin could see her only from the back because at the moment Gloria was in the bathroom, teaching Josito how to pee.

"So it won't grow shut," she added, showing José how to shake it three times at the end.

She scratched her bristles of hair that, as they grew longer, rounded up her skull like she was a bear cub. "Don't you know that?

"And if you think that it was ME who tried to pick HIM up, then . . ." Gloria said, zipping up the diminutive jeans fly. "OK! And now you know how to pee all by yourself!

"All right, I'm SORRY, OK?" Gloria added with forced selflessness. "I had no idea that he meant so much for you . . ."

(I DON'T GIVE A SHIT!

I DON'T GIVE A SHIT!)

Then Gin could hear her own voice, a tiny, teeny, choppy one: "Do you at least have his phone number? Because I DON'T!"

Gloria was wiping Josito's nose on a piece of tissue: "He

promised . . . OK. Blow! Now! That he'd call. And now the other nostril!"

And then she resolved to run into her room where she seated José on her bed, tying his shoes.

Just to make sure Gin wouldn't be able to tell.

Which is that he – when he hanged up his coat in the foyer and pulled his sweater over his head and removed the leather vest he'd had under the sweater, and pulled off those tight-fitting jeans of his, and liberated himself from the G-string he wore underneath the jeans – that he had the ABSOLUTE PERFECT COLOR. Exactly the color that Gloria wore inside her, desperately wishing to have it on her skin. He had a warm-brown color, the kind of color that sweetens under your touch like honey because a million tropical suns are hiding underneath.

Chapter 16

The Razor

In the morning Gloria wrestled Josito out of Gin's arms and brought him to the neighborhood kindergarten on Avenue B while Gin, still half asleep, lifted her eyes up and shut lizard's lids over them.

I DON'T GIVE A SHIT!
I DON'T GIVE A SHIT!
I DON'T GIVE A SHIT!

She let this sentence lull her to sleep like it was a child's pacifier, and when she woke up shortly before noon, she still half believed it. To her great relief, she found out she was home alone, with Husband her only company. As soon as she sat up on her mattress, Husband gave a yip and commenced to chew her big toes. And so she decided to make use of that peace and quiet, she decided to cut her veins open, she most likely doesn't have AIDS but that's purely good luck nowadays . . . and she already started to imagine how the funeral parlor people (or, perhaps, coroners?), dressed in space suits, would lift her up from the reddened bathtub, with disgust and extreme care, but she didn't find any razor in the bathroom, just the little electric device Gloria used to shave her legs. And so she went out to buy it but then, just a couple yards from the main door, squashed in between a dogshit and a beer bottle cap, a razor was lying. It wasn't even rusty.

Gin carefully picked it by the end that wasn't sharp, she was careful not to wound her fingers, she didn't want to get AIDS from this razor, it was clear that this razor got dulled while somebody was using it to get coke ready for snorting, on the surface of a little pocket mirror. With this razor's blade he was slicing the crystals that were too large, making them tiny, and then he arranged the white dust into glistening lines, and the lines got reflected in the mirror, un-Earthlike just like a marble staircase – they already let him peek at that illusory world behind the mirror, and then that someone was making tiny incisions on the tips of his fingers with this razor, he wanted to test what pain feels like when you're high on coke, and when nothing was left of those white crystals, then he started desperately licking that mirror, making sure not a single speck of dust was left on it, and then he started licking this RAZOR, and as he was shaking a little, he cut his tongue, and this little wound did hurt him, the cocaine high was ebbing away, and he, all cramped up, rolled himself up into a ball like a porcupine whose quills, unfortunately, grow on his belly, and –

And Gin, her mood uplifted thanks to the disgusting fate of that razor, carried it home, getting the tips of her fingers acquainted with the razor's surface. Her thumb and forefinger were almost touching one another, the razor was very thin, it reminded her of a condom, that dam that divides life and death, that divides bodies – and at times like these it's advisable to divide bodies with a latex wall; bodies have become fortresses, desperately lonely, standing on a bluff above a river . . .

Gin filled the bathtub with water. She circled her wrist with that razor, very lightly, then a little harder, but the latex wall of her vein gave way a little under the razor's edge, bouncing it off. Gin was surprised by that resistance. Her body refused to become part of eternity; it refused to be permeated by anything; actually, the body itself was so usefully divided into rooms and compartments and enclosed spaces. Organs wanted to be separated even though they functioned together. Even the walls of her veins fought back.

Suicide presents a problem. It's not easy to execute. The bubble we got born into isn't so easy to burst.

Not talking about the fact that after death, they zip you up into a black plastic bag. Perhaps they do it in spite. So you can't get fused with the Universe no matter what.

Gin zapped out of the bathroom, and before the water had time to trickle off her, she threw herself on Gloria's paintings.

She picked the canvases off the floor, from the walls, from the top of the fridge and from the bed – and holding them by the edges, she cut them from top to bottom.

Like when you tear your shirt into strips so you can bandage a car-crash victim.

The razor (it was probably still high) hungrily bit into the canvases. It tore thick threads, made even thicker by paint, from them. It cut through the strokes of Gloria's brush. It negated her compositions. It cut the roaches that got stuck to them in half.

After a while, in a colorful mess on the floor, precisely the same branches and vines were twisting like the ones that Clyde had on his head.

Chapter 17

Harlem

On each of the seven milk crates that Gin put down into the first layer of that year's snow on the corner of Avenue C and 7th Street, there is an inscription, hot-ironed into the plastic:

ILLEGAL POSSESSION OF THIS CASE VIOLATES THE MILK CASE RECOVERY ACT N.J.P.L. 1982 CHAPTER 213. VIOLATION OF THIS ACT IS SUBJECT TO FINE AND/OR IMPRISONMENT

Those seven crates, picked up who knows where, contained the essence of Gin's whole life. Actually, her whole life, too, now seemed to her stolen and illegal. A coffee mug that had MINE written on it. A 12-inch skillet. A teapot. Shoes. Several plastic roach traps she had bought just a few days ago, which she now felt obligated to pick up from the corner and from under the sink, so they wouldn't stay there for Gloria to catch roaches with. Three cans of tuna and half a green pepper that smelled of vitamins. A fragrant soap in a thin plastic bag.

Several photos people had given her. A bunch of letters. A marriage certificate. A rainbow bed sheet, stolen in her New York apartment number six. A long-sleeved T-shirt on which three tigers with touch-and-feel noses were sitting.

Gin's whole life was standing on the corner, squashed into seven illegal milk crates. It looked cold and uncomfortable, its corners sticking out of the geometrical holes in the crates. It was slowly being covered with hesitant, huge flakes of snow.

And when Gin hailed a taxi and squeezed her crates into the trunk, they left dry, dark patterns on the sidewalk.

"Hi," Gin said, making herself comfortable on the back seat, "116th and Powell Boulevard."

"Park Avenue?" the driver asked. "And what street do you say?"

"NOT Park Avenue. 116th and Powell Boulevard. Powell Boulevard, that's the continuation of 7th Avenue. North of Central Park."

"I still don't understand you," the driver turned to her apologetically. "What did you say? Central Park West?"

"7th Avenue," Gin articulated as clearly as she could. "Avenue Se-ven. Street one-one-six. You can go up on the FDR."

"What, you want to go to Brooklyn?" The taxidriver got all frizzled up. "At this hour? Well, I don't know, I'll have to go to the garage—"

So Gin leans toward the hole in the plastic partition, in the partition that divides the front seat from the rear, the driver's bubble from the passenger's, and yells at the top of her lungs: "Jee-zus fuckin' Christ! Just go to Harlem!"

The driver didn't say anything for a while. He seemed all lost in deep thought. He looked like someone who really likes to work. Like someone who works much too much. She could see that he really meant it when it came to making money; she could see that time and distances had turned into dollars in his head a long time ago. That his horizons, rather than blue, became decidedly greenish. That somewhere above his horizon a greenish bank note with a one and six zeroes on it was neatly glued to the sunny skies. Jean-Pierre looked like he loved water sprites, just for the color. That he avoided parks and nature whenever possible because the green hue of the woods, all piled up so carelessly, painfully reminded him of the stashes of money he didn't have yet. Fall was like a stock market crash for him.

Jean-Pierre looked like his brain didn't contain gray creases but, rather, greenish mobster rolls. That under his jet-black skin not red but dollar-green blood was throbbing.

Jean-Pierre Lefrac's temple vein got dangerously overfilled with that green blood of his. It began to contract spasmodically.

Jean-Pierre had been driving since 5 a.m. that morning and he was in no mood for surprises. He wanted everything to fall into categories. He wanted everything to be simple. Easy to understand.

I pick you up on Houston Street and 6th Avenue. You're going to 58th Street. Six bucks. On Broadway and 56th Street I pick up someone else and on the Upper West Side I get a fiver, without a tip but so what. I drive through the Park from west to east –

But he'd never dreamed that – here, on Avenue C (where he wouldn't bother to go, anyway, only he was driving that Puerto Rican guy with a shaved head and baggy pants with their crotch somewhere at his knee, baggy pants at least four guns could fit under – he could have killed Jean-Pierre dead with at least four guns without a blink . . . Jean-Pierre put all dudes like this one into the "nigger" category even though he was just a bit grayish, and this one did pay in the end, that's true)

Jean-Pierre wasn't just ready for THIS, for a WHITE girl who'll make her way inside his cab –

Without a word, Jean-Pierre pushed a button that opened the trunk of his cab. Then he waddled out of the car.

He circled it in a gait that testified to what the number on Jean-Pierre's hack license had already revealed to Gin: he'd been living in the space between the steering wheel and the front seat for six years or so. During that time, Jean-Pierre developed a gut of a shape that fit perfectly into the gap between his spine and the wheel. He grew into his cab and took on the shape of the space inside the cabin, the same way some unfortunate circus children were forced in the past to live in huge pitchers in order that they would grow into them and become pitcher-shaped freaks that could be shown to audiences for a fee. Jean-Pierre's gut was useful, after all: he could rest fast-food containers on it like it was a private little restaurant table. And although Jean-Pierre was still capable of turning the wheel without hurting his belly with it, walking wasn't that easy at all. His belly lacked something to lean on.

Jean-Pierre solved this problem by opening the car trunk as wide as it would go, plopping his gut on the edge of the metal.

He stretched his arms inside the trunk, took a wheezing breath and threw out Gin's box number one. It flopped sideways and a tiny radio, six apples, a book of poems by Halas and innumerable sweated-through T-shirts of Gin's flew out of it. The apples rolled away in the snow, each leaving a trail behind it. The book of poems flew flat across the snow, leaving a brush stroke in it.

"*Merde*!" Jean-Pierre commented, throwing out box number two.

"*Mon dieu*!" he said and got all sweaty, lifting up box number three. It was heavy as it contained Gin's collection of Zen stones.

"Harlem, my ass!" he added in English while getting rid of box number four. He paid no head to Gin who was waving her hands in the air, yelling that every taxidriver must go to Harlem, there's a rule for that, rule two-thirteen, and I have your medallion number and your hack number and everything, and that means you'll have to pay five hundred bucks for a fine, if you never heard of it, sweetheart, and if you want I'll file a complaint and it'll be, See ya in taxi court . . .

Box number five landed on the concrete and Gin fell silent for a while, wiping night cream of the Oil of Olay brand from the roach traps.

"No, miss, you crazy," Jean-Pierre said, leaning over to pick up box number six. "I no go to Harlem. I not crazy. Me, no."

He dumped box number seven to the general mess and closed the trunk. Before he had the time to make it three blocks north in the direction to 14th Street, his taxicab got as green with rage as were Jean-Pierre's horizons.

Gin was standing on the sidewalk on Avenue C and 7th Street and in the seven stolen milk crates (into each one of which somebody or something had branded with a hot iron that its illegal possession is subject to prosecution) the essence of her destiny was hiding, slightly mixed with snow.

She was looking for some taxicab but none were driving by at the moment.

Instead, that homeless guy Randy was approaching her from the south. In front of him he was pushing a cart, most likely stolen from a supermarket, and behind him, he was pulling a perfectly graphic, black-and-gray-and-white strip of tracks. All of a sudden, Gin felt incredibly close to him. That's because from the sides of the cart exactly the same milk crates were sticking as the ones that were lying at Gin's feet. Gin had one dark blue and three light blue ones, a brick-colored one and a vermilion-colored one, and one in the hue of healthy human stool. Randy's crates were purple and green, all sprayed over with weird silver symbols. Gin was quite sure that their colors were part of a scheme. From Randy's cart, a whole forest of well-used brooms was sticking into surprising heights. These were Randy's antennas. He always needed to be touching the sky.

"Hi, Gin!" Randy hollered. "Wouldn't you have some loose change on you? It's such a beautiful day today . . ."

Gin obediently started to rummage through her pockets. She put fifty cents into Randy's palm. It was all gray with dust but warm with high hopes.

"Wow," Randy said, wondering, and drew an aerial circle around Gin's mess with his thumb. "You going for a walk or what?"

"I'm moving Uptown," she explained. "Downtown's not that good for me."

"Uptown!" Randy beamed. "Up! Into the sky! That's where we all move. All the time!" He lifted his eyes and cast an upward glance that wasn't pious although it looked like one, all the way up his brooms, to the place from which snowflakes were falling.

Then, with a lot of huffing and puffing but without asking for a pay, he helped to move all of Gin's boxes to the bus station on 14th Street.

Harlem.

Har-lem.

Ha-a-lem.

Gin was testing the word on her tongue. And not just on her tongue: under it, too, and on her palate and on the back of her teeth. She tested how one's mouth opens wide at the breathy first syllable, how the tongue then lifts up to the soft palate – that's the moment when you're all ready to pronounce that "r," but then you reconsider in a split second and you prolong the "a" instead: you pronounce that "a" twice, one right after the other, like a stammering waltz. Ha-a-lem.

It seems that white people don't even know how to pronounce Harlem the right way, and then they like to hate the place just because they've robbed themselves of the magic of its name.

When you pronounce Harlem "Harr-lem," the word loses its rhythm, it's halved by the hard New York "r" like it was a chainsaw, a machine gun report. In its white-man style pronunciation Harlem carries with it all the terror that white men feel from it. It sounds like a desperate white motherfucker in a sweated-through suit who, by some fatal mistake, by some unfortunate turn of his destiny's wheel, found himself in the three-digit streets above Central Park: in those streets whose three-digitedness is so obvious that from the words "Hundred-and-" only a mumbling "Hun" is left in the mouths of those who live there. In Harlem nobody lives on "Hundred-and-

Sixteenth Street"; they live on "Hun-Sixteen", and that mumbled "Hun" serves as a reassurance for them, reassurance that they are really at home there.

The bus was making its way up Madison Avenue and Gin was stroking her mouth with this word.

Ha-a-lem.

On the lips of every passenger on the bus the potentiality of this word was sitting in a specific shape. She tried to imagine that word on the lips of a businessman who got on on 42nd Street (he stretches his lips in an unnatural way, he trips over the very first syllable; he simply doesn't possess the rhythm, the sliding motion of the tongue and all, he feels like he was trying – his Brooks Brothers suit and all – to do the hip-hop in a black nightclub on Leonard Street, but the music didn't do shit for him).

An older white woman with an armload of shopping bags from Food Emporium got scared a bit at first but then she let herself be talked into it – and in front of Gin's mental ear Harlem appeared, long and thin, like a turd, trying to make its way out through a fear-constricted asshole. ("But I don't live there, I don't!" the little lady adds right away. "I will get off at 95th!" And she shivers because she knows that the spirit of Harlem, some kind of gooey specter or God knows what, makes its sneaky way down year after year so that one day . . .)

But the farther Uptown they climbed up Madison, up that spiral of Randy's, up the ladder of streets, the more populated the bus became with people of a completely different sort.

People carrying huge radios in their hand. People whose hairdo consisted of geometrical patterns or words like DEATH, REVENGE or X shaved into the closely cropped hair on their skulls. People who bopped down the aisle of the bus in hip-hop jeans with their crotch down on their knees and in untied "con" sneakers. People in whose mouth the word Harlem swung on three lazy, rhythmical waves. These people belonged.

On 116th Street, Gin was welcomed by Talibe, his surprised

half-smile framed by the scratchy door of apartment #5C (from which the well-known smell of African inedibles, oriental oils and incense sticks was emanating).

"Hi," Gin said, feeling embarrassed.

Talibe glanced at the seven boxes with his wife's life extract in them, then he lifted his gaze up to her, fingered the good-luck charm on his chest, and stammered: "*Mais chérie* . . . What you do in Ha-a-lem?"

And in his mouth, even though he didn't really speak English, that word possessed a three-syllable gracefulness, it performed a little waltz on his tongue. Gin tripped over the sky-blue box number six and proceeded, to Talibe's great chagrin, to kiss him on those lips that knew how to pronounce the word Harlem.

Chapter 18

God of the Garage

Gin was standing on the rainbow-colored oil slick in front of Alex's garage, decked out in a purple Dior coat she had found in the summertime on a pile of garbage on the corner of 56th and Sutton Place. She had just managed to avoid Alex's groping paw. But, of course, Alex had mastered a whole array of pawings, and now, when Gin's rear end didn't stick out of her sweater so seductively (as he called it), he started a new method of inconspicuous, stealthy sticking of his hand under her coat.

A few drivers, shivering with cold, stomped on that rainbowy oil slick, getting the soles of their boots covered in it, and sharing the horrors of last night with each other in several languages. Thick clouds of yellow fog wafted from the garage because Ramon the car mechanic, a gauze mask on his nose, was presently yellowing the cars. The fog settled on everything: on the spare parts strewn all over the place, on the floor, on Ramon's eyebrows that stood erect above his mask like some humongous golden scarab's branched antennae. Even the rainbow in front of the garage got its share of the yellow drops, as did Alex's pantleg and a cobweb in a corner by the gate.

Gin's day partner Fakim hasn't showed up yet. Although there was at least seven minutes left until the five o'clock shift change, Gin started, like a real cabbie, to tap her wristwatch nervously, throwing accusatory glances at Alex.

"You're right!" Alex said, moving closer to her. "That son of Allah he come always late. Every day!"

(Gin knew it wasn't exactly true, but she'd be against herself if she defended Fakim now.)

"But if he's late another one minute, he the whole hour have to pay. Fifteen dollars! I will be not nice to him. And the fifteen dollars you get, Gin! Because I will not let some son of Allah rob the money off my best chauffeur!"

Alex's paw was long and stealthy; right now it was exploring Gin's rut just above the laced rim of her panties.

"My BEST chauffeur, Gin!" he repeated significantly.

And then he continued without missing a beat: "You know what that Mexican did to me?" (Alex invariably referred to Ramon as "*etot Meksikanetz.*" Honduras must have been a blank spot in Alex's mental world atlas.) "One day early morning I come here into the garage, it wasn't five in the morning yet, but sometimes I cannot sleep, you understand, Gin, because I have this haunting feeling that something rotten in my garage is happening, and that night something was telling me, go and look what those motherfuckers are stealing from you, in your own garage, and of course: I don't yet have time to park, and I see that Mexican running away with a bag this big – a bag of what? Spare parts, what else? It is clear to me right from beginning, Gin. Open the bag, you motherfucker! I yell to him, and he, when he sees me, runs away like fucking rabbit, but I run after him, I snatch the bag from him, and from it falls away a big-big-big pile of headlights and sparkplugs and tail-light covers, and screws and everything, so I punch him in the teeth, until he falls into the big mess, and I tell him, Now you pick up this all! One after the other. And quick. Ball joints. Nuts. Thermostats. For brakelights and headlights you get one in the teeth, for brake plates you get two, and for each screw I can see in this pile I give you FOUR because you screwed me over, you fucking no good son of Mexican bitch! And then I tell him: Now you think I fire you, right? So you croak somewhere in the street. But don't worry, Alex is not like that. I just deduct all these shits from your pay, and, by the way, do you know that I was champion of Soviet Union in boxing? You don't know it, you dummy? Now I every day come here, EVERY DAY, when you not expect it, and I make you my own personal punchin' bag, until I box all that stealing away from your head. Until you beg me to forgive you! Until you kiss my legs from gratitude! Tell me, where would you spend winter, if it isn't for me? In shelter, so they will cut your throat? On park bench, so you freeze to the death? Here you have beautiful, cozy, heated taxi garage, I have it here only for you all. You understand, Gin? And he do this to me!"

Alex shook his head dejectedly and made a motion as if kicking a pigeon that, cooing in a low voice, hobbled dangerously near his loafer. The pigeon jumped up, fluttering its wings. But since the time it became a part of the taxi garage it has unlearned how to fly. It collapsed back to the ground and limped away, parting the oily rainbow with its tail feathers.

"And from that time, Gin, whenever I show up, the Mexican is so afraid he hide in the engine, not even his legs are sticking out, but I always pull him out and give him one in the teeth. And because he never has the smallest idea when I show up, Gin, I am in this Mexican's eyes – well, why should not I say it: I AM GOD! Because we also never know when the Almighty is watching us. When his punishing hand will fall upon us. I am in my own garage GOD, my dear Gin!"

Meanwhile, seven minutes have passed. It was 5 p.m. on the dot. From the lights on Eleventh, Fakim Fakem took off. He imprudently parked right next to Alex. Alex threw himself on his door, pulled Fakim out of the car the same way a magician might pull a bunny out of a 10-gallon hat, and yelled while shaking him in his grip: "That how you return from your shift, you no good Arab motherfucker?! You pay to her for whole hour she lost. Fifteen dollars! Right now! I don't wanna hear nothing – gimme the money!"

Gin, from behind Alex's back, motioned to Fakim not to take this so seriously. But Fakim wriggled his way out of his boss's embrace, straightened his T-shirt on his back with a cormorant-like motion, walked around his cab with the gait of a driver who just finished a twelve-hour shift, tore off the Coors Gold Beer can that served as a radio antenna from the car and hit Laila the dog with it.

While so doing, he mumbled his own nickname incessantly, the same way a Buddhist monk keeps chanting the magical syllable "om."

And that's how a brand new era began for Alex's garage: It could be called the Tow Truck Era, that later, thanks to Alex's despair, turned into the Era of Alex, King of All Pushers.

This is not to say that until then Alex's cars didn't ever break down. According to the unofficial statistics, even the newest garage cab breaks down at least once in two or three weeks and then returns to the garage in a less than glamorous manner, hooked up nose down to the rear end of a tow truck, like a defeated Yellow warrior. And Alex's Yellow herd certainly didn't belong among the newest. The day drivers as well as the night drivers have long ago gotten used to the fact that once in a while something goes wrong with their car, and, save for two or three apoplectic drug users, nobody complained about it. The car runs, then it quits running, if you happen to have a passenger at that particular moment, you kick him out with a curse, then you open the hood to see whether the problem is fixable with a few magical motions. Then you call the garage and, sipping coffee you've bought in a corner deli, you wait for them to come and fetch you. An incident like that is not pleasant, to be sure. Obviously, you lose some money. On the other hand many find it an almost welcome distraction from the blurry Yellow tediousness of your mundane job.

Alex's drivers have learned by heart every trouble that could be expected to pester this or that Yellow car, and drove accordingly. From the intensity of the warning sounds in the chassis, the axles or the engine many of them could recognize the exact minute when it was advisable to return to the garage. Then, with a victorious air, they made it to 47th and 11th in a cloud of blue smoke from the transmission, or they rode down from a little slope on 10th Ave with a stalled engine, sometimes dragging a tailpipe in an explosion of sparks. They arrived without any brakes whatsoever and managed to come to a stop on the curb, barely avoiding a crash with the humongous green dumpster.

To make a long story short, each and every one of Alex's autos suffered from time immemorial with annoying but, for an old hand, predictable flaws. Flaws that Ramon kept fixing, and because they kept repeating themselves to death, he got really good at fixing them.

This time of peace and relative troublelessness, however, ended the moment Alex became God. The drivers couldn't count on the engine's warning sounds anymore. Not that these sounds disappeared, they were exactly the same as ever before. Only now they wouldn't allow you to predict what would happen in the next quarter of an hour, or even in the next minute.

Alex's cars began to break down at a rate that even the most experienced senior cabbies couldn't recall having seen before.

It seemed that, as soon as Alex decided to become God, Ramon decided to become Satan. He concentrated all his resentment against Alex into tiny little gremlins who he then dexterously placed into the carburetor, the battery, the tires or the transmission. That's where the gremlins sat quietly, awaiting their chance.

Alex's cars began to break down in an almost poetic manner.

On 3Y50 the horn quit working. Fakim Fakem was going crazy, when, stuck in heavy traffic, he couldn't express his feelings sonorously. The car, though, perhaps in order to make up for this frustration, blew its horn on its own whenever he made a right turn. Every attempt to fix the horn ended up the same – unsuccessful, even when Ramon was not around. As soon as the driver of 3Y50 made it to the garage, the horn did what it was supposed to do, and Alex kicked the driver back into the street. In fact, even other car problems mysteriously disappeared the minute the wheels touched the asphalt of West 47th Street and the neighboring blocks, only to reappear immediately after Alex yelled a few insults at the driver and sent him back to "go to hell to make money."

Transmissions didn't break down gradually, as they should: first, it has trouble shifting between second and third gear, then even first gear emits a strange humming sound, and only then the car quits running. Transmissions broke instantly, with a yelp of pain. When the car was towed to the garage and examined for three hours, it became evident that all it needed was the adjustment of a few tiny screws. The next day the transmission got messed up again, in precisely the same manner.

The battery didn't warn you that if you park for a little while to shovel down a plate of lo mein in a Chinese restaurant, it wouldn't allow you to restart the car when you sat back behind the wheel.

Tires didn't go flat during lovely weather in some quiet and safe neighborhood but invariably in the worst slum a taxidriver ever entered, or when a snowstorm whisked through town.

During the torrential rains, snows and hurricanes that the winter of that year was rich in, a lot of Ramon's gremlins decided to go berserk. The windshield-wiper control kept breaking off just when it began to sleet. The chauffeurs arrived at the garage with useless wipers and an inch-thick layer of snow on the windshield. Their heads were stuck out through the window and icicles grew in their beards.

The heating system froze and the ventilator filled your cabin with bluish exhaust fumes.

When you put on your left signal lights, the right ones started blinking.

The high-beam lever turned the radio on.

And in most taxis, something strange happened to the meter. Sometimes, when the car hit a bump, the fare disappeared from the meter, replaced with a big, fat zero and a turned on "vacant" light. Of course, this happened invariably when the cabbie was approaching his destination somewhere in deep Brooklyn, a cheap customer in the car, who "refused" to believe that the meter, before it turned itself off, really had showed $18.50, "because he always pays twelve, or doesn't he?"

The reality began to resemble Gin's old nightmare.

The yellow roof light that distinguishes an empty taxi from a loaded one, went cuckoo. Around five o'clock in the evening, when EVERY New Yorker wants a cab, it refused to turn off, although the meter was on. This meant that hopeful potential customers threw themselves in the middle of the road, convinced they were hunting down an empty taxi. On the other hand, late at night, when passengers are scarce, the lightbulb decided to go off permanently, making the potential passengers too lazy to even raise their hand.

The doors refused to open or close, and many a passenger suffered through a ride holding the door latch to keep from falling out as the car sped up the avenue.

The trunk locks got a taste for breaking, usually in the middle of the hustle and bustle at Kennedy Airport. Desperate passengers with their luggage trapped in the trunk, ten minutes to takeoff, pounded mercilessly on the closed trunk, or on anything remotely yellow, and on their cabdriver, threatening to sue them all.

The front seats usually got somewhat loose and shifted freely back and forth. When a driver stepped on the gas a bit he slid back so much he could barely reach the wheel. When he hit the brakes, he also hit his chin on the steering wheel.

These, however, were only the most innocent jokes of Ramon's impish spirits. Very often the spirits didn't even waste their time on silly kid stuff of this sort. Instead, they simply stalled the car out. As far away from the mother garage as possible, of course.

Alex barely got any sleep at all. He stayed in the garage overnight, battering Ramon, picking up the phone that rang incessantly, and dispatching tow trucks to the four winds.

Then it dawned on him that he simply couldn't afford tow trucks anymore. He decided he'd push the stalled cars back to the garage with his own Buick. He had to buy a map in order to do that. He didn't know the City quite as well as his drivers did. Often he got lost and drove around Queens or Brooklyn for hours before he found the disabled Yellow.

Then, invariably, he yelled a few insults at the driver and pushed him back to the garage.

This troublesome trip without the engine, lights, power brakes and power steering on, without all the technology that, under different circumstances, made a driver's life easier but now turned against him, wasn't made any less difficult by Alex's bragging: "I am best pusher in the world! Put it to neutral, my darling! We be in ten minutes home! As sure as my name is Alex!"

"Remember this African half-wit, Gin, yes, that tall-tall one, do you know what happen to him? No?" Alex asked a rhetorical question and his profile, for that moment, looked like a falcon's. "Yes, I kick him out. All way. Because do you know what he do to me? No, you not able to imagine that, Gin! He drove somebody to Pennsylvania! And in a total, complete hole of town somewhere in Mechanicsburg his car breaks down on him. 5P68. Can you imagine bigger motherfucker, Gin? And then he call me: It don't run, he says, please, please, send somebody get me! And I tell to him: Mechanicsburg, right, can't you find a one fucking mechanic in whole Mechanicsburg so he will fix the cab? Are you REALLY such dummy? And then – do you know what I did then, Gin? I tell him, yes, yes, yes, I'm going there to fetch you, I am on my way, I am speeding to you, I'll in two hours be there – and then, Gin, then I let him wait two days there! Don't go anywhere, I tell to him, don't leave my car alone for one second, don't you know that in Mechanicsburg mechanics steal spare parts from Yellow Cabs because they like yellow color too very much? And he didn't step away from that car, believe it or not. Hungry, thirsty, frozen and unshit, he wait there for me, like stupid dummy! And he goes: Can I have cup of coffee now? But I tell him: As soon as we back! And without any accident I pushed him on the highway all the way. I am the best pusher in the world, you can believe that, Gin! And then I kick him out. Don't ever stick your snout around here, you stupid African, I tell to him, because what I am supposed to do with a motherfucker who don't even know that with 5P68 he to Pennsylvania just cannot go?"

It is not clear whether Alex had the slightest suspicion that the formidable Era of Yellow Cars That Broke Down All the Time and Everywhere was the doing of Ramon's gremlins.

Half of the cabbies left his garage – and those more stable, or more loyal, or more stupid, Gin included, stayed. Perhaps they were too lazy to look for a new boss, perhaps they were fascinated by the ways in which the cars broke down, or perhaps they were pacified by Alex's promises that in no time he would provide brand new and absolutely perfect vehicles for their butts to ride around.

Ramon still lived in the garage, garbed in the same pair of soiled overalls, so soaked with gas that they have long ago become unified with his skin into a single stinking mass. Scared of Alex, he crawled so deep under the cars' hoods that not even the heels of his oil-saturated sneakers showed – and as soon as Alex left the garage, he proceeded to plant a few fresh gremlins here and there, and then he lay exhausted on a sheet of newspaper on the garage floor with his finger stuck into a Corona beer bottle's mouth. The bottle became his pacifier.

Sure, he enjoyed less peace than before.

And whenever Alex, God of the Garage and King of All Pushers, pushed one of the sick cars into his garage, Ramon's face stuck out from under a hood. And it was hard to tell whether certain irregularities on that face were merely the result of Alex's punching, or whether Ramon, under swellings and bruises, sneered at him with a victorious air.

Chapter 19

Comebacks

And that's why Gin now spent several hours every night in the company of the gremlins, usually at places where she wouldn't be parking at all if she was luckier.

The car – naturally – stalled out only in the least pleasant streets, after all, it was programmed to do that, but it sometimes seemed to Gin that, in addition to everything else, Ramon's gremlins were fucking with her soul.

Her Yellow, which was constantly falling apart, guided her way through all the neighborhoods she ever lived in in New York City.

She had to do some emergency parking less than half a block away from the house in which she had lived through her pasta feasts. She fought the idea for a minute but in the end she couldn't help herself: she simply had to ring the bell of that . . . (that junkie! that jerk! that . . . man who wasn't so easy to forget) but a woman opened the door.

The car died on her in the East Sixties, and after an hour or so it began to seem to her that the stench of seven cats was penetrating into the cab. The stench of seven cats that lived, ate, shit and pissed in a single concrete cubicle from which the only window leads to a shaft, tiled in grass-green.

The car refused to work in Greenpoint, Brooklyn, and Gin just couldn't fail to remember how Manhattan – then – stretched its skyline toward her like welcoming arms.

The car went out to lunch in Chinatown and so she locked the taximeter in the trunk and went to see whether that photographer who had helped her so much so long ago still lived under the same roof through which stale dead sperm cells were seeping toward him.

The car took her for a walk in the Bronx, as well, and Alex – truly mad at her for even going to such a middle of nowhere, because only them niggers live in the Bronx and she's got no business driving them niggers in HIS taxicab! – would hardly believe that, while he, the rescuer, spent two hours trying to find his way to her through the ghetto, Gin managed to visit a certain drummer with whom she had lived for a while long ago and who, on one hand, really and truly pissed her off all the time because he often decided, in the middle of the night, to sit down behind his drums and wake up the whole building, but then, soon afterwards, he made up for it by bringing the same drumming rhythm to the fucking that followed.

The car made it possible for her to watch the blue ocean pensively from the middle lane of Belt Parkway right under the Verazzano Narrows Bridge that complemented the color of the sea with two fragile-looking neon-blue arcs. The car's whole electric circuit went haywire, so Gin had to leave her Yellow right there and then, and wander half a mile to the nearest phone booth. When she came back she found out that somebody had crashed into her Yellow from the back a bit, it did make sense, after all, the car was barely visible as it sat in the middle of the highway with its lights out. Then she just sat in it, expecting another bang any second; she sat there, parting the traffic with her cab. The river of cars flew swooshing by, wild and angry, and she felt like an unfortunate boulder, flung by the hand of one god or another into the middle of a mountain stream.

And that was one of the very few moments when Gin's thoughts ran away across the ocean and into Europe; that was one of the PERFECT stops she experienced in New York City, a perfect stop, made even more powerful by the movement of dozens of other cars just a few inches away from her. A whole bunch of memories, distant in both space and time, got replayed in her head with great intensity, making so little sense that when the King of All Pushers arrived in his Buick to save her, Gin had to flutter her eyelids really fast and make sure the lights of passing cars wouldn't swipe across her face.

Ramon's gremlins must have been stronger than her own recollections. Almost every night, they made her spend hours and hours in places generally considered unsafe. And they made her visit her INNER timescapes, too, timescapes that she wouldn't dare to enter otherwise.

Those magically claustrophilic spaces underneath highway overpasses, under the subway el, at the bases of bridges and in the armpits of exit ramps!

That formidable mass of iron, concrete and asphalt, those steel constructions, arches, ropes and connecting beams that tied the City to itself, to distances, to the skies! Those shiny-bright primary colors – blue, yellow, red – somebody painted the steel with, making the whole City look like the work of a colossal sculptor of the constructivist period.

Those corners at the bases of arches and under highway crossings, right there where they were touching the Earth. Those miraculously dry places, filled with brown-gray, greasy big-City dust the ancient origins of which reminded her of the Cro-Magnon caves. Those tiny spaces, each of them with a majestically arched ceiling, those tiny spaces that can hold one lousy gray mattress, one New Yorker with a history and one bottle of brandy.

People from the deepest depths of New York constructivism, all gray with dust, shuffled on shaking, dusty legs toward Gin. Dust covered the palms of their hands, their eyes, the blisters on their feet oozing with puss. There was dust in the creases on their faces – faces outside of sex, outside of age, outside of race – the dusty creases on their faces copied the creases of their gray brain matter so their thoughts, every bit as dusty as themselves, could live right on their foreheads.

Those dead-end streets of Brooklyn and Queens, sticking above the City's highways and main arteries, their ends all wrapped up in razor wire to make sure that suicides, attracted by free fall and speeding cars, wouldn't have it so easy.

Those masses of concrete that made the movement of others easier but didn't work that way for you because you reached them from the back somehow. The concrete walls at the rear end of streets. Neighborhoods, gutted by main City arteries.

Gin now spent hour after motionless hour in spaces made for the purpose of being driven through really fast. Their vibration inoculated her head with the rhythm that can be heard only by those who for one reason or another had to stop in a City where everybody rushes and runs somewhere. The electric waves in her brain that got activated by that rhythm were awfully reminiscent of a very pleasant, repeated and never-quite-completed death.

It almost seemed to her that the cars that swooshed around her were an abyss, some kind of motionless fluid against which Gin, at sixty miles an hour, kept falling and falling and falling.

And while she was stuck, let's say, in Williamsburgh, Brooklyn, right next to the river, and Manhattan's skyscrapers stretched their distant lights toward her the same way a snail stretches out his eyes on stalks, Gin would climb out of the stalled-out car and pace back and forth down the street, the same way lions in a zoo tend to walk around, only the wires of HER cage were imaginary, they resembled stretchable rubber threads that kept her in the space right around the Yellow invalid –

They prevented her from sneaking around a corner, they didn't allow her to cross the street, they ordered her not to come too close to the other end of the block where some guys in hooded sweatshirts were stomping with cold; and they advised her not to stroll through the light of a street lamp – not just because that might make her a better target for a whimsical bullet from a local gun, but mostly because of that monstrous shadow the streetlamp's light would stretch Gin into – a shadow reminiscent of her own puffed-up cadaver.

Gin was scared.

And so she marched through those neighborhoods in which her car decided to croak on her, back and forth on some seven or eight curbstones, the curb being a tiny footbridge that divided the wrinkled, pock-marked, crumbling asphalt of the sidewalk from the wrinkled, pock-marked, crumbling asphalt of the road. She marched in her stiff, inelegant, would-be courageous gait back and forth and forth and back, for so long that everything she met on her way got engraved in her memory.

A cigarette butt, half-squashed with a shoe sole.

A shattered crack vial with a bright blue cap.

A piece of wax paper that once carried a Burger King burger, completely worked into the asphalt.

A spit-out stepped-on chewing gum.

A plastic bag that once was full of pot.

Gin walked back and forth, waiting for Alex to rescue her, and all that –

Bag
Chewing gum
Wax paper
Crack vial
Cigarette butt
Crack vial
Wax paper
Chewing gum
Bag –

got worked into her thoughts the same way it had been worked into the asphalt of the street, all details included:

The plastic on the bag that once had pot in it was a bit pierced through in places, all slightly yellowed from the squashed herb, and the little Ziploc zipper on it had a tiny red stripe next to it. But now the zipper was open and the gaping edge of the translucent plastic was reminiscent of a carp's gaping mouth.

The chewing gum hadn't lost its stickiness as yet, even though its color was gone for a long time already. Trampled on by dozens of sneaker soles, it looked like a squid that had died on the asphalt.

The Burger King wax paper was all torn and limp; little bubbles on the asphalt penetrated through it; it covered its area of the sidewalk like an ancient, peeling latex paint.

The crack vial, that tiny tube made of fragile transparent plastic, got shattered and resembled a thick cobweb now. Those little shards that fell off it sparkled a little each time Gin, her eyes down, passed by them.

The cigarette butt was soaked in water and all brown, and a couple of grains of tobacco that had fallen off it already had the time to stretch into roundish brown spots.

And Gin couldn't help herself, she had to wonder whether all that might be part of some scheme, the same way hooded sweathirts are part of a scheme, and the heavy gold chains on the neck of drug dealers are part of a scheme, and the crotchless panties of whores, or the oversized, spotless, untied sneakers homeboys wear . . . whether the cracks in the asphalt of the sidewalk (the ones she just passed) those spots where the asphalt is caving in and crumbling apart or where it's bubbling out into space like tiny, tit-shaped volcanoes –

– whether all that might be a sign, a secret script, difficult and ancient and uncrackable, some strange script that, day after day, reveals something to people who inhabit these streets.

It seemed to her that some message was hidden in the way plaster was coming off the walls of buildings, exposing the brick. It seemed to her that graffiti, the dynamic street art that gets changed all the time – sprayed over, erased, covered by newer and newer layers of itself, the art that seems menacing to some but at the same time is so colorful, shiny, silverish and rotund, joyfully pregnant like a fifteen-year-old black girl – that graffiti, too, carried in it some mysterious codes of the City, codes that she never understood.

From her sick car she would watch, day after day, the colorful heaps of garbage, the sealed windows of dead buildings, the graffiti, the paths of mangy wayward dogs who stick their muzzles into black garbage bags, yipping with delight –

– and after a while she got quite positive that all those things she sees around her are the fingerprints of a powerful Time God; that it's an unfamiliar, fragrant, completely foreign language for which she has no textbook.

Gin's husband Talibe had homogeneous black skin with dark-blue highlights on his elbows, knees and knuckles; his skin looked like the highest-quality black coal. His skin was perfect, smooth and uninteresting.

At least for Gin's eyes, there was absolutely nothing written on his skin.

But Clyde –

(at that moment in her thoughts Gin had to set her jaws, throw her head backwards and keep repeating to herself I DON'T GIVE A SHIT!)

– there was something written on his skin.

The pattern of his complexion consisted of tiny little dots of various hues of brown, like ancient oak-spangle ink, diluted with water.

These dots were not round, they had little bristles on them, little tails and tentacles; they reminded her of amoebas, of squids, or of spilled fragments of tea leaves.

On the skin all over Clyde's body something was written in a script she'd never deciphered – the letters were much too small and Gin couldn't read them without a magnifying glass.

On the skin all over Clyde's body, a long and fascinating novel was written. But Gin didn't even manage to read its title page.

Chapter 20

King of All Pushers

"Jee-zus fuckin' Christ, Gin," Alex bellowed through the night. "God fuckin' damn it!" He screamed so loud that the homies loitering on the corner began to turn their heads to see what's going on. "Why the fuck you go right here? When your car break down HERE? You would have to go some other place where it would not break, fuck it! How many times I have to beg you for this, Gin: don't go terrible fucking places like here – OK, put it in neutral, sweetheart, we go to the garage!"

When one is being pushed back to the garage in a stalled-out car, up and down ramps, past street crossings, over vibrating bridges . . . it's not a pleasant experience.

Nothing works in the car.

Often not even the headlights but that constitutes only a slight contribution to your conviction that you'll be dead within the next second. The power steering and power brakes don't work, it's really hard to turn the wheel, and if somebody accidentally jumped in front of your hood, you'd have no choice, you'd have to run him over. When, late at night, you're speeding over steel bridges whose metal beams rattle under your wheels even more menacingly thanks to the fact that your car doesn't make a sound, the Universe closes above you and sucks you in, you're racing through space on an unchangeable trajectory just like you were a cosmic object. The uncontrollability of your own motion permeates you; within a couple of minutes you get all sweaty even though it's freezing in your car; you get all sweaty with fear – not because you might crash into something; you might get killed, you might get into a skid in the super-narrow lane in the middle of the Williamsburgh Bridge and the car, with a power you had no idea it possessed, would bore through the railing and land, yourself included, in the waves of the East River that, when the weather is at its coldest, get covered with thin razors of ice before dawn —

— no, you're not afraid of that, not really, the fear that makes you moist with sweat is much more universal: it's fear of the fact that destiny has no steering wheel; it's fear of the narrow slot that enables you to glimpse the future – it's the same terror that makes some of us scream like crazy for the last few split seconds just before a car crash – only this terror is slow; it's stealthy; it's the reverse equivalent of the terror that snatches you when your car gets stalled out in the middle of a highway and, surrounded by the avalanche of speed, you're forced to sit motionless – you die —

It's fear of your own powerlessness.

And so, during the innumerable pushing trips back to the garage on 47th Street from wherever the car had stalled out, the erotic action between Alex, God of the Garage, and Gin, his employee, did get consummated, after all.

The hand on Gin's behind was replaced by the touch of Alex's car's bumper on the bumper of her car; Gin's powerlessness in the role of the driver of a stalled-out car somewhat resembled sexual submission in bed.

She became a boat with no helm, a frigate with no sails, a glider with its wings all torn. And with every jerk, with every thrust of Alex's front bumper into the bumper on the back of her car, Alex was giving her new energy: he was passing on to her the power to move on, to keep going.

Gin, all covered with cold sweat, was speeding through the middle of the road – at a speed she hadn't chosen, to a rhythm she didn't like. And every time her Yellow, after a pilgrimage brimming with peril, happily landed in front of Alex's garage, the intensity of Gin's relief verged on erotic fulfillment.

Chapter 21

She and He

Talibe's good-luck charm lay on the top of a chest of drawers, out of reach of the curious Gin, who wasn't allowed to as much as look at it too closely, so it wouldn't lose its power.

A yard away from it, Talibe was presently screwing.

With his consistent thrusts he pushed Gin into the corner by the bed, until her head was all but trapped between his love and a sloppily plastered brick wall through which Harlem penetrated into her skull, taking her thoughts away.

The center of her body belonged to Talibe.

With his velvety, ebony-colored, pencil-shaped dick, dressed in an ill-fitting, smelly, lubricated, disturbingly light-blue rubber of the Trojan brand.

Talibe kept thrusting and thrusting, mumbling "*Chérie, chérie, chérie*!" whereas Gin, who already knew that this was one of the few situations when Talibe actually listened to her a bit, said: "We gotta pay the phone bill."

"*Chérie, je t'a—*"

"378.26. And almost all the long-distance calls are yours. I'll run and pay it, that's no problem, but you gotta give me the money."

"*Oui, oui, oui*," said Talibe whose English worked only when he was sitting or standing, and then he began to speak Mandinge.

The harmony of sounds and movements made Gin come pretty big time, a tropical ocean washed over her and tiny neon-blue fish bit her feet until they tickled. "Oh, man, do I love him!" a thought shot through her head and she tried to make that moment last forever, to imprint Talibe's face on her palms, to let the Mandinge language penetrate her more completely than the police sirens wailing outside, than the screams of kids in the street, the dirty snow, the phone bill – but the neon fish hadn't swam away yet and that gentle and hoarse language began to sound suspicious to her – perhaps Talibe is yelling at her now, what does she know, sometimes she yelled at him too, tenderly, in Czech.

She stroked Talibe's tiger shoulders. "I don't want to bother you, but . . . we owe 378.26 for telephone and it's all calls to Mali!"

"*Oui, oui, oui*!" Talibe pushed her farther and farther into the corner, even closer to Harlem, that fragrant exotic neighborhood, "*oui, oui, oui, oui, oui*!"

"So you'll give me the money right away? 378.26."

"*Oui, oui.*"

"And tomorrow I'll go and pay it."

"*Oui, oui, oui*!" Talibe moaned. Then he fell down on her like a cut-out bamboo and kept repeating: "*Chérie, je t'aime, je t'aime, je t'aime!* Today I make you baby, baby, BABY!"

And his father's pride wasn't the tiniest bit hampered by the negligible fact that he'd just wasted the juices of life into an ill-fitting, light-blue condom of the most common brand.

Chapter 22

Kenny

For Gin, that place was mentally surrounded by blue wooden barricades with POLICE LINE DO NOT CROSS written on them. And so she'd hardly dare to visit her old garage if it wasn't for Ramon's gremlins. They dragged her to the corner of 10th Avenue and 21st Street where she had to stop at a red light, and her car sighed, burped and stalled.

But then again . . . it was past eleven . . . and all that had happened almost a year ago, so she pulled the key from the ignition and staggered the three-quarters of a crosstown block toward the west, along that electric short-circuit that, to her surprise, still gave a few sparks somewhere deep inside her.

In the low, acoustical garage space, several sick Yellows in different stages of being gutted were hanging on lifts below the steel ribs of the ceiling.

Gin took a bashful look around the ceiling, the walls and the floor, all of which was speckled with yellow dots. These garage spaces reminded her – with their mood, their grease and their dust – of those spaces hidden under highway ramps. They resembled them thanks to the same logical loop that makes the yellow color of taxis similar to the blue of distances.

Gin's stomach got all queasy with an under-the-sea feeling. She felt a bit like she stepped into the belly of a canary-yellow killer whale. But she squeezed in under the Yellows, jumped over two or three puddles of colorful grease that were seeping into the gravel on the floor, and then brought that slush with her up the stairs and into the dispatcher's booth.

And there, bent over backwards in a chair, clad in sneakers on which little red snakes of oily liquids were weaving in and out of less viscous green ones, mixing with them and dripping to the desk top in the form of electric, color-changing drops, Kenny the dispatcher was snoring loudly. Gusts of hot wind from a heater periodically flattened his eyelashes. In this position, Kenny looked like a baby, like an overgrown muscular angel. Gin tripped over the burden of delayed tenderness, falling against his thigh.

"Hello, Miss Gin!" Kenny hollered cheerfully, without revealing any signs of surprise, as if they saw each other just yesterday. "Hello, hello, how ya doin'?"

And he fine-tuned the corners of his lips into a charmingly dolphin-like smile.

"But it's sooo easy, Gin!" Kenny explained to her above the wide-open hood (and she was almost envious of that hood, she wouldn't have minded changing places with it). "It sooo easy to fix! What kind of boss have you got anyway? Can't he as much as change the gas pump?"

Kenny, leaning toward the engine from the side, thoughtfully wrinkled his brow and with a single click of his fingertips he unscrewed the bolt on the carburetor cover. He took something out, blew into it and then examined it against the light of the street lantern. "Shit!" he decided, darting away.

He came back two minutes later with something similar, and stuck it into the carburetor. He screwed the back on with a single click of his fingertips. He patted Gin's Yellow on the fender, smearing it with black dactyloscopic creases.

"Turn the key for me, OK, sweetheart?"

The engine started purring like a contented kitten.

"Well, I guess I—" Gin started saying.

But Kenny dove under the hood again, and – leaving greasy marks on the wiring that innervated the engine – pronounced thoughtfully: "But that's weird – Step on the brakes for me, will you?" He circled the car. "Do it again. Nothing???" He squeezed his way under the dashboard, between Gin and the wheel, and pulled off the plastic cover. It fell under her feet. "Can I look at something, darling? Just a sec!" And he jerked at a few wires and levers.

A colorful heap of car intestines cascaded to the floor.

Gin didn't have the stamina to watch that surgery any longer. It seemed to her, just like it always did on similar occasions, that her car was bleeding, that it cried quietly, that this kind of operation should be performed only with sterile instruments and under general anesthesia.

"Kenny . . . would you like some . . . coffee . . . or tea?" she said, hanging onto a straw. And as Kenny absent-mindedly nodded his head at the word "tea," she grabbed that opportunity and escaped several blocks away, to the nearest corner deli.

"Well, Gin, when you connect the brake lights to the signal lights," Kenny explained to her in between blowing on his tea and noisy sips, "and when a tiny, inconspicuous wire leads from the windshield wipers to the starter switch, so your car stalls out every time a couple raindrops fall and you turn the wipers on, and when the battery cables get cleverly doctored and they're hangin' on a single tiny little wire thread, and sometimes the charge does get through and sometimes it don't, and when it don't, then your car stalls out, and you feel like a stupid motherfucker, 'cause no matter how many times you check the contacts, you won't find anything 'cause that doctored part of the cable is covered up so well that you can't possibly find the trouble until you squeeze every quarter inch of every fuckin' wire with your fingers, and when – but I'm not gonna bore you with all that," he concluded, noticing Gin's haunted look, and waved his hand, "I mean, if somebody fucks up the car like THAT and you can still START IT UP and make more than four blocks with it . . . a mechanic like that is a GENIUS, and next time you talk to him, Gin, tell him this: If he wants to work for my garage, I'll make the owner pay him fifty bucks an hour, and every time he's tinkering, I'm gonna go down on my knees in front of him and worship his big toes. I've no idea WHY he fucked up this car like that but he's . . . he's an artist. I mean, Gin . . . maybe you should give some thought to switching garages, I'm tellin' ya!"

Kenny straightened up, patted her Yellow and added: "OK – and now go and make money, sweetheart. I want you to be rich!"

"How much do I owe you?"

Kenny frowned, making the furrows on his forehead grow thicker again. Then he pulled his whole forehead two inches up and pursed his lips, waiting for a kiss.

Gin stood on her toes.

Carefully, as if not to burn herself, she touched her lips to his. Kenny's mouth captured hers. Just for a split second. But Gin still had the time to feel an electric wave move down her spine at the speed of lightning. The wave shook the whole sidewalk and made the midnight-blue sky above her descend a couple hundred yards. That was because the minimalist kiss carried with it the hugging power of Kenny's arms, even though Kenny's arms were behind his back right now. He was making sure he wouldn't make her dirty.

Chapter 23

Anchors

And that's how the network of anchors and lifebelts grew thicker on Gin's mental map of New York.

These were the spaces that seemed hospitable to her; street corners that built themselves in front of her mental eye each time somebody pronounced the combination of two numerals.

55+7

14+2

96+5

The grid of the City, that humongous multiplication table, seeped into the creases of her brain.

Manhattan got speckled with little shards of adventures that never lasted long enough – the depth of every look had to correspond with the beat of the street lights. Red-and-green-and-yellow made Gin's nights rhythmical.

Street corners she'd gotten to know, curbs made wiggly by people's steps, puddles, potholes (that one on 23rd and 5th, for example: every car fell into it, their mufflers sparkling as they hit the scarred asphalt) – for her all that turned into climbing ropes, ship anchors – dependable friends she always knew where to find.

By becoming familiar to her, the City developed a hard-to-explain kindness.

But the most important anchor on the map of New York became Kenny's lips. The seven marked nerves in her body still remembered their embrace. And the tiny creases on Kenny's lips began to fit perfectly into the tiny creases on Gin's lips.

Chapter 24

The Magic Triangle

From 4th Street, next to the corner where it crosses Avenue B, an orange glow, crackling and smoke were emanating.

A couple yards away from a burning car, the plastic milk container (which the guys at the Houston Street gas station must have filled up with gas for him despite all regulations) still in his hand, Randy the homeless man was standing, high flames reflected in his dark pupils. His eyes now – finally – radiated light, the big light he had inside him but nobody could see.

"That's the magic triangle!" Randy was yelling, with his right hand choreographing the flames the way a snake charmer choreographs a basketful of cobras. He was jumping up in place like a happy pingpong ball. "That's the magic triangle! God's eye! God's eye!" For a second, his vision got projected into the fire: the middle flames were shooting the highest. And then the God's eye went blind and blackened out – and the acrid smell of burned fake-leather seats got penetrated by the cherry lights of police cars. They circled through the curtain of that smoke, prickly white, blue, red; they tore the space into colorful shards, they cut into the thick column of smoke like chain-saws.

Eight police officers got out of the cars. They surrounded Randy, kicked the container out of his hand and squeamishly spread him on the hood of the nearest car. One of them grabbed the back of his neck in a sliding, well-practiced motion – to make sure Randy wouldn't get stuck in the door as they were stuffing him into a police car. Randy repeated in an increasingly surprised voice: "God's eye! Really! You don't believe it? God's eye!"

Immediately afterwards, six fire trucks arrived at the scene, effectively blocking all traffic.

Chapter 25

Taxi Stories

Every real taxi story is like a short-short mystery novel with the first and the last few pages torn off.

Couples of lovers and spouses at various stages of yelling at each other get into your cab. Why they are yelling at each other – well, that you don't know even though you can often get a clue, based on the pissed-off sentences that make it to you from behind the partition. But when it comes to where the whole situation is leading – that's what you shall never know. The guy angrily throws a fiver on you, then catches up with his wife (or whatever) on the sidewalk, and squeezing both her hands behind her back, he hisses: "Just you wait, you fuckin' whore! I'm gonna kill you!"

A naive cabdriver, one who has spent, perhaps, half a year or a year on the streets, just blows off his head. He stops at the first corner, dialing 911 from the public phone booth there, and then tries to explain to a tired, jaded, bored, but nevertheless professionally patient voice on the wire that at such-and-such a number on such-and-such a street West a husband is about to murder some nice-looking petite brunette.

Once the cabbies find out, however, that they invariably get told to wait and see how the situation develops, and if that man doesn't stop murdering her, then they should call again, yes, 911 again, yes, sure – the cabbies give up on being saviors.

The second stage in the life of a curious cabdriver is the study of daily papers.

Day after day he buys all the tabloids New York has to offer, and only when he DOESN'T find a picture of his female passenger of yesterday in *The New York Post*, accompanied by the headline IMPALED WITH PEACE PIPE FROM NATIVE AMERICAN HISTORY MUSEUM or something of this caliber, when *New York Newsday* DOESN'T contain an article titled MEAT CLEAVERER SAYS "YOU PIG" AND CHOPS UP GIRLFRIEND, when even the tiny little briefs at the edges of *The Daily News* pages DON'T mention a dead body of a woman discovered in the wee hours of the morning in a bathtub on the Upper West Side – only then does he calm down a bit.

The problem is that this naive, caring cabbie-savior believes in newspapers only for a spell.

Then one day, it's a Saturday, he gets hopelessly caught up in a traffic jam near Union Square. The jam that blocks all the traffic within the radius of five crosstown and ten uptown blocks is caused by about a million police troopers, twenty ambulances and fifty fire trucks that are trying to trump each other in hooting and circling their vicinity with hellish signals in piercing colors. The whole scene looks like Armageddon. On street corners boys and girls in fashionable baggy jeans are standing, their feet still jerking with the rhythm of the Palladium nightclub, discussing things in a heated manner: "Naah, don't gimme that shit, man! I heard a twenny-two from deep in there some place—" "That was a forddy-five, you mahfah! I can tell—" "Yeah, that's what I matha-fuckin' heard, too, you asshole! But a whole lodda time later. You know what I'm sayin' man? That other gun went off first—" "And all that blood everywhere, I was—" "Yeah, they're gonna find a bunch of stiffs down there, man!"

The next day the taxidriver buys *The Post, Newsday, Daily News, The New York Times*, even, but there's not a single line anywhere about a shoot-out in a disco nightclub. The journalists just didn't find it worth mentioning, it seems.

And so the taxidriver sheds his naivety, just like a snake sheds his dead skin.

He begins to understand that the cops in New York City DON'T want to hear that at house number XYZ on 73rd Street somebody might be stabbing some petite brunette to death right now.

That the journalists DON'T monitor all the police channels there are in the City. That every major car crash DOESN'T attract a whole flock of reporters. That it's, after all, quite possible to get shot, thrown next to the sewer, discovered, autopsied and buried without anybody reading about it in the paper.

At this phase of getting used to the City, a Yellow Taxi driver gets the goose bumps. But, for some reason, these goose bumps feel kind of sweet.

He realizes that he won't learn very much about the life in the streets of New York by merely reading the papers, listening to the radio and watching television.

He realizes that HE HIMSELF is the most knowledgeable expert on the City, dubbed the Big Apple.

That – even though he knows neither the beginnings nor the ends of stories that get revolved on the back seat of his taxi night after night – he could easily dream them all up.

Which makes it even more interesting, of course.

"Young, long-haired redheads shouldn't be driving cabs," Geoffrey said with a thoughtful air, twirling, to Gin's chagrin, a strand of Gin's hair on his fat index finger. The ancient greasy dust on it enhanced the visibility of his dactyloscopic creases – one could read them just like on a police card. "Women in general shouldn't be driving cabs. And men shouldn't do that, either—" He let go of Gin's hair and proceeded to adjust the spiky bracelets that decorated his wrists.

A thirty-pound chain that was swinging on his neck hit the tabletop with a thud. "In this City, only pitbulls should be driving taxis. Pitbulls with a helmet on their head. In a bulletproof vest." Geoffrey himself had begun to resemble a pitbull, an oversized one and without an overlong pedigree. His stubborn face was framed with a leather aviator's helmet, studded with metal, and on the middle fingers of both hands he was wearing steel boxing rings.

Several taxidrivers, more or less at random, had gathered at a quarter past 1 a.m., when business wasn't worth shit, in a restaurant rather famous for its lousiness. It was called Munson Diner, and it had been operating for the better part of eternity at the corner of 11th Avenue and 49th Street. On the salmon-red, scratched and peeling tables, inch-long, overfed cockroaches with a healthy shine on their shellcovers were roaming, looking every bit as well-developed as those on Gloria's painting. The bathroom was permanently locked and the key to it was hanging on a huge chain right above the grill, jealously guarded from anyone who didn't order at least a cup of soup. In front of Munson Diner, though, there were always a few parking places to be found – and, after all, taxidrivers somehow preferred the West Side, anyway. They gladly forgave the diner for a few roach legs in their omelettes.

"Pitbulls in a bulletproof vest, Gin!" Geoffrey was spitting out at the moment. "And that means you, too, Miss Chang! Don't you think that you're ever safe, with those little dimples of yours—" he aimed his fat finger at the middle of Miss Chang's cherub-like face. "They'll get you, anyway, never mind you drive the day shift."

Miss Chang (who required that everybody put that "Miss" in front of her name, frowning menacingly from the visor of her hat at anybody who dared to omit it) pouted and grew taller in her chair.

"No-bo-dy will tell me what to do, Geoff!" she said in her correct, grammatical but somewhat chopped-up English that sounded like little bells falling down a staircase (which drove Miss Chang nuts but she had no idea how to fix it). "And if you think you can be sas-sy with me just be-cause I'm a woman, then—"

Miss Chang put her coffee cup back down into the little brown puddle on the saucer and made a menacing gesture toward Geoffrey with the spoon. But she overdid it and wound up hitting him right in the nose. The companions around the salmon-red table gave a unanimous "Ooooh!"

"Don't be like that, Miss Chang!" Geoffrey was rubbing his nose until the round pink scar on it went purple. The story had it that a German Shepherd once bit Geoffrey's nose off; they sewed it back on but a bit askew. "I have nothing else in mind but your well-being, girls."

And he opened his watery, light-blue eyes as wide as they would go. Geoffrey's hit-man style gear masked a gentle soul, belonging to a soft-hearted guy of not-exactly-fast thinking capabilities.

"Oh boy, I could tell you things, oh boy," the discussion was joined by Ashraf who, up until now, had been crouching in the corner and stirring his coffee with a spoon to the rhythm of some wild, though inner, music. "I been driving – wait a minute – more than fifteen years, and not one year, not one, weren't so many taxidrivers killed. What I seen with my own eyes, stories you wouldn't believe."

"Like?" Gin prompted.

"Well . . . like I driving one day – boy, I could tell you things!"

"OK, so tell us."

"Like you taking your bassanger somewhere and he doesn't wanna bay—"

"That hap-pens to me once a week on a-ve-rage," Miss Chang said.

"I could tell you things, oh boy," Ashraf repeated three more times before reclining his rather heavy face of an Alexandria storekeeper back toward his coffee and started stirring it like he'd gone mad. Jee-zus, I hope I won't end up the same way! Gin thought to herself, after fifteen years of driving "bassangers" who don't always "bay" me! Ashraf, who'd bought his own medallion some ten years ago, belonged among taxidriver-owners, the lords of this profession. On the roof of Ashraf's shiny stallion the number 3E54 was proudly shining – and all the way up, on top of that dandelion blossom, a sheet-metal eagle was permanently lifting off, attached by its talons with three steel nuts. Neat stickers on the car's window informed everybody that Ashraf is a member of Independent Taxi Owners' Union, that his vehicle was air-conditioned, and that he was "Available for out-of-town calls."

Judged by his car, Ashraf really belonged among the lords of this notoriously serflike profession. The inside of his taxi, which served as his money-making device, his apartment, his mistress, his savior, his only love, was made fragrant with oriental incense sticks. Ashraf had screwed a tiny chiselled plate to the dashboard; it carried an Arabic-and-English edition of the Koran. It was attached to the plate by a decorative chain to make sure that it wouldn't – Allah forbid! – fall on the floor while that Yellow clipper of Ashraf's was negotiating the asphalt waves. But in contrast to his car, the palace, Ashraf looked like a homeless oaf. Summer or winter, he was decked out in a greasy padded coat that doubled up as a blanket whenever Ashraf, late at night at the taxi parking lot at Kennedy Airport, fell asleep on the front seat in a fetal position while waiting for the TWA red-eye from the Coast. And he washed his feet only on one occasion: that is, when he dug a carefully rolled-up prayer rug out of the trunk of his Yellow and retreated to perform his worship behind the embroidered curtain that the Pakistani fast-food place on 39th Street and 8th Avenue had set up for its faithful customers. All the time that Gin knew him it seemed that Ashraf could function socially only in truly short time spans, lasting, as it seemed, no longer than one change of the traffic lights. Sometimes, for as long as thirty, forty seconds Ashraf was a charming companion – and then he got switched off. He got shut off. And he sank again into that viscous Yellow pudding that his life had become.

During the fifteen years he spent "on the street," even though wrapped up in his comfortable metal can, the rhythm of the City imprinted itself into him, as if Ashraf himself became a traffic light. Ashraf never ceased to stomp his right sneaker, and with the corner of his eye he kept checking the reflection of the blinking neon light that informed the whole world they were sitting in the Munson Diner. That pink tube looked suspicious to Ashraf, no doubt about it. Whenever it lit up with a flutter, he stepped on the brake pedal under the table.

"Oh boy, I could tell you things!" Ashraf glared at his surroundings menacingly for a few seconds, then he reclined his head and again focused his whole attention on the private tempest in his coffee cup.

A cadaverous Puerto Rican woman, her hair dyed blondish-red, clunked into the Munson Diner on seven-inch heels.

"Good afternoon," she greeted everybody in a hoarse voice, pulling her miniskirt down over her bluish thighs. "I need the key! The bathroom key!"

Kasif, a Pakistani who served here as a cook, waiter, cashier and busboy rolled into one, devoted his full, indeed superfluous, attention to a hamburger that sizzled on the griddle.

"The key! The bathroom key! D'you hear me?"

Kasif flipped the meat patty, watching little drops of fat bubble out from under it. "The bathroom is out of order, ma'am!" he said in a tough-dude voice.

"I'm out of order, too! Gimme that key!"

Kasif looked around to see how many people were watching, then he sighed and, leaning across the bar, handed her the key. It was attached with a heavy chain to a wooden log of a decidedly phallic shape. The bottle blonde grabbed it with a motion that showed she was well acquainted with such things and clunked toward the toilets. Ashraf's gaze slid down her calves and got seriously scared of her bright red pumps.

"Gee-zus, I'm never gonna come here no more!" Geoffrey commented on the situation. "Why does a woman have to shoot up junk in the bathroom of a dump like this, well, that's beyond me. And you girls, how can you just look at all that and—"

Immediately afterwards he hurriedly got up and ran away because Miss Chang flew herself at him, her fingertips turning into the talons of some oriental bird of prey.

"Wo-men have the same right as men do to shoot up he-ro-in," she screamed. "Or smoke crack! Or drive a ta-xi! And if you say once again that—"

"OK, OK," Geoffrey was smoothing the situation over. "I didn't mean it so—"

"In this count-ry I have the sa-me rights as a man! The-o-re-ti-cal-ly! But you, you men here—"

"I didn't mean that—"

"The sa-me rights! I'm go-ing a-way!" And Miss Chang banged Ashraf on the shoulder. "You will drive me ho-me, o-kay?" Miss Chang didn't have her cab. She only drove in the daytime.

Ashraf gave an absent-minded nod. He threw a single on the table, the pyramid-side up – that was Ashraf's homage to his native Egypt – and waddled toward the exit. Miss Chang scolded Geoffrey with her gaze in place of a goodbye and ran after Ashraf. From the back she looked like a man who you wouldn't want to see from the front. She was wrapped up in filthy baggy sweatpants and a checkered shirt from whose sleeves only her fingers were sticking out. Chang, as a habit, stuck her thumbs through the hole behind the cuffs, using these makeshift semigloves for steering her taxi. As she walked, she was bopping from side to side like a sailor of the seven seas. Gin could tell that this movement didn't come naturally to her, she must have spent months practicing. Now, as she caught up with Ashraf, she slapped him in the ribs with her left hand so hard that Ashraf gave a gasp.

"She's fucking him!" Geoffrey sighed knowingly.

Geoffrey gazed at their lonely Yellow vehicles, parked right behind the window, then at his coffee, then at Gin: "We are working here like goddamn slaves, Gin, because you or me, we're DUMB. But there are pros out there, believe you me, who can make more than a Wall Street banker with the help of this lump of Yellow shit. Yeah, with this heap of Yellow shit you can make a heap of money, can you believe that? All you need to do is know the ropes a bit and you make a THOUSAND! FIFTEEN HUNDRED! in a single day. They have a booklet—"

"You mean in a week . . ."

"In a day! Shit, why do all redheads have to be so dumb? I'll bring that booklet and show it to you: THE OFFICIAL GUIDE TO TAXI RATES IN NEW YORK CITY – and in this OFFICIAL booklet, Gin, everything is printed, black on wh—"

"In an official booklet?"

"It ain't easy to unteach you your stupidity, is it, Gin?" Geoffrey sighed, making his coat of armor rattle. He was rubbing that bitten-off nose of his with his enormous dactyloscopic creases. "An OFFICIAL booklet like that can be printed for a few bucks, Gin, Jee-zus, when were you born? And everything is in there, black on white: From Kennedy Airport to Manhattan – $320! From the West Side across the Park to the East side – $70! From the Vista Hotel near the World Trade Center – in that hotel, by the way, only the greatest dumbos in the Solar System stay – anywhere in Manhattan: $150, Brooklyn $230."

"A booklet with prices. Fine. But what about the meter?"

"Well, you gotta outsmart the meter, Gin. If you or me weren't as dumb as we are, we'd be millionaires by tomorrow. Sure, you need a bit of a faculty. There are pros out there, Gin, who hold a piece of black tape in their palm, cut exactly to the right size so it covers the meter's display. Just imagine: you go to the airport, you wait in line like a good boy, you don't jump the line, nothing, you don't attract anyone's attention to yourself, you're perfectly legal – and then, what not, a little Froggy family is rushing to your cab. Their only English is '*Man-a-ton, 'otel Algon'in*'. You get them in, turn on the meter and in the split second before the $1.50 shows on the display, you cover it with your black tape and you explain to them that you're *'désolé'* but the meter isn't working. And then you show them in that official booklet that a trip from Kennedy Airport will cost them only 320 bucks."

"But what if—"

"The only thing you gotta do is push that button on the meter, right then and there, at the airport, so that the light on your roof goes off. Everybody who's looking at you from the outside must conclude that you're perfectly legal, my dear Gin."

"But what if you make a mistake and—"

"Well, you just must not make a mistake. That's the trick: deciding, in half a second, who you can pull this one on and who you can't. Not every idiot with the face of a week-old calf from Oklahoma is a dumb rubberneck, my dear Gin."

"But what if you do get caught? What happ—"

"What happens if you get caught? Well, what d'you think? What can they do to you? They give you a summons, you gotta appear at the Taxi and Limousine Commission, and then they sentence you to paying $500 for a fine. Big fuckin' deal. Then you jump into your machine, go to Kennedy, and all you need is two calls to *Man-a-ton* to make up for all the money you've lost. That's how it is. By the way, remember this: in Rome, when you're going to the airport, you pay double. That's why it's easy to convince them Dagos that instead of 30 they owe you 60. The only thing you gotta be careful about is Cosa Nostra. They, too, often look like they can't count to five."

Geoffrey fell silent.

Then his gear began rattling on him as he turned toward the window. He gazed over the blinking Munson Diner sign and through the colorful little will-of-the-wisps that sat in the semi-transparent glass, into the yellowish darkness in front of the joint.

"Sengane is coming," he said pensively. "And this nigger, I mean, this African, I mean this African African American, just to be PC, will certainly broaden your horizons, Gin."

*

Gin often watched in wonder the various ways in which members of various nations get reborn while climbing out of their taxis.

Blond Russians, with much huffing and puffing, slid out from behind the steering wheels, then placed their palms on their butts and straightened their backs with a screech like their spine was a rusty coil.

Pakistanis and Sikhs must have learned the back straightening techniques from collapsible rulers.

Americans who, after years of driving, tended to grow into their taxis, taking on the space between the steering wheel and the front seat, often didn't even bother trying to convince their own butt they're not sitting on it anymore. Counterbalanced by a well-developed gut, they waddled away from their machines into the garages or eateries like hemorrhoid-plagued ducks.

Hispanic Yellow drivers kept checking their flies and stuffed their shirts and T-shirts inside the belt while the biggest worry of Orthodox Jews, as it seemed, was to arrange their beards as neatly as they could.

West African drivers jumped out of their machines on straight legs, like every joint of theirs had a well-oiled spring in it.

Sengane entered the Munson Diner with the gallop of a race horse whose oats had been spiked with heroin.

"Hi, Gin!" he greeted her, then his gaze moved over to Geoffrey: "Hello, whitie!"

Geoffrey generously forgave him for that compliment. "I'm just about to tell this here miss how you wasted that guy, you see—" And he winked both his eyelids at Gin.

"Man! Didn't I tell you that yet?" Sengane flapped his arms in the air and yelled that he will have one well done. "I tell everybody and nobody want to believe. And it's the truth, really. OK. Once I'm in my taxicab driving a nigger to Harlem—"

Geoffrey, with the diction of a kindergarten teacher: "A black man."

"I picked him up right in front of the Cat Bar, on 54th and Broadway, and he says he wants to go to 126th and 2nd. I was suspicious of that right away, 'cause it seemed like he had to think about where he was going, you know. Well, and right after that nigger makes himself comfortable in my cab—"

Geoffrey: "A black man. Don't teach this here missy bad words like that. This here missy, she don't know words like that. She's from Czescoslowakia."

"I don't want to know words like that!" Gin chirped in – and she smiled at Sengane. It appealed to her that in his English only a suggestion of an accent remained. If only her own husband stumbled over this language a little less drastically! At the same time she felt that, thanks to Talibe, she was connected to Sengane with a strange bond of intimacy. Sengane, of course, had no idea.

Geoffrey's comment, it seemed, made Sengane a bit annoyed as it interrupted the flow of his story: "Nigger, that's what he was, Geoffrey. An American. A whitie like you is not gonna tell me who's a nigger and who isn't a nigger." Sengane slammed his fist on the tabletop: "Say, both of you: He was a nigger!"

Geoffrey: "OK, he was a nigger."

Sengane: "You say it, too, Gin!"

Gin: "He was an asshole."

Sengane: "No. Say that he was a nigger."

Geoffrey: "Come on, just say it."

Gin sipped her cold coffee and shuddered: "I won't say it."

Sengane: "Come on, say it."

"You know, I . . ." Gin said in embarrassment, "I just don't wanna use words like that. I know that every other person says it like that but I—"

Geoffrey: "But that's NOT an attack on black people when you say of someone he's a nigger. There's black niggers and there's white niggers. You don't know shit about all that, Gin."

Sengane: "Niggers, they are Americans. Who were slaves. Who are not from Africa. I mean, they are, but only those whose grandfathers let themselves be caught. In Africa it's different. But here in America, sorry, but that's white blood that makes niggers niggers. Come on, Gin, say it!"

Gin stammered: "But I think that . . . historically . . . I don't think that white people have a right to use that word at all, say it aloud, I mean, because . . . because . . ."

Geoffrey and Sengane exchanged a long, pitiful glance above her head.

"OK, then I'll have to teach you," Sengane remarked. "Nigger, nigger, nigger."

"Leave me alone already. Just tell the story."

"OK – Where did I finish? – OK. The minute that NIGGER got into my car, he looked already suspicious to me. Usually NIGGERS like this NIGGER are happy that someone's taking their ass to a middle of nowhere like that, so they shut up and leave me alone, but this one NIGGER was sitting on the back seat like somebody nailed him on to a cactus or something, he kept wiggling and all the time he kept asking some stupid bullshit. That's what niggers do when they want to sneak away on you without paying. They try for you to lose your attention. So I'm saying to myself: Sengane, you must be vigilous! And so when this nigger told me to pull over to the curb, I stop in the middle of the street and I say to him: It's OK. Here, a bit closer to the curb, he says. And I say again: It's OK. Go closer to the curb, he repeats again, and I don't move one bit. Yeah, right, I'm thinking for myself, I'll park like a jerk two inches from the sidewalk, so we're in nobody's way while you're murdering me. But he took his knife out anyway! I'm gonna carve you up, you stupid African, he tells me, your guts will be sticking out. Gimme all your money."

Kasif threw a plate with a hamburger and french fries in front of Sengane. A second later, a bottle of ketchup came flying, performing a pirouette on the table top. The smell of burned beef rose to the taxidrivers' noses.

"I'm gonna have one myself," Geoffrey yelled.

"And what do you do, Gin," Sengane asked her rhetorically, while waiting for a huge puddle of ketchup to plop down on the meat patty, "what do you do when some nigger pulls a knife on you and he wants money? What do you do?"

"I give it to him?"

"Bull-SHIT! No! You run away. You get out of the car and you run away. This way you're free from the law and you can't ever be found guilty of anything. What did you do, defendant, when that nigger pulled a knife on you? Please, I ran away, Mr cop. Do you understand: You're not running away from that little knife of his. You get out of the car and you run away from the law, do you know what I'm sayin'? OK, so what do I do in this situation? The only smart thing: I get out of the car and I'm running away. But I'm running away REAL SLOW! I'm running away so slow that even the fattest motherfucker must catch up with me, even if he didn't try. OK. And when that stupid nigger with his pen knife caught up with me, I put a better knife into his figure."

Sengane put down his fork, reached inside his pocket and lovingly stroked the blade of a menacingly shaped hunting knife. Gin stretched her hand toward it and soon afterward she felt its weight in her palm. Little lights were reflected on the blade, they got scattered on scratches and little scars on it, tickling Gin's pupils.

"And was he gone right away?" Geoffrey asked suggestively.

"Oh, no!" Sengane rejoiced, sinking his teeth into his dinner in a somewhat cannibalist way. "Oh, no – what do you mean, gone? I stab him two times, three times, five times. He still didn't fall. Instead he started yelling: 'Help, help! Murder! Police!' And I say: 'That's right!' And I stab him and stab him, and while he's lying on the ground I still stab him, until blood started coming out of his mouth – and I stab him and stab him – Oh, oh, excuse me!" Sengane interrupted himself in mid-sentence. He jerked his knife out of Gin's palm and, as if drawn by a magnetic field, proceeded toward the bathroom. From its door the Puerto Rican woman with reddish-platinum hair had just emerged. The back light was undressing her from her skirt that she kept pulling down to her knees. She still looked a bit wiggly but a satisfied sneer was now flooding her ragged face.

Sengane welcomed her with a happy bellow. He pushed the heroin beauty back into the tiny room and for ten seconds everything was silent.

Then they could hear: "O-o-oh! Good pussy! Good pussy! That's a good pussy! O-oh!"

Geoffrey reached across the table for Sengane's unfinished hamburger. "He's fucking her," he sighed knowingly.

Chapter 26

Cobwebs

"*Chérie*," Talibe said one morning – that is to say around one fifteen in the afternoon, gulping down cold palm soup, "I marry you, yes?"

"Well, yeah," his African wife answered cheerfully in her heavy Slavic accent, "it was very nice of you, I know."

"*Mais* I have one cousin—"

Gin didn't freak out. She didn't know what was coming. She was just the tiniest bit surprised at why Talibe should, so early in the morning, talk about some cousin at all. ONE COUSIN certainly didn't belong among Talibe's relatives. Even the word "brother" meant not much more than that they belonged, probably, to the same tribe. But even that wasn't for sure. Gin had already met several dozen of Talibe's brothers: they flicked in front of her, then disappeared, and when Gin dared to ask about the well-being of this brother or that one, Talibe at first had no idea who she was talking about and then he waved his hand: "Oh, this one? *Mais* he move long ago to Michigan!" As a matter of fact, all you had to do in Harlem was come out into the street and you'd discover that everyone was a brother of sorts. Limamou, who'd been driving a gypsy cab in Harlem for quite a while now, told her about a customer who pulled a shiny gun on him, stuck it to the nape of his neck, conducting the smell of steel into Limamou like he was an electric wire, and said: "Black brother, I kill ya dead, gimme all your motherfuckin' money!"

One cousin, that must be somebody who came more or less from Africa and who Talibe drove in his taxi into Flushing, Queens, last night.

"One cousin," Talibe continued. "More handsome than I. Very, very handsome. I ugly. He most very handsome taxidriver. *Mais* in Brooklyn. He make forty a day, most. And he needs send money to Africa. He no work permit, illegal, you know."

Gin took a spoon out of a used Folgers Coffee can (that now served as a kitchen cabinet) and sank it determinedly into Talibe's breakfast. The soup tasted like fried orange termites, parboiled in turpentine. Until the end of my days I'll eat on the fire escape, she thought. She went to the bedroom to get a sweater.

"*Chérie*!" Talibe yelled after her. This was unusual, he almost never raised his voice. "I your husband, *non*? *Mais* you no listen! I talk, you listen what I talk, *tu as compris?* You to my cousin get married. You this make for me!"

Gin dropped her sweater on the floor and then followed it, slowly sliding down the side of the refrigerator. She sank to the linoleum and dropped her head between her knees. No, she wasn't fainting fashionably like a fair heroine in a Harlequin romance. She only kind of lost her balance, thinking about all the BS she'd have to discuss with Talibe in the hour to come. In the City of New York, some culture shock was laying in wait beyond every street corner – the little Park Avenue ladies who screamed bloody murder every time the taxi hit a pothole; "tough" Wall Street executives who used silver tubes to stuff cocaine up their noses on the back seat; Chinatown where she struggled with chopsticks and a bowl of chow-fun noodle soup, and all the waiters retched every time a Westerner touched his face with his left hand; the unwritten laws of the Harlem ghetto where many a decked-out resident was purely begging to be ogled at but at the same time a curious stare was a crime punishable by instant shooting.

Gin should have been used to culture shocks.

But she simply refused to believe that they would occur on a more or less daily basis and in her own kitchen.

"But Talibe! I am already married! To YOU!"

"He no have money, you know? Forty dollars a day, never more. And his family he has in Upper Volta, I want to say Burkina Faso. Problem, in Burkina Faso, you know?"

Gin had never heard about a single country in Africa in which there wouldn't permanently be a "problem." But she decided to keep that comment to herself.

"I can't have TWO husbands! Jee-zus Christ! Don't you understand?"

Talibe gave her a look of chilly appraisal. Personally, he was convinced that Gin could have a dozen husbands, should the need arise. He could easily imagine her in bed with Limamou, with Traore – pretty much with any of his acquaintances. He didn't even get mad at that thought anymore. Anyway, Gin isn't going to actually sleep with her second husband, that's not the plan. Now he tried to concentrate on this deal, a deal a friend had secured for him. It's not going to happen overnight but in the end Talibe might make as much as seven thousand dollars.

"Here we are in America, Talibe!" his wife was presently screaming. "I can't get married two times, or three times, or eight hundred and twenty times. I'd get DEPORTED, don't you understand? Everything is on fucking COMPUTERS, don't you fucking understand? If we were in Upper Volta or in West Sahara or in Crocodile-on-the-Nile-istan, well, I'd marry all the cousins, male or female, you ever heard about. If it makes you happy. But this is AMERICA. Can't you fucking understand?"

"*Mais* he very, very handsome," Talibe said.

Talibe's apartment stood, pretty much, in the middle of the ghetto (that is, if we don't listen to those experts who say that

116th Street isn't quite Harlem yet, that only on 125th a cemetery begins, slowly turning into a morgue somewhere around 145th). In order to enter his apartment you had to climb up a marble staircase, smelling of gallons and gallons of dried piss, decorated in the corners with the green bile left by junkies and the orange bile left by junkies-cum-methadone addicts, strewn with cigarette butts and empty pot bags – and syringes so decrepit that not even the most desperate of junkies were willing to shoot up with them one more time, and used condoms, and crack vials, empty of course, but equipped with orange, purple or pink caps, all that in several stages of brokenness. On the second mezzanine several bullets got embedded in the plaster, forming a cute little semi-circle. Gin had no idea what their motive, target or success rate was but they sure looked dramatic in the soft, sickly light the cracked cream-colored windowpane let inside. The peeling paint on the walls was made more lively by colorful curlicues of graffiti. Sure, they all looked a bit unfinished and indecisive; the spray-paint artists didn't pay quite as much attention to them as they did to the murals on the more visible outer walls.

(Graffiti in New York, by the way, seemed to be born right from the plaster: It grew out of the gray concrete of highway overpasses like some strange decorative mold . . . It sprang up, within days, on any fresh surface; even at places where the artists couldn't get in any other fashion but hanging down from a rope by their feet you could soon spot huge, round, fat, silver-rimmed letters. Gin, who spent her nights sailing down rivers of concrete didn't once see anyone actually spraying graffiti. But the designs on every corner, every street, every highway kept changing all the time, like growing colonies of iridescent bacteria. Like the sand dunes in the Sahara desert, shaped by the wind into newer and newer patterns that were the same for thousands of years.

Perhaps this desert theory had a meaning of its own on 116th Street: In Harlem there thrived certain adjustable life forms – plants with amazingly deep roots that can reach down for the water of the Earth, thorny cacti that store moisture inside themselves, fast-legged ants who have half an hour to find food on the hot surface of the sand before they die of dehydration.)

Gin knew she was no desert flower, even though she would like to be one. And Talibe was deathly afraid of Harlem.

So he turned his place into an oasis. A sweet-smelling and life-giving one.

The door leading to apt. #5C had peeling paint on the outside, and the silverish curlicues on it read PUSSY and KILL – but Talibe painted its inner side celestial blue and decorated it with pictures of his whole family: about thirty-five people whom Talibe hadn't seen for at least four years. His grandfather, grandmother, father, mother, brothers, aunts and uncles, and also his beautiful sister with four children like little steps, the children Talibe missed so much he could cry.

Talibe's apartment had beautiful, spiffy, wall-to-wall carpeting. Its windows were perfectly washed but covered by heavy curtains because, after all, they only led out into a reality he didn't want to live in.

Talibe's apartment smelled sweet. Day in and day out Talibe burned three scented sticks he'd bought in a botanica on 116th and Park Avenue, owned by a certain Rasta. The sticks were supposed to purify the air by getting rid of lousy smells and witches, so Talibe would wave their little flames around the whole apartment day after day, wafting their cleansing smell into every corner.

In the bathroom, right above the spic-and-span tub, there was a whole pile of fluffy towels and the metal faucets were all sparkly. By polishing the faucets, Talibe fortified his place against the dusty, dangerous reality of Harlem, a neighborhood filled with unknown smells and strewn with colorful garbage, plastic cups, papers, bags – things children in Africa could play with but here they were festering by the sewer grates.

Talibe swept his apartment daily.

He swept away the wail of the police sirens and took it out in a black plastic bag, all the way to the garbage can that was squeezed in between two blue Greek columns in front of the building. From behind the dresser he swept out the never-ending fights of his upstairs neighbors. He collected Gin's dumb ideas on a large dustpan, and flushed his unrequited dreams down the toilet, in the form of used rubbers.

Talibe's cleaning binges were awfully similar to purifying his house from the presence of bad spirits.

All around Talibe's living room, on the clean, sweet-smelling, wall-to-wall carpet, several Africans – about fifteen of them – were sitting in classical tribal positions. Dressed in richly embroidered long shirts called *boubou* they drank green tea, which was served, as tradition prescribed, three times into the same plastic cup, and they gnawed on cola nuts that reminded Gin, both by look and by taste, of horse chestnuts soaked in turpentine.

The light of a tall lamp reflected off their noses, cheeks, temples and foreheads in so many different ways that even Gin's untrained eye could clearly recognize they weren't of the same tribe.

They talked, really loudly, African creole of which she understood only a couple of words here and there.

As the only woman nearby she was appointed to serve tea and pile up (with her RIGHT HAND!) newer and newer cola nuts on a little tabouret in the middle of the room. In her spare time she was supposed to pretend she was cooking dinner in the kitchen. Talibe had decided to splurge and have food delivered from a recently opened Senegalese restaurant on 117th Street.

Gin was not supposed to enter the conversation. Which was easy because nobody paid any attention to her anyway.

They were discussing Gin's second wedding.

In among shards of words she didn't know, the word "Ouagadougou" emerged out of Talibe's mouth, hanging in the air for a while.

Then it fell.

"Ouagadougou!" Limamou yelled out, hit his knees with his

fists and began to laugh. "Ouagadougou! Ouagadougou!" he screamed. "Ouagadougou! Ouagadougou!" He went down on all fours and then collapsed, head-first, on the carpet. "Ouagadougou!" he bellowed, wiping tears from his eyes with the tip of his thumb, wriggling like he was a shaman in a trance or a fish on a hook. "I've never heard anything like that! Ouagadougou! You will kill me!"

Soon all the advisers were rolling around with laughter, among spilled green tea and kola nuts. The whole conversation was reduced to one four-syllable scream.

Gin searched with her eyes for the dark brown eyes of Talibe's. They were narrowed with anger. Silently Talibe kicked her out of the room with a single motion of his head.

Members of few nations carry their name so unchangingly, docilely and publicly as Europeans do. In Africa people deal with their names in a much more generous manner. They often have one name while they're little babies, another one when they grow up a little, and still another one after they've gone through initiation ceremonies and become men and women. When an African decides to move out of the village of his birth to another, he often changes his name for this occasion. It's not because he wants to hide and act like a desperado. For various residences, just like for various ages, various occupations or even various moods various names are fitting, that's all.

Even though the naming ceremonies significantly differ based on the tribe, apparently, in most of West Africa their principle is the same: Every man gets his SECRET name, whispered into his ear by the tribal shaman, or his father, or his grandfather. It's a name no one else must hear. It's a dangerous name and when pronounced aloud it carries in it its owner's death, but at the same time it accompanies him throughout his whole life, protecting him. That name is the essence of his self, and whenever an African thinks about his self, he addresses himself in his thoughts by his secret name. All other names are just additions, they don't carry his identity in them.

And so it shouldn't be surprising that many an African, upon departure behind the ocean, chooses a completely different name, one he'd never carried before.

It's his "Western" name – but, of course, only a fool would write an American-sounding one into his passport. The best is to choose a name that sounds very African but reveals absolutely nothing about its owner.

Africans write into their passports – perhaps out of laziness, perhaps out of nostalgia – the names of rivers, mountain ridges or villages in their homeland. The syllabic clusters in them sound exactly the same way the immigration officers with a trained ear imagine the "Africanese" of a certain land should sound.

And so throughout the United States perhaps thousands, perhaps tens of thousands roam whose names, if translated into English, would be Hudson River, Empire State Building, Arizona Texas or Hellville Wisconsin.

It turned out that Gin's future second husband chose as his American name the name of the capital of Burkina Faso.

"I marry to you in Manhattan. *Mais* you marry to my cousin in Bronx. And not to be afraid of anything, *chérie*. We have magic in Africa you don't believe, I show you. And nobody knows anything bad, nobody, nobody. My cousin get his green card. You understand what I speak to you, *chérie*?"

Talibe squashed Gin between his thumb and forefinger and then squeamishly threw her between a hard place and a concrete wall. She tried to explain to him that that whole plan of his is total bullshit because whatever the clerks at the Borough Hall won't find, the computer at the Immigration Service certainly will, and this whole thing is not about getting Ouagadougou to marry, it's about his getting a green card. However, Talibe was equipped with a rare ability not to hear whatever he didn't want to hear. He announced to her sternly that if she doesn't marry Ouagadougou he, Talibe, will have to divorce her and marry some other woman – some woman who will willingly give her hand in marriage to any of his cousins.

"And I know many woman like this, many!" Talibe gave a worldly wave of his hand. "It is web, *chérie*, you know. I help you, you help my cousin, and your girlfriend if she need green card, maybe my cousin he will—"

Visions of complicated, multi-dimensional, hopelessly entangled and never-ending webs, thanks to which all the people will help each other so they ALL can get to America, haunted Gin even in her dreams. She dreamt about fishermen's nets with square holes in which a whiting called Gin was hopelessly wiggling; she dreamed about honeycomb nets in which she sank into a sweet and sticky substance; she dreamt about doilies crocheted out of black and white threads, about rectangular nets and 3D nets, about mosquito nets, about resonant spider webs in which huge spiders with mandibles like Caterpillar excavators were sitting, whetting their appetite for Gin. While, a smug half-smile on their snouts, smearing the ropes of their webs with KrazyGlue.

"Don't worry about nothing, *chérie*," Talibe cheered her. "We have magic in Africa . . ."

He reminded Gin more and more of a spider as the days went by.

When it comes to magic, however, he wasn't telling her the truth. Talibe couldn't be sure of any specific African magic, and even though Limamou swore to him that he knew everything about green cards, including the right magic that will bring them to you, Talibe didn't believe him so much anymore. Limamou had been living in Harlem for almost eighteen years already and so far he hadn't managed, magic and all, to bring his own wife over here. "Bah!" Limamou used to brag on every possible and impossible occasion. "Bah! That green card of yours, those never-ceasing worries of yours, you're just like women! You people just sit at home in Africa, in all comfort, you wait in line for a tourist visa, that's all. Is that what you call trouble? It doesn't take longer than a year or two, when you know which strings to pull, and as soon as you're here, then—"

It was true, after all. As soon as a person made it here, to America, even though only as a nonentity without a social security number, without a driver's license and without any rights – well, then it's sink or swim – and Talibe was truly grateful for the life belt the Harlem African community threw to him day after day. The African community of Harlem was an alliance of people who would, at home in Africa, barely say hello to each other, but here they were glued together with their need for unity in an enemy land. The Africans recognized one another immediately – after all, they were substantially darker than American blacks, their faces swallowed light much more hungrily. The African faces were so dark that in subdued light their features were hard to read, even though, Talibe believed, they shone with an inner fire that penetrated to the surface in glistening pearls of the skin structure. And so they recognized one another – and immediately started to speak to each other in the African creole.

But they also knew how to hate each other, and Talibe, thanks to Gin, made a lot of bad blood for himself in the community. He shouldn't have shown her off to them, he knew that now and was mad at himself about it, even though he had no idea how to keep her a secret anyway. The West African community of Harlem resembled, judged by its nosiness, gossip and public secrets, a truly strange and truly tiny village in which women were practically missing. The news that Talibe had married a redhead taxidriver flew through Harlem faster than the white puffs of dandelion seeds.

All of which meant that Ouagadougou represented a great hope for Talibe. He had to prove to them somehow that his wife was good for at least something.

Otherwise, they'd think he was a fool.

Limamou was right, after all, when he said that immigrants of Talibe's generation had it easy in America: Limamou himself had entered this continent, hanging from a hook on a shipyard's crane, nailed into a huge box of bananas. It wasn't possible to travel with cans, they provided a rather monotonous and salty diet, even if you didn't forget to take a can opener with you, and because they didn't go rotten so fast, they often got totally lost somewhere in depots and shipyards, so that it took forever for your skeleton to make it somewhere, and you often didn't even know where exactly. Limamou, as he said, had to spend over ten weeks in the shipyard in Dakar, bribing all the guards daily, choosing his box – one with wood as soft as possible to sit on, with its boards as far away from each other as they came, so light and air can get inside – and seven times he made sure where that ship of his was headed before he descended on it with the assistance of the shipyard crane (on the rope of which he was swinging for at least half an hour). The problem was that the United States didn't import too much stuff from West Africa, and the impatient security guards at the shipyards were trying their best to put you on any boat, never mind where it was going, and get rid of you in this way. Oh-oh, didn't Limamou hear about cases! Like that one about a certain desperate guy who, after a year and a half of sailing (of course, out of the box already) ended up exactly in the same place where he'd begun his journey: in a shipyard in Senegal, and from the ship his journey made a beeline for the jail in Dakar. Or, a relative of his had himself nailed into a box of mangoes, just because he liked mangoes, and after a suspiciously short sail he debarked – in Norway! He lived in Norway ever since and he apparently was doing quite well, but Limamou shuddered at the mere thought of northern winters that penetrate every bone of Africans' bodies, so they get arthritis within a year and pneumonia within two weeks – and he was already congratulating himself on his farsightedness as he was swinging on the rope above the ship that would take him to the American paradise, when, in one of the sunrays that cut through the darkness in the box like thin golden guillotines, he saw some bright-green shape coiling.

A well-developed green viper was trying to emigrate in the same banana box.

"There are occasions in life," Limamou liked to elucidate philosophically, "when magic works one hundred percent, and there are others when you can't rely on magic." This, evidently, was the latter case. After hours of laying in wait while every, every! shadow in Limamou's box was coiling and hissing poisonously, Limamou killed the snake with his fist. The bananas were bitter and green, only during the trip did they slowly ripen.

Well, whatever happened, Limamou would say, when his ship landed at Elizabeth, New Jersey, the weathered box, made of tropical wood, contained – except for the thinned-out Limamou, banana peels, two big gas cans that were originally full of water and now brownish yellow pee was splishing in them, and a huge pile of what a decent man won't talk about – also the white, chewed-off skeleton of a viper whose power now belonged to Limamou.

"Yeah, you are a snake, aren't you?" Talibe said, but not aloud.

The situation into which Talibe let himself be manipulated just begged for some unnatural powers, but at the same time Talibe was afraid it belonged among those situations in which African magic doesn't work. At least he couldn't remember any recipe to follow when YOUR WIFE IS MARRYING YOUR (DISTANT) COUSIN IN THE BRONX BOROUGH HALL, AND THE COMPUTER MUST NOT FIND OUT ABOUT IT.

He couldn't depend on Limamou and he knew that. He went for advice to the Rastafarian who had a botanica on 116th Street and Park, and this was the advice he got: "Shit, mon! We didn't get to that in my Island Magic 101 course, mon! But as we're talking about it, how 'bout checkin' out my Universal Track Sweeper, mon?" He picked up a box from a shelf and added: "I know a mon he rob houses for twenty years, mon, and he always sprinkle just a pinch of the Sweeper, mon, just a tiny little pinch, and he only got caught once, and that's just 'cause he was out of it, mon!"

The Universal Track Sweeper was a greenish brown dust

with a bitter and acrid smell, and it cost more than three La Guardias. Talibe had long ago begun to measure prices with the distances he had to drive in his taxi to get that kind of money. But he would gladly return to La Guardia Airport ten times or more, if only he could be sure this magic would work.

Talibe was taking his cousin Ouagadougou (from whose eyes the dried cow shit of his home village was falling in flakes, he thought with an air of worldliness) to the Bronx Borough Hall on 149th and Grand Concourse. From a little box with magic inscriptions on it he threw little pinches of the Universal Track Sweeper behind their heels. Better something than nothing at all, he reasoned mournfully.

Gin's knees were buckling with terror and the rattling of the train, as it was making its way through the slimy tunnels, was turning in her imaginative soul into the horrendous earthquake that will sweep her off the face of the Earth one day not so far from now.

It wasn't easy to tell what Ouagadougou was thinking. His face looked like he didn't have a clue what was going on around him. They had to show him three times where to sign the register, then he grabbed the pen like it was a hammer – and his signature resembled dried-out rat's droppings.

"You kiss him very, very much, *chérie.*" Talibe waived his hands disapprovingly, angrily casting the last bits of the Universal Track Sweeper around the subway station.

"I have to kiss him at the City Hall, don't I? That's normal, isn't it?"

"*Mais*, you kiss him. Very—really! With ton . . . tongue!" Talibe blurted out, and if he wasn't black, he'd turn crimson. He wasn't used to talking like that.

"Maybe I liked it," his half-wife said brazenly. She grabbed the confused Ouagadougou by the hand and intertwined her fingers with his. She formed a black-and-white chessboard. Talibe began to stutter.

"*Mais . . . mais* . . . you must not be me so . . . unfaithful, *chérie*, it . . . I Muslim. I will not tolerate you . . . I will not allow. I-I-I—"

The very same evening Gin followed Ouagadougou to his Brooklyn apartment where they – while his three roommates smoked in the kitchen – descended to the bed of love.

It was a mattress, thrown on the worn-out parquet floor.

So far, Ouagadougou didn't own a good-luck charm to protect him from bullets. But it took him about fifteen minutes to remove some kind of magical contraption, made of shrunken snake skin, from his ankle.

They turned off the overhead light, so the contrast of their bodies wouldn't disturb the wedding night.

They didn't talk very much.

Even if Ouagadougou did speak English, he wouldn't have a clue what to tell her.

He took off his pants. He'd only started wearing jeans a short time ago, as one of the concessions he made to this continent. They got on his nerves.

With his hand, which would like to have the practice of a womanizer's, he checked in between Gin's thighs.

Gin emitted a deep sigh.

Ouagadougou got up, pulled those damn pants back on (so as to hide his confusion) and stumbled to the switch.

Electric light had its advantages, after all.

In its yellowish glow he saw an image he'd never seen before.

Wedged between the labia on Gin's private parts, a protruding, wet, pink bump was sitting. He'd heard about such a thing quite often. But he'd never seen it. The girls of his tribe were initiated when they were about thirteen years old: the older women sliced off their male part with a knife, as tradition prescribed. The genitals of the girls of his tribe consisted of a sewn-up unity, of devoted meekness; of a hollow into which their husband sowed his sperm – and after some time his son came out of the hole.

The girls of his tribe were beautiful, dark, smiling and inaccessible. The ritual surgery removed from their bodies some kind of control switch, a lump of flesh that would turn them on and make them unable to say NO.

In the yellowish glow of the American lamp Ouagadougou examined the pink genitals of his new wife. They seemed overgrown and unruly to him. They didn't look at all like the neat scar in the dark skin of girls he'd known so far.

The beautiful maidens of his tribe wanted nothing but a son. But Gin could be manipulated.

It was enough to touch with his finger the pink protrusion between the thighs of his white wife, and Gin began to moan and wiggle, almost as if he was hurting her, but a little differently. She mumbled something in English. Ouagadougou didn't understand very well but he was sure it was an invitation into the unknown depths of her loins.

In a rather experienced way, with two worldly fingers, Gin pulled a light-blue condom on Ouag.

It wasn't easy to fantasize about sons.

Chapter 27

Talibe

Gin was climbing up the pukey stairs toward apt. #5C, in her hand a huge chain of keys to all the locks Talibe's door was equipped with, in her heart an arid desert. She hadn't seen Talibe's taxi in front of the door, which made her feel a little better, but after a while she concluded that he must have parked a few blocks away. Talibe didn't trust 116th Street one bit, he was afraid the locals might know him. He refused to park here since the time his taxi got decorated with silver-and-blue graffiti in the short while between four-thirty in the morning and half past eight.

My husband will be home, Gin thought, he sure will be home – and she was already numb with terror. So far, Talibe didn't really show any interest in the sex life of his wife (even though, once in a while, he would complain that a few smacks with a club over his head would be better than having a wife like his *chérie*) – but he'd sure never believe that she would make a fool out of him in front of the whole African community.

Just as she was passing apt. #4C, a phone started ringing one floor up. In the mezzanine she quickened her pace because after the first two rings Talibe still hadn't picked it up.

When she was turning the fourth key in the fourth lock (the lowest one, the one slightly sprayed over with the second L of the word KILL), the phone rang for the sixth time.

Gin kicked the door open.

"Is this Miss Gin?"

"Yes."

"How are you?"

"Fine. Who's calling?"

"Good. Good. That's good. This is Limamou. How was the night?"

So it's already beginning, a thought flashed through Gin's mind. It's gonna be like that for months, what am I saying, months – for YEARS from now on. Until I'm dead and buried not one of Talibe's friends is gonna look at me without sneering. Why the hell did I do that?

"I'm fine," Gin managed to say, "but if you want to talk to Talibe, I must tell you Talibe is not at home right now, I don't really know where he is, I've myself just—"

"Good, that's good that you were fine. What was the business like?"

"Business?"

"In the taxi . . ."

"Well, yesterday I didn't—"

"Good. Yes, that's good," Limamou repeated absent-mindedly. "How about your health? Are you all right? Strong? Healthy? Nothing wrong?"

(Is he trying to hint that I caught something from Ouag? Or what?)

"Well, yeah . . . Why do you . . . Wanna leave a message for Talibe?"

"And you had a quiet night, I hope," Limamou continued, undistracted, his small-talk interrogation. "Nobody gave you a hard time in the taxi, nothing bad happened, the car didn't break on you, everybody paid . . . How much did you make, by the way? Was it all right?"

"Well, I didn't—"

The rest of Gin's sentence was drowned in a beep and a

synthetic voice of a lady who said: "PLEASE-DEPOSIT-FIVE-CENTS-FOR-THE-NEXT-FIVE-MINUTES-OR-YOUR - CALL - WILL - BE - TERMINATED. PLEASE - DEPOSIT—"

"*Merde*!" Limamou whispered, then something clicked and the pay phone at the other end of the line gave a contented gargle.

"Limamou . . . hello . . . where are you calling from?"

"Harlem Hospital. Talibe is here. At night somebody shot him."

Gin was never good at cross-country running, let alone City-street running, but she made the one-point-something mile to 135th and Lenox Avenue in under seven minutes. On her way, she managed to trip over a baby carriage, take down some guy who blocked her way, asking for a cig, and get called a "goddamn motherfuckin' white bitch motherfucker" by a gypsy cabdriver who used up quite a bit of his brake pads on her account, at least judged by the screeching.

At the main entrance, at the information booth, she jumped a whole line of visitors and made her way to a window called A-M.

"Wait a minute!" a woman behind her back said. "There's a—"

"FOFANA!" Gin screamed into the hole in the plexiglass.

"—line here!" the lady finished, sinking her two-inch long, red-and-gold striped fingernails into Gin's sweater.

The girl behind the window didn't hear her well. "Es like Sylvia?" she asked and turned her ear in the direction of Gin's shouting. "That's the other desk!" She made a gesture toward the hole named N-Z.

Gin, who was now being dragged backwards away from the window by the woman with vamp nails, couldn't come up with any nice word beginning with an F. Not even formaldehyde. "Eff for . . . FUCK!"

The hands of the black beauty behind the plexiglass began

to dance on a computer keyboard. "Eff-oh-eff-eigh-enn-eigh? I can't find him here. When was he admitted?"

"I . . . I don't know. At night. In the morning."

"He's not registered yet then. What's his disease?"

"He got shot."

The line behind Gin emitted a collective sigh. The angry lady extracted her nails carefully from the fabric of her sweater.

"Look at that! White folks dying of lead poisoning too, not just us niggers," a legless old man on a wheelchair commented quietly but clearly.

And that hoarse whisper followed Gin on her way to the elevators, bouncing off the cream-colored walls, and in tens of thousands of little echoes invading the creases of her brain.

Talibe was lying in a bed, half-hidden behind a plastic curtain, pale as death. For the first time in her life, Gin could see little odd-shaped dots on his skin, connected together with amoeba-like limbs and thorns. For the first time in her life Gin felt that all over his skin there were messages written in an unknown language.

Suddenly – and painfully – Gin felt the need to read the hieroglyphs on her husband's skin. She was suddenly sorry for all the bad stuff she ever did to him. Within half a second she promised to herself that she'd never make fun of Talibe because of the tribal spirit on whose account she has to take a crisp new sheet out of the dresser every day. That she'd never again strike her forehead in exasperation, questioning how anyone at least half-sane can gnaw on something as terrible as cola nuts. That she would learn –

"Hello, *chérie*!" Talibe said and flashed a moronic smile.

He was covered by a thin hospital blanket through the fabric of which a bandage around his whole stomach and chest showed. Both of his wrists were fastened to metal bars on the sides of the bed, and plastic tubes stuck out from every which place in his body, dripping variously colored liquids either into him or out. Around Talibe's head, on little pulleys, a bunch of machines were standing, beeping loudly.

And at his feet, half a yard away from his long, thin, beautifully shaped big toes, about twelve of Talibe's brothers, cousins and friends were standing, eyeing Gin with reproachful contempt.

"Mrs . . . Fofana?" the doctor said, having read the name three times from Talibe's chart. Even this guy, though obviously smart, had a hard time connecting Gin and Talibe. "Your . . . husband . . . after getting shot . . . made it to the hospital in his . . . automobile and then he walked all by himself all the way to the Emergency Room. It seems pretty amazing. The very fact that he didn't lose consciousness shows he has a real strong will to live." He patted Talibe on the mesh blanket and Talibe gave a moronic grin. "Do you know something about medical sciences?"

"Not much."

"Your husband, Mrs . . . Fofana, lost an amazing amount of blood from internal bleeding. In similar cases it's very common for the lungs to collapse; they fill up with blood very quickly, ceasing to supply oxygen to the body, not talking about the fact that the pressure of the blood from the abdominal cavity on the pericardium often causes a cardiac arrest. On the other hand, a quick lowering of the blood pressure in the brain – MRS FOFANA! Your husband is OUT OF DANGER now! I operated on him myself – I mean, with my colleague Weissbaum, who's our best GSW specialist. Your husband couldn't have chosen a better hospital, believe me! Here we have three, four cases a day, and people with much, much worse shot wounds go home perfectly healthy. Here in our hospital—"

The doctor looked at his watch, then at Talibe, then at her. "Now it's twelve fifteen. Your husband is on morphine. He's stable. Can I invite you for lunch? MRS. FOFANA! Are you interested in medical science?"

"Man, that's funny, Gin, that's really funny!" Dr Whitehead

said, sinking his white front teeth into a third fried chicken leg. "You mean that whole marriage of yours—"

"The marriage isn't fake at all!" Gin frowned. For the last hour at least she'd been swearing to herself that Talibe was the only love of her life. "Talibe married me because—"

(She wasn't at all sure why in God's name Talibe married her but the physician started speaking so quickly that she didn't have the time to get embarrassed.)

"When your husband was coming to after the surgery," he said, pulling with surgical precision the crusty skin off a chicken leg, "he started shouting something. In French. I'm not boasting, I'm far from it, but, you know, I thought, why shouldn't I dust off the few lousy idioms I've learned in high school, so we began to talk. Do you speak French, Gin? Well, I don't really understand how you could communicate but . . . never mind. Anyway, your husband kept talking about some children or something. MES ENFANTS means my children, doesn't it? Who, he kept repeating, is gonna take care of my children . . . How many children do you two have?"

"These are his sister's children. In Mali. In Africa. Talibe used to send them money because – because – I guess you know about families like that."

"I see. I almost started thinking . . ."

Dr Whitehead was eyeing Gin – in a decent manner – only from the neck up but it was plain that he was trying to figure out how she was equipped between the legs. Gin had noticed a long time ago that her marriage with Talibe often makes people do just that. In front of Dr Whitehead's inner eye Gin, spread out like a frog, is lying on a delivery table, a child's head, then shoulders, then belly, sticking out of her loins. And the child (white? black? brown? striped? polka-dotted?) welcomes the light of the halogen lamp with screams in some unknown African tongue.

Gin put her hand down on the greasy plastic, right next to the paper coffin brimming with torn-off limbs of poor little murdered chickens. "You wanted to tell me about his wound."

"Yes, yes, that's right," Dr Whitehead admitted and chewed

thoughtfully for a while. "You know, here in Harlem, we're absolute gun experts. Your husband couldn't have chosen a better hospital, even if he drove for two thousand miles with that wound of his. Guns, that's what we know best. I mean, I never had a gun in my hand in my whole life but I know more about bullets than a hit man, believe me. Snipers, so to speak, often don't even get to see the final product of their work. But us here, Gin! Your husband got only one, in the stomach, from a short range, even though not point-blank because in that case you can see a ring on the skin. I suppose I can tell you now: it's a miracle that he's alive. Had he lost consciousness, which is a miracle that he didn't, then maybe some doctor from the coroner's office would've invited you for this chicken lunch – Jesus, Gin, forgive me, I'm kind of – I mean, all you have to do is tear the peritoneum and it makes a mess in your belly you can't believe. In his case the bullet hit the stomach – and you should see the mess a single hollow-point bullet can make when it ricochets in your body. You should see what your intestines look like; surgery, Gin, is nothing but groping elbow-deep in sh– and when it's just a bit far gone in the way of digestion, you sometimes feel like cutting off your own nose and throwing it on a pile of dung."

For some reason, Gin now could see cola nuts and palm soup, as they travel, stinking, through Talibe's digestive system.

"And don't forget internal bleeding, when it mixes with the content of the colon. In his case, the spleen was hit, too, so we had to remove it, it's not easy to splice the spleen up, not talking about the fact that you don't have enough time for that when – but that's no problem, you can live without your spleen; half of Harlem is alive and kicking with their spleen removed as the consequence of gunshot and stabbing wounds – but what I was trying to say was: When you imagine the whole ocean of viscous shit spreading in front of you on the operating table, and you have to plunge your claws in it pretty much elbow-deep, then – Forgive me, I – He was shot from a .25, I can't give you the bullet right now, the hospital has to keep it for the cops, what if, I mean, just WHAT IF some detective or other did get interested in his case? Or do you think that a murder attempt still attracts the attention of the law enforcement in this City? But I don't mean to bore you with that . . ."

He pushed the chicken coffin closer to her.

"I don't know," Gin stammered. She was struggling to keep down that little bite of chicken leg she'd unthinkingly swallowed at the very beginning of their conversation. "I don't know how to thank you properly," she said, tears rising into her eyes almost as fast as the half-digested chicken rose back into her pharynx. "For saving him. For giving him his life back."

"There are things I really like about being a surgeon, Gin," the doctor said, tearing the last ounce of meat from the pinkish bone with his white incisors, "and this is one of them. All you have to do is IMAGINE that pile of shit on the table – and how you claw around in it, for four, five hours, or seven hours, or twelve hours – trying to catch your breath, sweating and swearing, praying all the time for him not to be a last minute croaker because then all your effort would be in vain. This is the time when you think about him like he is WORK and nothing else. You don't think of him like he's a human being. You think about him like he's a whole pile of guts and intestines and stuff – you gotta take that one out, sew on that one . . . you understand, Gin? But then you sew him all up, you try to make sure every stitch looks really neat so one day he can boast about that lovely scar he's got – and the next day you go see him and you know what, Gin? There's a HUMAN BEING lying on the bed. He smiles or cries, he thanks you or curses you, sometimes he's a nice guy and sometimes he's a jerk. But you know what? You – a nobody, an unimportant little doc, a surgeon from the Emergency Room who doesn't even have his own private practice – you've turned a pile of shit into a human being! So you can't believe your own eyes, you feel like the Creator . . . At least for a bit, I mean . . ."

Dr Whitehead's beeper went off for the third time, so he made an apologetic gesture and got up to go. "Oh, don't let me forget, I got something for you." He fished out something from the pocket of his unhealthy-green surgeon's frock. "I mean, it's against the rules but what isn't . . . This is what your husband had on his neck. You know it, don't you? What is it? Some African mojo bag?"

An object she hadn't been allowed to as much as take a close look at entered Gin's palm. The three little scrolls of goat skin inscribed with stuff only the tribal shaman was acquainted with. It was the good-luck charm that made Talibe bulletproof. Its sweat-stained string was severed with surgical scissors and the old leather was caked with Talibe's blood.

"Oh shit!" Gin whispered.

Chapter 28

Color White

For some immigrants horizons broaden after their arrival in America, for others they get narrower. Talibe belonged among those whose horizons got narrower.

Right now they were SO narrow that Talibe barely dared to peek through his eyelashes at all the color white around him. The surplus of piercing white light in the hospital room made his pupils constrict to the size of pin heads, the pins pricking his consciousness. Talibe squinted his eyes like a wild cat but even so the white whips of light penetrated his eyelids, brandishing the creases of his brain.

Talibe's life had long ago shrunk to the size of a morbidly clean apartment, a couple of friends and his taxicab. He was convinced that he wasn't going to stay in America for much longer – but he has to hold on for at least another several years so he can take good care of his family. All his hopes and desires were now dwelling in amateurish snapshots of some thirty-five people, taped to the inner side of the door of apartment #5C.

Talibe squinted his eyes into the color white of the hospital room. Its walls were made white by a coat of shiny latex paint. The bed legs were creamy white. The nurses wore frocks designed to prick his eyes with every white thread on them. His own body was rolled in a gauze bandage, white as snow, which burned and chilled him at the same time. Even the hospital mesh-blanket was white. The color white – even here, in Harlem – symbolized cleanliness, sterility, and Talibe himself felt unbearably dirty when he was surrounded by all this anti-color. It seemed to him that he was growing smaller hour by hour, that his head was shrinking because of this color white, the same way his pupils were shrinking because of white light. It seemed to him that all that color was choking him, laying heavily on him, it seemed to him that he was sinking deeper and deeper into it like it was a dangerous snow drift. And when the rectangle of the door frame flew open and the pale face of his American wife appeared in it, Talibe almost howled with terror. It came out as a tiny sigh.

"Talibe!" Gin yipped out just like every day – at least ten times since he's been here. "Talibe, HOW ARE YOU FEELING?"

Talibe shrugged his shoulders. It came out as the straightening of a crease on his blanket.

"Hi, *chérie*!"

"Hello!" the circle of Talibe's friends murmured. Not very enthusiastically but in unison.

There were usually ten to fifteen of them. They were standing in a semicircle around Talibe's bed and, with the exception of his own toes, their hands and faces were the only source of that sweet, soothing color that didn't prick his eyes. They made their way in, one by one, every morning, and they stayed, engaged in loud discussions, until the head nurse threw them out some time around midnight.

Talibe looked horrendous.

"You know what was the first thing your husband asked me, Gin?" Dr Whitehead said a few days ago. "He asked me: Did you give me blood? Well, I had to tell him, what else can you do, after all, he sucked up at least five liters, otherwise he'd die on us in the OR. I don't like to reveal this to patients, you know, everybody's afraid of AIDS – but this wasn't what your husband was worried about, Gin. He says: And did you give me BLACK blood? *Le sang noir.* We were talking French. Do you mean black man's blood? I say, and I can't believe my own ears, so I tell him: Well, I just don't know, we got no tests for black blood so far, we test blood for HIV and hepatitis and – well, you'd have to ask my colleagues, the hematologists, they'd lecture you about it for an hour, but for BLACK blood, if you please, we don't have no tests, I guarantee that, even though I'm not a hematologist, I'm a surgeon!" Dr Whitehead said angrily, inadvertedly spitting a thin, angry thread of saliva into Gin's face. "And if you're really so TERRIBLY concerned about getting BLACK blood, you should've told me right away, while I was elbow-deep in your guts. I'd have taken my claws out of your stomach and I'd have made sure that they dyed that goddamn blood black for you!"

"He's from Africa, you know?" Gin squeezed in apologetically. "And in Africa blood is – You can imagine: ancestor worship, magic, animal sacrifice, tribal bonds and—"

"And me? I'm not from Africa?" Dr Whitehead articulated indignantly. "Just look at me, look at my squashed-out nigger face. I'm BLACK which means I'm from AFRICA. Which tribe am I from – well, I don't know, I'm no Alex Haley so I suppose I'll never find out where the toubab got my great granddaddy but I'm an AFRICAN, just like your husband. And some full-blooded new arrival with his Black blood can kiss my – Jee-zus, excuse me, Gin, I just—"

"How much blood is there is a human body? Ten, twelve liters? Something like that?"

"*Non, non, non,*" Dr Whitehead articulates painstakingly in his high school French. "*Pas dix*. Much, much less. Between four and five liters."

All my blood, ALL the blood that's flowing through my veins, all my blood isn't mine. And I'm not even allowed to know whose it is—

Talibe could painfully feel every little blood cell, every little blood cell of his new blood that (most likely!) was white, he felt it grow bigger and divide in his body, he felt it infect his system, he felt the color white, masked by the red, crawling all over his body; it was an intruder; not even the INSIDES of his body were safe from that blood, that color.

That color which, in Africa, only the angel of death is wearing on his mask.

"Talibe! Talibe! Come on, talk to me! You can talk, can't you?"

"*Oui, chérie . . .*"

"Talibe, give me your hand. Give me your hand! Put your hand out and give it to me!"

"I'm . . . cold, *chérie*!"

"I'll warm it up! Can you feel how hot my hands are? Just touch my hand!"

"*Mais* I'm cold."

"OK, so hide your FEET under the blanket. I'll cover them up for you. And give me your hand, you hear me?"

"Leave me alone, *chérie*."

"Talibe, you'll be fine in a few days. In a few days they'll let you go home. That's what the doctor said. Give me your hand! I mean . . . smile. At least smile at me! Talibe!"

"I am cold, *chérie*!"

And twelve or fifteen Africans at the foot of Talibe's bed watched Gin's actions, talking in a tongue she couldn't understand.

To her ears they sounded like a mad swarm of hornets.

The rest of the incident happened very swiftly.

Gin's eyes got filled up with tears – it was an uncontrollable tidal wave – and they rolled down her cheeks and fell on Talibe's blanket, on the spot where his elbow could be seen through the holes.

Immediately afterwards Gin was lying on the floor, her wet nose stuck to the linoleum. Limamou was lying on top of her.

"Never, never, never, NEVER!" Limamou filtered through his teeth, "NEVER!!! must a woman cry over her sick husband. It's like you are crying for him! Do you want to kill him? Do you?"

Talibe's countrymen started yelling at the top of their lungs. But not in English.

In the next second the security guard, attracted by all that noise, pounced into the room. He was an obese Puerto Rican with a million fat folds undulating under his uniform, with an eighteen-inch nightstick and a dark gray face.

"What d'you think you're doing, nigger?" he screamed, picking up Limamou off Gin. By his shirt collar. With exactly the same motion a cat picks up her kittens by the skin folds on their necks.

"What d'you think you're doing? What do you have IN MIND? Are you trying to rob her? To rape her? Or what? That's why I'm here, to prevent you from doing that! You're never gonna stick that nigger face of yours into this hospital again! I guarantee that! You stupid fucking nigger!"

And like the well-trained cop he was he struck Limamou's knee cap with his nightstick.

"He didn't mean it that way!" Gin yelled out, getting up from the linoleum.

But the guard had already marched Limamou off behind the corner of the corridor, and to the elevators.

Chapter 29

The City, Circles

New York neighborhoods – or hoods – seldom have well-defined boundaries. In fact, the opposite is true: for God knows how many decades the whole New York has been fighting over where one of them begins and another one ends.

If you tell someone that you live on the Upper East Side, the person in question measures you with his gaze, then lifts up his eyebrows and asks: "HOW Upper?" – that's because there's a borderline of at least twenty, thirty blocks that, in theory, still belong to that neighborhood, full of bored old ladies who, as the law requires, meticulously pick up shit from under their dogs' rear ends, but in reality it's Harlem already.

The inhabitants of 156th Street certainly consider themselves Harlemites although north of 155th Street Washington Heights officially begins. On the other hand, most of the people who live, let's say, on 207th Street and Broadway, will probably insist that they live in Washington Heights. Possibly they don't even know that this northern tip of Manhattan is called Inwood on the map.

New York neighborhoods grow larger or shrink, they crawl like rainworms to the north or to the south, they send little tentacles into their vicinity, they go "up" with surprising swiftness, or they die out into ghettos.

Very seldom can they be defined with exact coordinates of the streets and avenues.

New York neighborhoods resemble circles.

They resemble circles; their almost magic power locks their inhabitants inside them, they lure a certain type of people (with their financial possibilities, their social class, their world view or their sexual orientation) to move to them – and then they slowly, imperceptibly change these people, they mold them into what they never dreamed of becoming.

New York's "hoods" are like circles that grapple you and suck you inside themselves.

And of course, hood is also something you pull over your head and you hide behind – and it certainly doesn't broaden your horizons.

And so it happened to Gin that, after she moved out of the East Village and landed on 116th Street, two circles started fighting over her.

East Village – that was art.

Harlem was rhythm and power.

Harlem wasn't a charity-ridden neighborhood at all. Only the most desperate people dared to sleep in the streets. Junkies at the stage of total decomposition when their whole body and soul was a single festering ulcer. Folks that were shit-faced drunk. And – naturally – the dead.

Once Gin was passing by a pile of newspapers and heaped up garbage on Manhattan Avenue and 119th. By the sidewalk a homeless man was lying, asleep. At first sight it looked like he was resting peacefully. He was lying all curled up on his side, his face buried in some rag, and it seemed that there was no difference between him and dozens or hundreds of others who also sleep, in the early afternoon hours, on a piece of cardboard, covered with filth and the Universe.

But there was something weird about this guy.

People didn't walk over him, tripping over his legs, even

though he had stuck them, one completely bare, one clad in a sneaker so holey that all his toes were sticking out anyway, covered with a bluish-gray gauze of dirt, all the way to the curb. People circled around him, keeping far away, often choosing to cross the street rather than having to get too close to him; they felt his aura. His aura was death.

Then Gin saw another man like that, at the church steps, right across the street from the place she lived with Talibe. FIRST CORINTHIAN CHURCH was announced by the sky-blue shades of letters in the dusty plaster that once had been sky-blue, too. The metal letters had fallen off a long time ago, leaving only their imprints, fresh and clean, with a few holes left after the bolts. The church door had metal bars on it like it was a prison cell, and it was secured by a heavy chain whose one end reached to the ground, and that man who was lying there had tied his wrists with that chain – he was holding that chain and that chain was holding him. He was stretched, head down, across several low steps in front of a chained-off church and he was feeling comfortable, death for him was a pillow stuffed with goose down. It was raining and his hair got plastered to the sidewalk like his head was a shattered medusa.

Gin walked through Harlem alongside splendid blocks of houses, now burned down or sentenced to die a different death, and windows, sealed with gray cinder blocks were shedding gray tears, others tried to smile – that was when somebody painted on the metal sheets that were nailed over the windows beautiful intricate shades, pretty curtains or flower pots filled with firetruck-red fuchsias.

Sometimes they painted a sky with little clouds on it on the blinded windows – an impenetrable, dead sky that served here as a barricade. While in other buildings the real sky shone through the holes of windows, framed with burned bricks.

In some blocks the desperate people who wanted to live somewhere no matter what poked a hole in the cinder blocks with a sledgehammer, and then they lived in those houses until they froze to death. Or until the police got them.

Gin sometimes felt a pang of desire to live that way, too, to bring her seven illegal milk crates into one of the dead houses somewhere around Douglas Boulevard and 118th Street, to make love to that neighborhood skin on skin . . . and then she got goose bumps just from that thought.

And so at least she sucked into herself all those burned walls, the structure of the chipped-off plaster, the crenelated fortifications above which the roof used to hang, the caved-in ceilings, exposed beams and useless piping that made its snaking way from nowhere to nowhere along the gutted walls.

She sucked into herself the wet little yards in between buildings into which the sunlight could penetrate only in slanted rays, in the shape of holographic daggers – but nevertheless it made little winking spots on the bare bricks of the walls and on the branches of trees that grew here. They were the Chinese trees of heaven, trees that possessed the most exciting leaf smell Gin ever knew – it was a green smell with a tinge of nutty fermentation; people called them the New York City palm trees. That was because they took root, uninvited, absolutely, absolutely everywhere: They threw their branches open like arms from those wet little yards, they stuck their heads from third-story windows, they grew, branch by branch, through the thick bars of fire escapes, and wherever they met with metal, they hugged and kissed it with flat scars the shape of lips. New York City palm trees' elegant gray trunks and bright green leaves lit up the neighborhood like lanterns; their roots turned old bricks and bore through concrete. They slit apart, along the seams, that flat of concrete that almost hermetically covered all of Manhattan.

Perhaps this was what Harlem was about: the feeling of dynamic history. The history of this part of town was so strong and far-reaching that even vegetation remembered the times when Manhattan was still a forest-covered island.

There were few beggars in Harlem, and if somebody did beg after all, then only on huge "business" streets like on 125th. On abandoned corners begging wasn't begging, it was more like robbery.

("You must NEVER, EVER give a cigarette TO ANYBODY. In Harlem someone will want a cigarette from you on every corner but you MUST NOT give it to anybody. Not even when he looks like he really needs it. Even when he's nice and polite, you must not give it to him, and if he blocks your way, you must not give it to him DOUBLE! You give a cigarette to one guy, then you light it for him, he thanks you pleasantly and you're thinking, Fine, I'm a nice guy, ain't I? but from a distance two or three others are watching you and they work in tandem with the beggar: By not refusing to give him the cigarette you've placed yourself in the sucker category, do you know what I mean? And twenty yards later they jump you, beat you up – because they know you're a weakling, you're not gonna fight back – and they rob you like pros, so within thirty seconds not even your underwear is gonna stay on you.

And that beggar on the corner is gonna lean on a lamppost, smoking YOUR OWN cigarette!")

There were few beggars in Harlem, but the abandoned buildings around Gin reminded her of wrecked human beings.

She walked through Harlem, with no cigarettes, and it seemed to her that those mutilated buildings, their eyes blinded with gray gauze, were dancing a slow waltz on their frail legs . . . that they were sometimes leaning down, toward her, the three-yard-tall tree growing on their gutter included, whispering something. Sometimes she was convinced these houses were dying and the next moment she believed they were rising from the dead.

Harlem sucked Gin into itself, teaching her, bit by bit, how to be different.

In Harlem you mustn't give cigarettes to beggars.

In Harlem it always pays to know who's behind you, and how far away you are from the nearest busy corner.

In Harlem, experts recommended, it is advisable to hold your right hand in your jacket pocket all the time, so the passers-by will think you have a gun there.

In Harlem little flocks of boys that appear out of nowhere know how to kick you off the curb like pros, and while you're collapsing on the sewer cover, filch all your money on top of that.

In Harlem fierce mothers with baby carriages – three or four of them at a time – know how to block your way so quickly that you have to jump from the curb and land in a puddle if you want to avoid a collision with screaming toddlers. All that is accompanied by shrieking accusations you've probably called upon yourself because of some mysterious sin in the life of your ancestors.

Tough guys, their heads wrapped up in bandannas with the colors of this or that gang watch you with their eyes narrowed to the shape of lopsided Arabian daggers.

And twelve-year-old kids in Morningside Park are training their pitbulls with bread-crust-colored hair and studded collars how to tear and choke on command.

The circle that called itself Harlem functioned on the principle of power.

And hate.

If you wanted to survive, it was necessary to learn how to hate others, too.

To steal from them. To shoot them. To knock them down on the asphalt with your fists and tear them into pieces so tiny that they can't possibly do you any harm.

Only when Talibe was dying in the hospital, did all that dawn on Gin.

Chapter 30

Talibe

In Dr Whitehead's opinion Talibe was dying of non-specific and most likely combined septic shock, which, as it seemed, neither Ampicillin, nor Tetracycline, not even Vancomycin could relieve. Dr Whitehead was anxiously awaiting the lab results even though he didn't give much hope.

Talibe lost his appetite for life completely. He was lying on the white bed like a rag, he refused to speak, even in French, and invariably looked the other way whenever somebody leaned over him in a helpful manner.

Perhaps Talibe was dying of the five liters of that blood that wasn't his own.

Perhaps he was suffocating on whiteness.

But most likely Talibe was dying of the magic powers of his good-luck charm.

The good-luck charm, after all, possessed in it Allah's powers in the form of Koran quotations, as well as the magic of the shaman's incantations.

The good-luck charm, as soon as you put it on your neck, made your body impenetrable for any iron object – if you wore it, it was quite impossible, for instance, to cut yourself while cutting onions.

You weren't allowed to "test" the good-luck charm – cutting yourself with a knife or pricking yourself with a needle, trying whether the blade of a razor could penetrate the skin on your finger after all. But Talibe remembered his joy at the moment he was cutting something in the kitchen, the good-luck charm on his neck – and he almost cut himself really bad, but then the knife slid along his fingernail and not a single drop of blood came out of Talibe's index finger.

The amulet guaranteed that you couldn't be stabbed with a knife, it wasn't possible to chop your head off with a sword – as long as the sword wasn't made of bronze, of course – and only a silver bullet might possibly make a mess like that in your guts.

Talibe's good-luck charm made any surgery on his body impossible to perform (just imagine the look on the sawbone's face as he watches his scalpel jump off his patient's skin as if warded off by the repulsive pole of a magnet!) – and if surgery became inevitable, then it would be necessary to take the amulet off your neck at least a few days in advance so that its power has time to wane.

Bullets were NOT ALLOWED to bore into someone who had on his neck a good-luck charm made of fragrant billy-goat hide. Instead, they bounced off him like he was a trampoline, and bored into the heart of that unhappy man who'd decided to take a shot at him.

However, Talibe was lying here, gutted like a chicken without gizzards, and he knew that that motherfucker had shot him with a bullet made of plain old steel.

"There are cases," Limamou was fond of saying, "when magic works one hundred percent, and there are others when you can't rely on magic."

Talibe, though, was now absolutely convinced that he couldn't rely on ANYTHING.

He felt like a man whose whole meticulously drawn

philosophical system, a system he'd leaned on all his life, had crumbled under him without as much as a sound.

Culture shock from the American continent had caught up with him only after four years, but then it ricocheted inside his gut.

Was the whole American continent some kind of destructive power field, some enemy land on which reliable, well-proven magic from Mali refused to work? Was the amulet's power sucked out by the funny little door that beeps when you walk though it at the airport? Did Talibe's American wife smear his good-luck charm with her menstrual blood?

Talibe felt like a man who'd dived to the bottom of a lake, convinced that he can breathe underwater.

He'd plunged, like a paratrooper without a chute, on the American continent, and during his fall toward the Earth he couldn't understand how it was possible that he didn't sprout wings on the way.

Talibe, behind forcefully closed eyelids, was falling and falling and falling.

I'm never gonna get used to this, Dr Whitehead thought mournfully, and for a while he desperately wished to be a dentist. (Oh yes, you're quite right, Miss, that filling really IS a little lighter than the enamel, you're quite right. OK, so we'll have to drill it again and—)

Or they should hire somebody to take care of that. What do I know . . . An undertaker. A priest.

I'm never gonna get used to this, Dr Whitehead thought mournfully, I'm never gonna get used to the change in their face when I have to say it.

Hope.

Their face turned toward you like you were a demigod that can—

Then that sentence you gotta say aloud. (And if you practiced a hundred times before, it's not gonna come out the right way. Never.)

Then that little "I-don't-get-it" sound they make.

Then disbelief.

Then fury. Dr Whitehead got beaten up with the fists of more than one mother whose son he couldn't save.

And then, sometimes, tears, sometimes a whisper-quiet "Thank you, doctor," sometimes the salt-pillar gaze of Lot's wife, sometimes a threat – "See you in court!" – and sometimes an almost soldier-like about face! and a retreat with the head held high.

Dr Whitehead hated that.

Perhaps, instead of a surgeon, he should have become a dermatologist. And kick out everybody with a big black mole the minute they walk in through his office door.

"I've called Air Afrique," Limamou said matter-of-factly. "Transportation to Dakar, if we book it quickly, will cost around three thousand, and then he'll have to switch—"

Limamou had torn all the pictures that had hung on the inner side of the door #5C, and now he was busy getting them rid of yellowed little shards of tape.

"—then they'll have to put him on a freight plane because the Mali authorities make problems with transporting coffins, even metal coffins; it's almost impossible to take them on a passenger plane. The best would be if I could fly with him. But I—"

"I can't go to Africa, either!" Gin said. She was sitting on a chair, folded into a little ball, and she was experimentally trying to sink her teeth into a cola nut that had, for some mysterious reason, rolled from under the sink half an hour ago. "I don't have a passport, either. And – Limamou, are you sure you want to send him all the way . . . there? When we can't even go with him? For three thousand we could give him a nice funeral here and—"

"You've gone crazy, Miss Gin! Here! Talibe will not rest here, HERE it is not his land! And we must send him as soon as we can so—so his children can see him for the last time."

"You mean his sister's children? The ones he sends money to?"

Limamou gave a deep sigh. "Miss Gin, don't you know that? Didn't it dawn on you? In all that time? He was just saying that, his sister's children. Because he had to, you understand? Because that's nobody's business that he . . . that he had no choice but to go to America and make money for his family. Because Talibe was born in a poor country, Miss Gin. You Americans can't never understand that, what it is, to work all the time and not have enough money for—" Limamou picked the picture of Talibe's beautiful sister out of the pile and stabbed her face with his thumbnail so hard that a deep, crescent-shaped scar was left on it. "This is his wife, Miss Gin, and she was hanging here long before he brought you over here. I don't understand how it's possible that you didn't understand that!"

"But how could he . . ." Gin was gasping for breath. With this discovery, a lot of things began to make sense. (Talibe's unwillingness to talk about his life in Africa, $378.26 for the phone bill, his excited, caressing voice while he was talking Mandinge across the ocean, his strict refusal to introduce Gin, his brand new wife, to any family member over the phone.) "How could he . . . how could he marry me when he—"

"Miss Gin, Talibe is – was – a Muslim. Maybe you've noticed that. He can have four wives. Or five. Or ten. As long as he can feed them. And he had only one."

"But the law here in America—"

"You wouldn't understand that," Limamou waved his hand dismissively, peeling an invisible shard of tape off Talibe's wife's back side. "But I wanted to tell you this, Miss Gin: Talibe was a good husband for you, or wasn't he? He married you when you needed it, you got your green card thanks to him . . ."

"Almost," Gin chirped in.

"Because that's what I was going to tell you," Limamou proceeded slowly to the point, "Talibe used to send at least six or eight hundred dollars to his family every month. You knew that, didn't you? I'll give you the address. And I'll tell you which bank to go to. Because it would be good to continue doing that. At least for a couple months. Or years. You can't imagine what situation they're in. But his family . . . Talibe in America died, his children in Africa will go hungry."

For the first time since she knew him, Limamou looked straight into her eye. He had huge, velvety-brown irises with a few gray cracklines in them. To Gin, his eyes were reminiscent of rotting oranges in the process of being cut with a blade.

"Maybe you should do that for Talibe, Miss Gin."

"And don't call me Miss Gin!" Gin screamed, grabbing a chair from under her own butt and proceeding to shatter it on the linoleum. With each blow something fell off the chair. "Don't call me Miss Gin, OK, when you know I was married to Talibe!"

Then she stretched on the floor comfortably, hugged the shards of Talibe's chair, pressed her face to them and started crying.

"Tears, tears, tears!" Limamou commented, throwing a look of condescending pity at Gin. "Just like in the hospital. Tears, tears, tears. Why did you do that? Why did you cry over him? Didn't you know you could kill him?"

Limamou raked the handful of photos off the table top, spat into the kitchen sink and carefully walked around Gin on his way to the hall.

"Africans should never marry white women, never. It doesn't work. I told Talibe that much," he mumbled quietly to himself. But in English.

Chapter 31

Protective Circles

Gin walked out into the street and that day, Harlem turned into a neighborhood of bubbles. Of protective circles everybody lived in. That is, everybody except herself.

These were the circles defined by the radius of a hunting knife blade.

The circles of the range of guns.

Circles of the essence of the ghetto that irradiated from baggy jeans, from heavy hooded sweatshirts and untied sneakers known as con shoes.

The bigger circle they took when circumnavigating you, the safer you were in Harlem.

Gin's circle shrank all the way to her skin. She was wandering, half-blind, through the streets, and people didn't arc out of their way to walk around her, quite the contrary: they made beelines right through her, pushing her off sidewalks, the curb, the street, cursing.

They pushed her away from their own protective circles. It didn't matter where.

On the south side of 116th Street she stopped under the

sign FIRST CORINTHIAN CHURCH, looking up to the sky-blue shadows of letters. She held on to the heavy chain on the church gate for a second. It was the gate that had heavy bars on it like a prison cell.

Perhaps I, too, would know how to make a medusa here, she thought, just like that dead guy I'd seen lying here. And death suddenly didn't seem so awful to her. Just comfortable. Worry free.

The sky above the rooftops was heavy and gray, so dark gray, in fact, that the silhouettes of antennas and lightning rods shone white on its backdrop like sun-bleached camel skeletons. Once she had looked up in the sky on a gray and unpleasant day like this one, and she saw a blue balloon flying high across it; it was unbelievably beautiful as it negated all that grayness. Now Gin was checking every inch of the sky that was left above the rooftops, but there was no blue balloon flying on it. Today she'd almost believe that the blue balloon is Talibe's soul.

Gin grabbed Talibe's good-luck charm, its cut-open string and all, in her jacket pocket and squeezed it in her palm. The skin on it was made soft and sticky by numerous touches, and now it seemed to her that the good-luck charm was permeated with the dissolved heat of Talibe's body.

– Gin, come on, pull yourself together, will you?

She'd just walked absent-mindedly into the gap between two Harlemites, and those two big-shouldered guys had, both at the same time, leaned toward her, squeezing her breath out. "Drop dead!" one of them whispered – but at the same moment she was free again and just some adolescent giggles were following her down the block. These two jokesters probably thought she was gonna shit her pants with fear but –

– she didn't want anything else but to drop dead right now. Drop dead. Melt. Die.

Death, after all, must be a bit like melting. Stepping into the waters of the River Styx, motionless and steel-gray just like today's sky. Her wrist still remembered the tentative touch of that rusty razor, back there, in Gloria's place. How idiotic it seemed to her today – wanting to kill herself. (It doesn't matter what for.) And how her whole body resisted that touch of the blade: It had its reasons. It was (and still is!) neatly divided into drawers and shelves and compartments and – death, after all, is melting. Blending in. Disintegration.

How much closer to the City were those who were dying in it than those who lived in it! How much closer to 116th Street that dead guy by the chained church door was when his hair spread around on the asphalt, blending in with it! How much closer to the City were those who vegetated on the streets, those who spent their nights, half-frozen, on the grills of its guts, those who staggered through its capillaries, those who bore into the plastic bags of the City's ass with long poles, eating from it by the handful.

Death is melting, and that's what Buddha knew when he entered Nirvana under the bodhi tree. Gin understood why Limamou wanted so much to bury Talibe in Africa. Limamou was horrified by the idea that in his death Talibe should blend in with New York, with America . . . that he might seep into the soil of the continent that killed him.

Chilly wind from the west started to blow, bringing with it moisture and pink snow. It's spring! Gin realized. She was walking against that wind with difficulties, until she reached a street corner where that wind had blown pink Japanese cherry blossoms onto black plastic garbage bags, onto a whole mountain of black plastic bags. The pink petals were forming little drifts on every surface that wasn't exposed to the wind, they slid down the plastic and formed layers on top of one another, in the end creating a humongous, black-and-pink sculpture, filled with every smell known to humankind.

On the sidewalk a piece of cardboard was lying, and so Gin stretched on it. She liked the idea that somebody had already lain on it and imprinted a hollow in the shape of a human body in the cardboard like it was a straw mattress.

Dozens, hundreds of smells from dozens of kitchens of that tall apartment building above her were crawling toward Gin from that black-and-pink mountain. A few drops of rain fell from the sky and the asphalt exploded with a sweet-and-acrid smell. The cardboard under her tickled her nostrils with a warmish smell of that someone who had already imprinted the shape of his lying body in this flattened box that once held a washing machine, maybe. And above all that the smell of torn-off petals of Japanese cherry trees floated toward her.

That spring smell buried Gin under pink drifts as light as a breath, and she was thinking about the imprints of people and things. About the imprints of dead Harlem houses that stayed on the building next to them in the form of scars, naked walls and water pipes that made no sense anymore.

And she was thinking about how much of Talibe got reflected in her.

(Because they didn't love each other, oh no, and they couldn't get along, but they had been standing – here in Harlem – very close to each other for some time.)

From out of my body, crumbling, halved bricks are sticking. The sealed windows and doors that (after all) once led from you to me are hurting me now. And I will never know how to live without your imprint in me, Talibe.

"Get out! Get out of my place! You fuckin' whore! Just fucking get your ass off my turf!"

Above the blending-in Gin a guy was standing. He looked like he just jumped off a greasy Santa Claus poster. His hair fell in coils on his shoulders, his matted, white beard reached all the way to his belly, and the half-translucent petals of Japanese cherry trees had gotten caught in it. His eyes were even a bit grayer and meaner than the sky above him. And he smelled exactly like the little hollow Gin was lying in.

"Get off, get off, you fucking whore!" the old man spat out, empowering his words with a nasty kick.

Gin realized there's no way she could just blend in.

Chapter 32

Return Trips

In the garage on 21st Street the hustle and bustle usually began to calm down after 5:30 p.m. At seven, she believed, she wasn't gonna meet a single taxidriver there.

She was right.

In that yellowish space under the low, ribbed ceiling, in the space where she'd always felt like a huge killer whale had swallowed her, only Ramon the mechanic was left. He wormed his way from under an open car hood as soon as she'd appeared at the gate, then he rubbed his eyes, looked at her in the back light, and with a happy yowl he ran to welcome her.

Gin had become his benefactor.

When, several weeks ago, she conveyed to Ramon the message that he's cordially invited to join Kenny's garage and what salary he can expect there, Ramon didn't hesitate a minute. That very same evening, right after the unsuspecting Alex said goodbye to him with a jab in the teeth, Ramon packed up his extra shirt (not exactly clean) and a half-full bottle of Corona Beer, in an unheard-of bout of good-heartedness he shared his salami sandwich with Laila the dog, and then, weighed down with all the spare parts he could possibly carry, snuck away in a southward direction. Twenty-six downtown blocks later his life became a paradise.

Gin could hardly recognize him today. Ramon was decked out in a brand new, flashy pair of overalls with a bib whose under-sea green color was smeared with brownish oil streaks only in several places. His washed, trimmed and combed head was sticking out of the collar of his surprisingly white shirt. Gin couldn't believe her eyes – Ramon looked so much lighter and younger. He didn't sleep on the muddy floor on a tattered issue of a tabloid anymore. Under the table in the dispatcher's booth a comfortable and comparably clean mattress was waiting for him. Now, when he had a whole shower at his disposal right here in the garage, he took not just one but two showers a day; he frolicked in that refreshing stream of water that was lukewarm at first and then, true, pretty icy – but Ramon didn't complain about anything. He enjoyed looking at himself in an old, pock-marked mirror now. He became an almost handsome man. Less than a week was sufficient for all the deep layers of dust, sweat and oil to get off him, and now he smelled to himself and others with all the cleanliness that a huge bar of laundry soap had in it.

"Miss Gin!" Ramon yelled out, bowing in front of her, "my *benefactora*!" he screamed, not knowing what to do with his hands. "You saved my life, Miss Gin, you saved my life. Oh – *mucho gracias, mucho, mucho, mucho*!"

He was walking backwards in front of her and, incessantly bowing, kept singing her praises.

"Kenny here?" Gin asked, just out of embarrassment. She knew he was there.

"Hello, Miss Gin, hello, hello!" Kenny bellowed as soon as she climbed up the greasy stairs into his cubicle. He wiped his palms on his pants, getting ready to welcome her with a hug. But then he took a better look at her and his dolphin smile disappeared from his face. Gin's face was all puffy and a streak of mascara was sitting like a heap of soot next to the corner of her eye.

"Did something happen, Gin? What's with you?"

"Kenny, I—" Gin said, resting her butt on the metal table.

"What, Gin?"

"You know . . . some time ago . . . that guy got shot? I . . . me, I want to say—"

"You mean number twenty-three?" Kenny asked. "You knew him? That Polish guy? He was going from Kennedy to Manhattan, and his wheel flew off on the Van Wyck, so he locked the whole car and went to the gas station to make a phone call and on his way those four kids – That's the one you mean?"

"No, no, no," said Gin who realized only this minute that every taxidriver who gets killed on the job immediately gets an unofficial serial number of that year – and that number is then used every time his case pops up among the taxidrivers or dispatchers – at least until the end of the year. ("Number seventeen, you mean? That guy, he was really stupid, really stupid! Why did he think he was chasing after TWO guys? 'Cause they didn't pay him? Man, me, it's much better when they don't pay me five times over than when they stab me in the kidney once. He could've figured that out, couldn't he? OK, if it was only one guy he was chasing after, I'll say, fine, maybe I would chase after him, too, but two at the same time—" "Number eight, you say? Yeah, I used to know that guy, he was a bit funny, but then again, who isn't, in this line of work, right, and he drove for that garage on 10th and 45th, some seventy medallions in all, and not in a single one there was a partition until mid-last year – never mind they made it a law now – then you have no reason to wonder, cabbies who drive without a partition, they die like flies. And this one, they hit him over the head with a cobblestone wrapped up in a newspaper – I don't know, but me, I can't possibly imagine a more ancient lethal weapon, perhaps shooting him dead with a crossbow, maybe. Now, can you imagine somebody could hit your head with a COBBLESTONE and put you out when you have a partition in the car? Even when it's open? Me, I wouldn't drive without a partition, not me – you have no partitions in your cars, OK, I'm going to some other garage – and always, when midnight hits, I close the partition, and only if I REALLY, REALLY like somebody, I open it a couple inches so I can talk to him.")

Each one of the taxidrivers who'd lost their lives on the job got an unofficial serial number in this City, just to make sure that the living ones won't mix them all up. There were not so many dead Yellow Cab drivers – perhaps five, six or eight each year – but the numbers grew thanks to gypsy cabdrivers from Harlem, Brooklyn or the Bronx, some forty of whom perished this way each year.

But how was it with those who got just wounded behind the wheel and then, despite all the hopes and efforts, did die after all, in the hospital – how did these fit into this number system? Gin had no idea.

"No-no-no," she said. "This – about number twenty-three – I didn't even know that. I wasn't driving for a few weeks now so I didn't know. Not that I wanted to take a break but—"

"I've told you several times, Gin," Kenny looked her up and down with an accusatory glance, "a beautiful woman like you should only drive in the daytime. Why don't you come back to my garage, and I'll get you the absolute best Yellow that ever roamed through this City. For the day shift. DON'T drive at night, Gin. Do it for me. A lot of guys would shit in their pants at what YOU're risking. And you're a WOMAN, after all."

For a second, Gin was almost sorry that Miss Chang wasn't around right now to hit Kenny in the nose with a spoon. "That's not the point, Kenny, I'm not afraid, but—"

"Yeah, you're not, I understand that much," Kenny commented dryly and touched her knee with the back of his hand. Actually, he didn't. He just put his hand on the tabletop right next to her. Gin felt the electric charge surge through her. Immediately, she reproached herself. "Gin, I'm just talking about the fact that—"

"The guy who got shot . . ." She shifted a few millimeters away from the heat of his hand. "He must have been number twenty-two, then. Or . . . I don't know. He got one right in the belly. He made it to the hospital and—"

"Oh, you mean THAT guy—" Kenny reached a little deeper into the bottomless yet rather mistake-prone memory of a veteran dispatcher. "Two weeks ago or so? An African. From Nigeria?"

"From Mali."

"Another Banana Republic. What happened to him?"

"He was—"

"Was it that guy, wasn't it, who got shot by some motherfucker in Harlem right in the lung but he covered the wound with a piece of plastic from a box of cigarettes so he wouldn't get asphyxiation, and he made it all by himself to the hospital. Was that him? He used to work for this garage, if I remember right?" Kenny asked, pushed the knuckles of his big hand a little closer to her thigh and began to show mild signs of impatience. "Well, he must be a hero in the Yellow world now? I heard that in less than a week he got completely recovered, and as soon as they took the stitches out he's behind the wheel again? That guy, you mean?"

"He died this morning."

Kenny grew taller in his chair. "Really? No kidding? I thought that . . . I could swear I'd heard that he—"

"He was my husband," Gin said.

And she didn't start crying. In fact, she was a bit too calm. She just touched the tip of her index finger to her eye, and because it got smeared with black mascara, she wet her handkerchief and mopped the corner of her eye with it.

"Jee-zus Christ! Oh shit! Oh man! Holy shit!" Kenny was saying. "Why in fuck's name did this have to happen to you? Fuckin' shit! I'm sorry. Terribly sorry. I am!"

He wiped his palms on his overalls again, pulled Gin up from the table and hugged her tight. It wasn't an entirely spontaneous action but he couldn't think of anything better. "That's good that you came here to see me. Come on, cry! You need to cry. All the sad stuff has to get out. Cry!"

He closed the door with a kick because, after all, there's no need for Ramon to witness this scene.

"I'm here with you, so you can cry on my shoulder. Come on! Cry!"

Kenny's nose and mouth got entangled in Gin's red hair. At the moment, he wished with terrible intensity that he knew how to help her. He felt pretty helpless. He was breathing Gin, her sadness and her fragrance, and he was thinking that every woman means something for a guy but on the other hand it's been almost a year, and he never promised her a thing, women SHOULDN'T remind you of themselves like that (and his hand made it under her hair, in the back). Doesn't she have girlfriends? Relatives? That husband of hers was a real dumbo, I remember him, yeah, he did drive for this garage for two or three years, something like that . . . Can't she cry her heart out on somebody else's chest, Kenny was thinking, and smelling that fragrance of Gin's, the fragrance of electric wires through which high voltage was running. The electric circuit between them began to get connected again . . . Women shouldn't push their way so close to a guy's body, he thought, I'm just a man, after all . . . Doesn't she know it? "Cry, cry, cry, don't be scared, cry all you want, get it all out of your system!" he was cooing to her ear in a gentle voice, hoping that the dispatcher's booth door did get closed when he kicked it, that the phone right behind Gin's butt won't start ringing at this moment. He twisted his body – very cautiously – in such a way that he wouldn't offend her in her pain if, after all, he did get a hard-on (and he was thinking: such a weakling, such a jerk, yeah, a stupid fucking JERK, and she married him, I can't believe that!). He tried not to let the smell from under her hair get too close to him, he looked at his watch behind her back and wondered when the moisture of her tears will seep through his thick denim jacket, when will he feel the wetness on his shoulder, how big will that spot be, and when it dries, will it leave a salt mark?

Gin raised her head. "I don't want to cry, Kenny . . . please, I – I lived with him, I mean recently, I mean I just don't want to go back to that apartment right now. You understand? I just don't want to. Will you take me home? At least for a few days? Kenny . . ."

"But I live in Long Island. Almost an hour's drive from here."

"It doesn't matter. I—"

"And I have, Gin, I have two dogs at home," Kenny improvised in desperation. "They would bother you all night long. I trained them . . . I trained them to—"

"I really don't know where to go."

"But my dogs will tear you into pieces. They're bad."

"I don't care."

And so Kenny arranged her face in front of his, almost as if wanting to kiss her, he took a deep breath, looked into her eyes and said: "I'm married. Didn't you know that?"

"Oh my God, Gin, whatever happened to you?" Gloria yelled out, rushing toward her. "I haven't heard from you for months, maybe, I really started thinking somebody did you in, and then I met Randy – just a few days after you took your French leave – I guess you don't even know that the sawbones got Randy, he set something or other on fire or what, and on the fourth floor of the VA Hospital in the Bronx they're shooting those magical spirals of his out of his brain with massive doses of Haldol, I guess you didn't know that, or did you? But, I mean, even before this happened to him I ran into Randy, right here, on 6th Street, and he tells me in that sonoric voice of his, 'Your girlfriend Gin, she moved UP,' and he lifts his eyeballs up to the sky like somebody wasted you or something, so I grabbed him right away and I shook him and I say, Randy, WHAT DO YOU KNOW ABOUT HER? But he just keeps on ranting and raving, he says you're up. So I came back home TOTALLY frustrated, I REALLY believed you were dead, really! And when you disappeared from here like a fucking ghost and a terrible mess was everywhere, and my paintings all massacred! Man, I was SURE that was the end of you. How CAN you just disappear like that? How CAN you?"

Gloria rattled this whole speech off with the speed and stopping power of a machine gun, striding toward her with Hubby at her heel. "Come on, come to me, come on!"

And she embraced Gin tightly.

She was careful not to touch any off-limits zones of her body. She didn't want to remind Gin of her sexual orientation.

"You're not mad at me?" Gin stammered. That thing – what she did to her paintings – now seemed much meaner to her than what Gloria did to her with Clyde. (Even though it still hurt a bit.)

"I completely changed my style, Gin."

"I didn't—"

"Conceptual art. You know what I'm talking about?"

"Forgive me, please, I—That's why I had to move out. It was because—"

"Conceptual art. THAT'S IT. You understand?"

"—because I didn't know how to look in your eyes. After what I did."

"Only NOW I really paint. I had to lose all my paintings—"

"I . . . really . . ."

"—in order to have a new beginning. Right from scratch. In China, God knows how many centuries ago, painters would change their names five times in a lifetime, perhaps. And their style with it. And they made it big under each of their names and styles. Me, what I do now—"

"But you could have kept these paintings as a memory. If it wasn't for me—"

"Only NOW do I really paint. You need to have a CONCEPTION. NOT a vision. You see? A perfectly calculated conception. No more talk about inspiration and bullshit like that. Only then—"

"But I couldn't believe that you could do THIS to me. Aren't you a—"

"Only THEN it's art. Real art. We have to free ourselves

from the old ways. And then you gotta catch that conception, NOT a vision, with such a method that—"

"—a lesbian! Aren't you? It just didn't occur to me that you might be the one who—"

"You have to tell it in a way that's understandable to those who live in New York. I don't care if somebody in Arizona can understand it. If somebody in Chicago can understand it. You gotta paint with the GUTS of this City, you see. You have to HURT this City, the same way this City hurts you—"

"What kind of lesbian are you when . . . when you snatched my man? Don't you—"

"Because FRAGMENTATION is the key word. Can't you see that, Gin? Just look at the skyscrapers, at those with all that glass on them, how they get reflected in one another, getting their image shattered at the same time. Just look at people: They don't know who they are. Fragmentation of the mind. Now I'm learning to paint with sand. And dust. And my own sweat. With bark because bark, that's the shattered lives of trees. I'm learning to paint with glass shards. With pieces of dirty, rotten old RAGS! And with crumbled asphalt – just look at my nails: See how they're breaking off? That's from when I get that asphalt from New York. I scrape it off with my nails."

"I still can't understand why you did that to me!"

"Because this is LIFE! In this City. It's stomped on, shattered and broken, the same way. THAT'S how I paint. Now."

Gloria moved over to the easel and with jerky motions of a razor she tore her own canvas to pieces, the one that was smelling of insufficiently dried acrylic. "Life in this City is torn to pieces. And I finally started painting all that, Gin!"

"Did he ever call you?"

"Who? I see . . . No. No, he didn't call, Gin."

(Because you must never get to know that, Gin. That I'm still painting him. I paint him in such a way that he, if he showed up, would definitely not see himself on those wounded canvases.

But you, you might see him there.)

*

"I should go, I suppose," Gin said.

Only as she was edging her way through the door, did she add: "By the way, my husband died this morning. He got shot."

And she ran away as fast as she could, to make sure that Gloria's calling would reach her ears only from a distance, in the form of a completely inconsequential echo.

Chapter 33

Time

It most likely wasn't a very good idea, to collapse around eleven at night on a bench in the middle of Tompkins Square Park and sit there and stare at nothing in particular, because she presently heard a voice behind her: "Hey, miss, ya can use some sense, man!"

"Wh – what?"

"Got the best sense in New York City, man, ya can mark my words!"

"But I . . ." Gin stammered. It took a while for her to translate that sentence. Sense wasn't sense at all, it was sinsemilla, that virginal marihuana, most likely out of California – seedless marihuana plants, frustrated in their motherhood, which got translated into great smoke.

"You really need some sense. You have ten bucks?"

"But I—"

"You have FIVE bucks? I'm losing money on this. But I can see you really need some sense, man!"

Tompkins Square Park was drowned in darkness in which the Haitian pot seller's face was disappearing, too. From the top of his head the branches of a tree were growing, clearly cut against the ashy-red sky.

But the Zig-Zag paper in which his invisible fingers were rolling a joint, was emanating silverish light – and it smelled like a promise or a hope.

And presently marihuana was smoldering fragrantly, and that sense in it (or whatever it was), sense of life, sense of love, sense of EVERYTHING, was slowly burning off, piercing its way into their noses, their lungs, their brains, their red blood cells that were carrying it throughout their bodies. Sense was stroking all their cells.

That sense got inflated inside of her, filling her up, connecting her to the past, present and future somehow; death ceased existing because you could look behind it; and time seemed beautiful and lazy like a cuddly hairy beast.

Gin got on a bus whose lit sign right in front, made of flickering yellow dots, was shining HARLEM, nothing else, as if the passengers didn't need to know anything else, as if the word itself was a destination. And while the bus was carrying her up Madison Avenue, Gin was looking out at the flickering asphalt of the road (and every little grain of asphalt got imprinted in her, it existed as a smear in time, prolonged by speed). The bus rode over signs

LANE
FIRE

– they meant FIRE LANE but they were written in reverse because cars were approaching them from below —

— The bus braked with a thud, and a cop with a pale and worried face climbed up its steps. The driver, a woman, smiled at him.

"You can't go through here. You gotta make a detour to Park Avenue. Just back up – here – here – down to 102nd."

The road was blocked with tapes that said CRIMESCENE-CRIMESCENECRIMESCENECRIMESCENE, and the tapes were buzzing in the wind just like the strands of a spider's web, and somebody was lying on the sidewalk. Two gentlemen in long coats were sprinkling the outline of his body with a line of white dust, but the dust got mixed in with blood and it was slowly flowing south; the cold-tormented gentlemen in rumpled coats had to sprinkle more and more.

The bus driver put it in reverse, looking at the whole scene over the side-view mirror.

"He shot a bus driver. Right through the heart," the cop told her in a low voice. "But we got him."

And then the bus was blowing its horn and backing up all the way to 102nd Street – and the bus driver was smiling – this was an adventure for her: she was driving into Harlem through the night with a whole bus and without fear, just with her heart exposed like a target. Her mood got transferred into Gin; she, too, had her heart all exposed and – and (because today time was all times) the air was swooshing with bullets, spears, lances, knives and the poisoned arrows of the Indians – and an awfully long tape that said CRIMESCENECRIME-SCENECRIMESCENECRIMESCENECRIMESCENE-CRIMESCENE was rolling off a spool; it constricted the City like a sticky spiderweb, blocking every avenue, every street, blocking the connections between people – and on every sidewalk, in every traffic lane the glimmering-white outlines of the dead got piled up: the lines that time refused to erase.

The asphalt of the whole City was shiny with intermingling lines, and the dead – the ones who got shot, the ones who got stabbed, the ones who OD'ed on heroin, suicides that jumped out of windows, homeless men frozen stiff – all those were lying there right now, and because there wasn't enough room for them, their bodies intermingled in an almost erotic way: they had no choice but to hug one another because time refused to erase them.

Chapter 34

Ouagadougou

In front of the locked door of apartment #5C a tiny, sad little black bundle was crouching. Out of the uncombed coils of his hair the silverish I of the word KILL was growing.

Gin turned around and ran back down the stairs.

Because when the bundle got unfurled like a snail, the sleepy Ouagadougou emerged out of his shell, yelled out, "*Chérie*!" and made after her. He caught up with her in the second floor mezzanine under that arc of bullets, and squeezed her in his arms so tight she could hardly breathe. "*Chérie*! I wait here for you. I wait here for you. I wait here for—"

"I can see that," Gin answered drily, shoving him off her. It seemed to her that she'd gotten more than her rightful share of hugs today. She didn't wish to be hugged anymore. Time, made all elastic by marihuana, allowed her to experience ALL the hugs of that day, as well as all the hugs of all the days that came before that, leaving all kinds of dactyloscopic imprints on her body. The best thing would be, she thought, to lie down into a round grave, left after a dug-out lump of asphalt with a sign

LANE
FIRE

on it and let a gorgeous, variegated Tree grow out of her in the middle lane of Third Avenue.

"But I can't invite you in," she told Ouag now.

"*Mais* I wait here for—"

"In fact, this apartment isn't even mine." She was opening the fourth lock. Ouag rushed for the door like a flood.

"This is TALIBE'S apartment!"

"*Mais chérie*!" And he closed the door behind him with his backside.

"I can't invite just anybody—"

"You my wife, *non*? *Mais* you not want let me in? You my—"

All of a sudden, a disarming feeling of *déjà vu* flushed over her.

"*Non, non, non*, please, not cry!" Ouagadougou got terrified. Doesn't this woman know that when you cry over dead people, then every tear you shed falls right on their body, scalding them just like a drop of boiling water? Is she really so dumb she doesn't know that? Ouagadougou mused, leaning on the inner side of the door whose blue varnish still carried the marks of the tape that had fastened the pictures of people Talibe had loved to it – waiting for her to calm down. In Africa, when a woman starts crying, a man gets up and walks off. But here we are NOT in Africa, he thought with relief. He didn't feel like walking off. He was just shaking with a desire to check – again – how these American women are organized down there. Is it really possible to switch them on, just by pushing that button of theirs? Just like when you turn a switch and the light bulb starts shining? Ouagadougou decided that he rather liked electricity.

"Talibe was my husband. Don't you—"

"I your husband."

"But Talibe—"

"*Mais* Talibe not here," Ouagadougou objected with indisputable logic. "Talibe dead!"

And right away he got his nerve to grab that spot of hers.

It seemed to him that it was working. Really working. Because he'd have sworn that Gin had to suppress an erotic sigh before backing up to the refrigerator and screaming: "*Merde*!"

Ouagadougou was equipped with a dick a little shorter than Talibe's had been but amicably fattish in the right places.

Otherwise, his lovemaking style pretty much resembled that of Talibe's.

"*Chérie, chérie, chérie*!" he bellowed in the end. "Now I make you baby, baby, baby!" And he fell down on her like a chopped off bamboo.

Well, I'm not really unfaithful to Talibe, not really, Gin said to herself, because Ouag here, on Talibe's bed, is a perfect replica of him.

I'm not unfaithful to him, no, I'm not, and that's because all the time is happening in me at once, the present, and the future, and even those times that are buried deep in the past – perhaps it's so just thanks to marihuana but maybe it's that way because time isn't a single straight line. Time is a tree. (A Tree?)

Rather than a negation, Ouag was the continuation of those uncertain emotions that Gin had entertained toward Talibe (ever since the time their fingers formed a checkerboard under the yellow glasses with their drinks) – and which she now, not knowing what else to do, decided to call love.

Chapter 35

A Regular Yellow Dream

"If all cabdrivers like work as much as you like, Gin, I can pack up all and go back home to Moscow. Where, fucking, were you when you don't even tell me nothing?"

The spring breeze was wafting through Alex's hair, lifting it, with the result that today her boss reminded her of a tufted titmouse. Presently, he ran his fingers through his tuft. In part, it was a wasted effort to plaster it to his skull, and in part it was a desperate gesture, meant to illustrate how terrible were the tortures Gin was putting him through. "I even ask in garages to see if you are maybe unfaithful to me with somebody, you know that half the drivers left me now – but for Miss Gin – *nyi slukhu, nyi dukhu*. I think you get engaged at the circus like first woman taxidriver in the history who is driving niggers to Harlem in the middle of night and she still alive. Show me, you still have your little ass?" (Alex made a searching gesture with his right hand, Gin shifted her butt elsewhere, and ever since that moment she could be sure there would be a car left for her today.) "And you today are not the only one who does that to me, Gin. Remember Darko? That fucking Yugo was coming here maybe five times every day, he have no hack license and no work permit and I bet he have no driver's license, too, but he begged and begged all the time, to give him some work, we are all Slavs – so I let him talk me into it and I let him drive at night, with license of Fakim, that stupid fuckin' fuck, the devils should bake that Arab motherfucker forever in the hell, so, at least the Yugo could drive with his license, it wasn't so bad, sure, he didn't look very much like ZAMAN ABDUL KAHAN on the picture, he was more like blond, you see, but Darko, he not stupid, he started telling everybody with that terrible accent of his that he's a Muslim from Bosnia. What else do you do when your Slavic blood is coming out of your ears and there's ABDULLAH stuck on your hack license? You know, that Darko/Abdul guy was really unhappy about how he changed, he wanted to quit right the first day, he come here in the morning and says: I'm not complaining, not me, but at least thirty motherfuckers asked where I'm from. What business of theirs is that, shit, isn't it enough that I'm taking their fat butt where they want, motherfuckers? But then he got used to it and he learn how to live with that change in him and he find that he cannot hope for nothing better than Abdullah on his license. He listen to the news on radio all the time, just to be in the picture, and then he explain in detail to everybody how Serbian dogs cut his father's throat, raped his mother, one his sister is in a fucking camp and another one they sew rat into her womb. So he's now saving money up so he can buy a machine gun so he can kill all the Serbian dogs dead. And then he go to the bar and drinks all the fat tips stupid Americans gave to him – soon he gets off the taxi, he's from Slovenia, you see. And then he, my dear Gin, just disappeared for a whole week, *ego nyebylo*, so I say to myself, what I know, maybe his whole story about machine gun was truth, maybe I raise a hero in my garage – but then he come back, all green, his eyes like dried apples – and he tell to me some stupid motherfucker gave him two hundred for that machine gun, so he go out drink. And he make like that—" (Alex showed the most innocent shrug his leather jacket would allow) "and he says: It's not my fault. It's in my blood. So I banged him on the head, he fly all the way on 10th Avenue, and I say: I was champion of Soviet Union in box and this I have in MY blood."

The wind blew the partition in Alex's hair over to the other side and he tapped it to his skull with a sigh. "And now you, *krasavitsa*. Two weeks you disappear. Or is it three weeks? If you wasn't a lady I will hit you so hard that you'll can only make friends with fishes in Hudson River."

Alex regarded her for a long time with the watery-blue eyes of a deeply wounded lover. "OK, so what, go upstairs pay Gana for the shift. I give you the best car I have. I give you 3Y50. When you see, believe me, your eyes pop out!"

Gin deemed it wise to swallow a comment that, so far, whenever she had 3Y50, her eyes popped out all the time, as she was suffocating with exhaust fumes. She climbed up the stairs into the booth in which Gana was sitting regally.

"Hello!"

"Khello, Gin, khow are you?" Gana, her face that of a Sphinx, said, smiling at her absent-mindedly. "You working today? Yes?"

She stretched her left hand toward Gin and with her right, equipped with a ball-point, circled above the list of cars questioningly.

"3Y50," Gin said.

"Gotta gimme the money!" the grass-green parrot screeched quite understandably even though with a heavy Russian accent.

It seemed that nothing at all had changed.

With one exception. Above the office desk there was hanging, in addition to a collection of traffic tickets from the Taxi and Limousine Commission the drivers kept bringing in, also the Xerox copy of Fakim Fakem's (that is Zaman Abdul Kahan's) hack license. Under the picture that, on the lousy copy, allowed the darker aspects of Fakim's personality to be particularly visible, there was a sentence, written with a smudged blue marker:

STOLE A CAR!

"What?" Gin yelped, pricking Fakim with her finger. "Really?"

"Oh, you will have to ask Alex about it," Gana said carefully and dropped her head so she could add a note in Cyrillic right next to 3Y50:

"$95 – DZHIN."

"You don't even know what that Arab motherfucker did to me?" Alex roared. "That motherfucker, he just wait until I got the most beautiful car in whole world to him, the most beautiful taxi anybody want, a regular Yellow dream – and then he run away. One morning he get his taxi and in the evening – no Fakim. When he not show up after three days, even, I started asking about him at gas stations and so – you know how these *khuyi* often steal your car for couple days and they drive with it, make money, and what they make they put into their own pocket, and then they leave the car for you somewhere parked, and they run away to another garage before you have chance to kick their face. So I think maybe Fakim made this same trick with me, also – but you know what I hear? I hear he drive the car to California! When he got through tunnel to Jersey, he rip off the light on the roof and painted the whole car to be blue and—"

Alex's eye flicked toward the corner of 11th Avenue. It was pretty yellowish: dozens and dozens of Yellow cabs, their OFF DUTY lights shining brightly, were making their way back to the garages on the West Side – and Alex's profile got to resemble a hawk's while he was searching for his vehicles among the not-too-easy-to-read medallion numbers. He didn't find any. "Shit!" he decided, looking at his watch. "Sometime I think, Gin, that you – everybody from my drivers – should keep one my car like souvenir, and I could go packing back to Moscow."

"Didn't you report it to the cops?"

Alex turned his gaze upwards and was now watching the sky on which tiny, light clouds were racing, forming fast-changing patterns a bit reminiscent of I-Ching. "To the cops, Gin?" Alex howled in horror. "Did you go mad? Do you have fever? You are taxidriver more than a year and you don't understand, still, that the cops everybody who has anything to do with taxis must avoid like the bubonic plague? Even if a knife is sticking from your liver!"

Alex crept closer to Gin. "You were illegal immigrant, were you? I was illegal before I was legal, why would I not say, because of Russian mafia. And many things I learn since! You were illegal, also, you know this shit. You still today think, Gin, that you would in this City find only one, only one taxidriver, only one garage that is legal? Wake up, please. If everything I make is legal, I could go packing back to Moscow!"

At the same time the most gorgeous car Gin ever saw in her life got unstuck from the traffic lights on 11th Avenue. It wasn't the poor old model of Chevrolet that sits on the road all squashed like a toad.

It was a Chevy Caprice of the most modern design, one of those that not so long ago began to multiply among the New York taxis. Gin, while she was still speeding through the streets in the beaten wrecks that belonged to Alex the God and that could, for all she knew, blow up like a bomb any second, used to get envious of drivers of those divine machines. Those cars held the road like they were glued to it with KrazyGlue, they swung over potholes gracefully, and if they, with a passenger in the car, did fall into a huge pothole after all, you didn't bite your tongue, saying: "Oh, sorry – ouch!" – but instead you just remarked: "Oooops!" while you were falling into the hole on formidable shock absorbers, and then both the passenger and you would giggle happily because falling into potholes in those Yellows felt just like riding a roller-coaster on the beach.

Not speaking of the fact that there was plenty of room in the trunk even for the most corpulent luggage, and the back seat comfortably accommodated even the most corpulent passenger. And the seats were truly well-shaped, so that the six- or seven-day-a-week drivers would comment happily that in these seats their backs don't hurt at all, quite the contrary: the longer you sit in them, the less your back hurts – and a twelve-hour shift is better than half an hour at the chiropractor's.

These cars were BEAUTIFUL, they were simply GORGEOUS, the speed at which you were going wasn't shown by some dinky gauge you couldn't really see on the ill-lit speedometer. Your miles per hour flickered in huge blue ciphers on the display. With their elegant and aerodynamic shape of the cosmic age's spawn these cars looked like immigrants from an entirely different planet; they looked a bit like yellow rockets, and even though that aerodynamic shape doesn't do much for you as you are straddling from one traffic light to another, it still makes you feel good just to imagine that your interplanetary wheels are cutting through space, crowds and the night . . .

And more often than not the passengers themselves chose a car like that, picking it from a whole line of less extravagant taxis that got formed in the wee hours of the morning in front of nightclubs like Limelight or Nell's. There was only one kind of taxicab that could compete with them for passengers' favor – and that was the dying breed of veterans of which there were only seventeen left in the whole City, those veterans with their ancient beetle shape, their pull-down seats for SIX passengers and a renowned name: New York Checkercab.

"You're popping out your eyes, right, Gin?" Alex commented, patting 3Y50's perfectly yellow hood without a single scratch on it.

And for those few seconds Alex didn't look like a boasting pigeon for a change. He looked like a majestic golden eagle.

Chapter 36

Mortality

"Hello, Miss Gin, hello, hello, hello!"

"Oh? What're you doing here?"

"I came to see you, Gin. Because—"

"I can't believe that you ever crawl out of that garage of yours. How did you know I'd be here?"

"I know a whole lot about you, Gin."

"More than I'd like you to, I guess."

"Don't say that."

"And along with you every other cabbie knows too much."

"Nobody learned anything from me, Gin. I hope you know that."

"Because you are married."

"Well, that's a part of it . . ."

"So don't come here, please. To 47th Street. Unless you have something really important to take care of here."

"I do."

"Because if Alex sees me talking to you, he'll stop giving me cars."

"You have a thing going on with that mobster, don't you?"

"Give me a break!"

"I didn't know that in every garage you work for . . . I thought you were an honest girl—"

"A good thing you were honest with me. A year later I find out I've been messing around with a married man."

"I thought you knew it."

"And how was I supposed to find out? When nobody told me that? You don't wear no ring."

"How could I? I'm always elbow-deep in cars. But I—"

"Everyone's gonna put two and two together. Even here, in this garage."

"OK, let's not stand on the corner like that. Let's sit on the curb. Behind this car."

"That's even worse. It looks like we're hiding and we are on display here like in a shop window."

"Gin, I came to apologize. For what I've done to you."

"What have you done to me?"

"I mean, you know, what I've done. But I couldn't help myself. The only woman in the whole garage. And pretty. European. I just couldn't help myself, Gin. I wanted to be your first nigger."

"Can you see how everybody's looking at us? We'd better—"

"No, I can't."

"— —"

"When you came to my garage for the first time, waving your freshly hatched license, I didn't need anybody. The whole garage was just brimming with a hungry pack of taxi wolves. They all begged me on their knees to dig out a car for them. Every shift, they were pushing as much as ten bucks on me each. Because it was a GOOD garage, Gin."

"And, obviously, you let them bribe you."

"It's a very good garage. Because it's legal. More or less. While in your new garage, Gin—"

"I just got a pretty nice car from my boss."

"Oh yes, you did."

"Didn't I?"

"Come down to Twenty-First to see me one of these days. I'll tell you."

"What are you going to tell me?"

"Everything."

"What everything?"

"Well, everything you still don't know. After a whole year of driving."

"What everything don't I know?"

"A lot of things. Come down to see me."

"You think I'm dumb?"

"I didn't say that."

"But you think it."

"Just IGNORANT, dear Gin. There's a difference."

"Everybody's watching us. As we sit here."

"I'm trying to help and you—"

"I've noticed that. When I came to see you. A few days ago."

"That's why I'm here now. To explain . . ."

"Thanks. I understand."

" . . . That you don't understand a thing."

"Thank you."

"And I brought you something."

"Oh yeah?"

"You know I was in Vietnam?"

"No kidding! Mr Kenny is a veteran today."

"Not today. Since seventy-one."

"You went there—"

"At seventeen. I enlisted."

"You were dumb."

"I was dumb. But I brought this knife over from Nam. D'you know what it's called?"

"A blade?"

"A survival knife, Gin. A knife that helps you survive. And I really want you to survive! Sometimes it seems to me that you don't understand that . . . That this City is full of guys who—"

"Who don't even find it necessary to tell you that they're married."

"Sorry."

"It was my fault anyway, wasn't it?"

"Gin . . . I'm awfully sorry about what happened to your husband."

"Thanks."

"But you must understand that you are that much more vulnerable. You're a woman. They can shoot you. They can cut your throat. They can rape you."

"Thanks. It's already happened."

"I wasn't THAT terrible, was I?"

"I just meant to say—"

"You must be in terrible shape, I can imagine that. I myself have—"

"It was a fake marriage."

"But you had sex, didn't you?"

"None of your business."

"This knife was in Nam with me, Gin. See these notches on the handle? This knife saved my life four times."

"You mean – four bodies."

"Gin, in Vietnam—"

"I thought you were a car mechanic."

"I am. But in Vietnam everything was different. In Vietnam . . ."

"You want me to pop somebody? So I go to jail?"

"I don't want that at all. Don't be like that. I brought you this knife so—"

"So—"

"So you can keep it with you. It will protect you."

"Like a good-luck charm?"

"Whatever."

"So you brought it to me. Like a gentleman."

"I'm not a gentleman, Gin."

"I've noticed."

"But I never made you a baby."

"Because I blew at least fifty bucks on scumbags."

"Don't talk like that."

"And how am I supposed to talk?"

"You – really – loved me?"

"No."

"I think yes."

"Don't think."

"You're right. I didn't think. I should have helped you."

"Give me a break with that."

"So I brought you this knife. It was in Nam with me. Do you know what to do with it?"

"Stick it into a flower pot and worship it every morning?"

"It's easy but you gotta know the trick. You take it in your hand edge up. Like this, see? Now that's how you hold it, edge up. This is the worst mistake beginners do: they grip it the other way and it's much easier to wrestle it from them. Or they lose their grip on the knife and they cut themselves and freak out. But if you hold the knife like this, edge up, it's much easier to stab with it. From the low point up. Or the flat way, so it makes its way between the ribs. You turn your elbow to the side and—"

"You seem quite experienced."

"This knife saved my life four times."

"Well. Fine."

"Remember, Gin, your first day? When you showed up in the garage? And I just couldn't help myself and I gave you the car keys right away and I went out to the street to show you which Yellow one it was, and you sat down into it and stuck the keys into the ignition and you looked around for a while, but in thirty seconds you were out?"

"Go ahead. Make fun of me."

"And you look like a recent arrival from the Moon, and you're looking sooo cute, and you walk up to me and say: Kenny, please, WHERE'S THE CLUTCH? And I tell you: It's automatic, my dear Gin. We're in America, drivers are idiots. Lots of people couldn't even move a car that has a clutch. See how easy it is: You put the lever into D and the thing drives. In America ANYBODY can be a chauffeur. All you need is half a brain and one leg. You step on the gas and it drives, you step on the brake and it stops."

"My boss is gawking again."

"But driving is not the most difficult thing about being a cabbie, Gin. The hardest thing is to pick your passengers well. And so I wanted to give you this knife, Gin. I've had it on me for over twenty years."

"Hmm."

"This knife, Gin, means more to me than you think."

"What good is it gonna do me?"

"I just thought you might come to needing it. So you won't remember in a bad light your first—"

"Don't say that! That word! Please!" Gin yelled out. "Anyway, you weren't."

Against her will, she stretched out her palm.

And Kenny rolled his forehead into little furrows (that were not easy to forget), and put the survival knife into her palm. It was heavy, and its glistening blade reflected the blue skies and a cloud and a half.

The scratches and scars in the steel hurt the reflection of the skies, cut it into pieces the same way lightning does.

"All right, thanks," said Gin.

Chapter 37

Talibe's Good-Luck Charm

She tied the ends of the leather strap of Talibe's good-luck charm together with a square knot. She stood in front of the mirror in the house that now belonged to her and Ouag, and it seemed to her that the good-luck charm was burning her fingers. That it was the only thing which still retained the heat of Talibe's body.

With a wet piece of toilet paper she removed the caked blood from it. She dried it in her palms.

Then she hesitated.

She felt her femininity. Her womb that bled every month. What did Talibe tell her? – "I not recommend this charm. For REAL woman. They stop . . . every month . . . have blood. *Mais* you not real woman. It is not dangerous to you." – Gin shuddered and turned her head. Those words printed themselves in her mind so sharply that they sounded as if Talibe had just pronounced them behind her back.

Then she put the good-luck charm around her neck. The dark smell of goat skin washed over her. She took a deep breath and shivered. The heat of Talibe's good-luck charm shot through her body like an electric vibe.

At the same moment, Ouag peeked into the bathroom. Gin hoped he didn't see anything.

"The sheets need changing," she said drily.

"*Mais* why, *chérie*?"

"Because sheets need changing every day. Otherwise the spirit of the bed wouldn't like living in them. What kind of African are you if you don't know that?"

Ouag tilted his head to the side, listening to her English. He still spoke very little but Gin was convinced that he could understand her now. "The sheets need changing. Do you hear me?"

"*Oui, chérie*," sighed Ouagadougou and went over to the chest of drawers to get new sheets.

She didn't see much of Ouagadougou lately. It was part of the strategy she adopted after Ouagadougou shoved his way into her apartment the very first night after Talibe's death.

Some gadget clicked in Gin's skull and all of a sudden it wasn't hard for her to explain to Ouag, the very next morning, that she doesn't live in this apartment for free. That the apartment costs almost seven hundred dollars, which means that Ouag will have to pay. "*Mais, chérie . . .*" Ouag objected then. "No mah-ah-ah," Gin said resolutely, "only goats bleat like that. Seven hundred dollars. Every month.

"And, by the way," she added. "Was he your cousin? Talibe, I mean. Was he or wasn't he?"

"Talibe? *Mon cousin*? *Mais non . . .*"

"Well, that's what I could've figured out," Gin said. "In any case, I suspected that it was hardly his cousin I was marrying. You're probably not even from the same tribe; I'll most likely never get to know these details. Anyhow," she continued, "no matter what, Talibe left his second wife behind him. I mean, his original wife, and four children, I guess you know that. *Un, deux, trois*, how the fuck do you say four, *les enfants*. Do you understand, Ouag?"

"Oui . . ."

"And every months Talibe sent them at least six to eight hundred dollars. So we gotta continue doing that. At least for some time. At least for a couple months. Until everything settles down a bit after his death. Do you understand, Ouag?"

Gin grabbed Ouag's paw, entwined her fingers with his and curled it into a fist as much as it would go. The pressure made her fingers turn pink, but no change could be seen on Ouag's fingers.

"*Mais* it hurt me, *chérie*!"

"So you should take care of that, Ouag! Because if you don't send them money, Talibe's children will go hungry."

It was amazingly easy, forcing Ouag to sit behind the wheel of his gypsy cab for at least sixteen hours a day. He moved his clunker to Harlem and was beginning to understand its streets. The business wasn't exactly great, and Ouagadougou had to make money for Talibe's children. And for the rent for apartment #5C. And for food. And for the phone bill.

Some gadget clicked in Gin's skull and—

Every day Gin went downtown, to 47th Street, and then she drove around in Alex's brand new, never-never-land Yellow Cabs, which, at five o'clock sharp, sailed in gracefully from the street lights at 11th Avenue.

Every morning, on her arrival home, she shook twenty-dollar bills out of her sweaty socks, ironed them with her palm on the kitchen table and then she savored their greenish, pervading money smell. She cuddled with them. She put them into little piles of a hundred dollars each and hid those fragrant wads into brown paper bags that she then stuck – when nobody was looking – into the seven stolen milk crates that still stood in the corner of the living room, holding the essence of her life.

Chapter 38

To Survive

"The average taxidriver, Gin, gets held up about once a year. And you've been driving for over a year. So, statistically speaking, you're up for it. You understand what I'm saying?"

"But Kenny—"

They were standing under the metallic ribs of the ceiling, in the yellow killer whale's belly. Kenny was scratching the short curly bristles on his skull, nodding his head mournfully. "I've already heard of number 24, didn't you? So I think that you, too, might get in trouble . . . I mean, I really worry for you, Gin. I do. You know what I'm saying?"

"Kenny, I mean . . . Is it really so terrible when it comes to getting held up? How many Yellow Taxi drivers are there in New York, huh? Around forty thousand! So if everybody gets held up once a year, there would have to be forty thousand reports every year. And the number of reports—"

"Is more like hundreds than thousands, I know."

"So you see that—"

"But d'you know what that means, Miss Gin? I'd say it only means that cabdrivers don't trust the cops, that's all. So they don't even file reports. Somebody pulls a gun on you, takes your money, and what do you do? Would you feel like spending the rest of the shift filing a report at the precinct? While you know they almost never get anybody? What would you do?"

"I'd file a report immediately. Because—"

"Because nobody held you up so far, that's why. But I saw tougher guys than you come to the garage all shaky just 'cause some motherfucker stuck a gun to their heads and yelled: 'I'll blow your fuckin' brains out! Gimme all your money!' A few sentences of that caliber can get you into a pretty strange mood. And then you don't feel like telling the whole story to some fat-faced piggie who's gonna be stuffing his mouth with a donut as he's listening to you. And he'll make you repeat it three times at least, to make sure you're not kidding him."

"But there are also veterans, and I've met a couple, who will swear to you on their knees that nobody ever, ever dared to do anything like that to them in their whole life, and they're driving that baby of theirs around this City for twenty-six years."

"Yeah. And there are also smart-asses, every garage has a couple, who'll tell you three times a week that some nigger held them up somewhere. And, sure enough, they're not gonna make a report."

"That's just because they get a free shift from the garage."

"Well, usually they do, that's true, a little bonus so they don't chicken out. So they get reimbursed for the fact that they probably had to wash their underwear one extra time. It's kind of a gentlemen's agreement, and it does make sense, don't you think? But I've met a couple of those who didn't get no free shifts no more, and they kept saying the same thing."

"Paranoid maniacs."

"You know what, Gin? You'd make me really happy if you was a paranoid maniac, too, you know that? I know, for example, that you don't even close your partition at night. That makes it much easier to get you."

"It seems a bit . . . strange to me. You sit down in a taxicab and the driver is afraid of you? Is it normal? I think—"

"Well, I'd say you don't think very much, Miss Gin."

"OK, if you say so . . ."

"And, by the way, d'you really believe that partition is bulletproof? They keep talking about it. But it's not, my dear Gin. Or do you really think that half an inch, or, maybe, just a quarter of an inch of plexiglass can really stop a bullet? A bullet from a .25, well, maybe, or, at least, it slows it down so much it can't kill you. But a little bullet from a 9 ms, or something like that, one like that will swoosh through it like butter, and before it drills its way through your skull, it'll sing a song for you. I can't help it: I really think you should drive only in the daytime."

Ever since Gin began carrying Kenny's knife in her knapsack she felt – God knows why – much more vulnerable. It must have been the notorious bulletproof-vest syndrome: the very fact that our chest is protected lets us feel very acutely all the other body parts which are not bulletproof. Which are pretty penetrable for bullets.

Ever since the time they killed her husband, all the bulletproofness Gin had in her got concentrated around the blade of a certain knife. She wouldn't have any idea how to carve anyone up with it, but she still carried it in her knapsack like it was the pivotal point of her existence, like it was her totem or her sky.

Because that knife did have the sky in it.

Sometimes she took it out, freeing it from its leather sheath, and turned it in such a way that its long, wide, elegantly curved blade could cut little slices off the sky and bring them, their color changed by the metal into indecisively gray, right here, into her palm.

Sky in her palm protected Gin.

"And aren't you afraid, a woman, to drive a taxi at night?" her passengers would ask her again and again, until her head started spinning. "Really? You're not afraid? Do you carry a weapon? What if something happened to you? What then?"

And Gin, who was bored to tears by then, had a whole

bunch of answers ready for a series of questions like that. It ranged from: "Wonder why you're asking. Are you getting ready to hold me up?" to a rather comical scene built around the topic that it's not so easy to fight back against a robber in a taxicab. Where are you supposed to carry your weapon? In your pocket? In your sleeve? Behind the visor above the windshield? It's not that easy to notice what exactly is going on behind you while at the same time you gotta watch the road; in your sitting position you're not exactly operational when it comes to martial arts; and that partition – right here – while it's supposed to protect you, it also blocks your view of the passenger through the rear-view mirror.

"Just imagine the situation," Gin would joke with her passengers, at least with the ones she could be sure weren't ready to rob her. "Somebody puts a gun to your head and you start rummaging through your purse: 'Yeah, yeah, just a moment, wait, don't shoot! Just wait until I find MY gun, where the hell is it, oh, yeah, right here, between my hairbrush and my lipstick, just wait a minute, will you? All I have to do is load my gun and then, then I will shoot YOU!"

Whenever she managed to go through this act in a comic enough way, her passengers would double up laughing on the back seat, consequently giving her great tips.

"Uptown!" the passenger barks, getting his butt inside the cab. He's dressed in a tricolor padded jacket with a hood, although at this time of year, even this late at night, the weather suggests you should be wearing a T-shirt. Before he managed to make it to the car, Gin had enough time to notice his baggy jeans with their crotch down at his knee and perfect white sneakers manufactured by Nike. It was the version of a customer for whom a lot of drivers most likely wouldn't even think of stepping on the brake, especially if the hood revealed a dark kinky head rather than this bed-linen-pale face, framed by closely cropped bristles the color of overripe wheat. Hooded jackets and baggy jeans usually meant a problem. If she was to believe what cabdrivers say, it's not the easiest thing to get any money out of dudes that dress like this. Geoffrey might tell her: You'd be surprised, Gin, but these oversized sneakers are really great for running, never mind they're untied.

Gin, however, strictly refused to pick her customers. Not by their looks, not by their race. Not by the neighborhood they wanted to go to. Her cabdriver's radar didn't work that way.

Or, perhaps, she refused to turn it on. And she spent, in the Munson Diner and elsewhere, hours and hours fighting over things like that with her colleagues on the job. "What did you say, Geoffrey? That I shouldn't drive black guys? That it's not safe? You're a racist, you know that? But believe you me, my experience is completely different—"

"That's not true, I never said that," Geoffrey would rattle his chains apologetically, "I just said that there are certain types of people with whom . . . you gotta be more careful. You owe it to yourself. As a woman!"

"But you did say that!"

"Well, I just said that there are certain places you shouldn't ever go to."

"And you know what?" Gin yelled fiercely. "Once I picked up four guys right in front of the Island Club. On Canal Street. Four. All black like the night. And four, and all of them pretty big, they couldn't fit on the back seat, so one of them had to sit in front. And do you know where they were going?"

"You know what, Gin? I don't want to hear that. Let me see, is it still you, in flesh and blood, or is it just a specter of yours sitting here with me?"

Gin shifted so Geoffrey's touchy-feely hand couldn't reach her. "They were going to 125th and Lenox Avenue. If there's a heart in Harlem, Geoffrey, then it's Lenox and Hun-Twenny-Five, don't you think?"

"Weeeell . . ."

"And you know what happened?"

"I can't wait to hear that."

"Nothing! Nothing of what you might imagine, Geoffrey, nothing at all. They told me jokes all the time, I laughed my head off, then they paid me, tipped me, thanked me and ran away. In their pants with the crotch at the knee. In their untied sneakers."

Geoffrey was rubbing his bitten-off nose. He cast a blue gaze at Gin and said: "Where do you think you live, Gin? Are you still on the planet Earth? You're telling me here, and you almost shit your pants with joy as you do that, just 'cause you've driven four guys to Harlem and they paid you. Just wait, let me touch your forehead to see if you have a fever or something. Don't move, I said forehead. Are you still normal or what? 'Cause what kind of City is this if a cabdriver has to boast that an unbelievable story of this caliber happened to him?"

But Gin somehow didn't know how to feel scared. She was presently turning the wheel of the most wonderful Yellow she'd ever seen in her life, and that Yellow car wrapped her up in a hermetically sealed can. All she had to do was roll the windows up, and the taxi turned into a fortress, into a bubble. Gin was sitting in her fortified bubble night after night and those undersea monsters that had killed her husband couldn't reach her.

Then one day the door opened, this character penetrated her comparably peaceful times and barked at her: "Uptown!"

"Where do you wanna go?"

"Uptown, I said!"

"WHERE Uptown, that's what I'm asking."

"You can go up Amsterdam."

Gin got into the left lane. A split-second before the light flicked red she snuck through the yellow signal and they were slowly making their way westward along 77th Street. At the end of the block, the traffic light flicked green right now, standing, like an unripe orange, against the sky over the Hudson that, thanks to some miracle, could be seen in between all the buildings. The ghost-like halo around the traffic light shattered the space around it into shards of unlikely psychedelic hues.

The street was completely empty, it was a Tuesday night,

almost 2 a.m., and so Gin didn't rush toward that green light. She lazily strolled down 77th Street, avoiding puddles left here after yesterday's rain, and only when the traffic light flicked orange (and that color was hanging up there for a moment, as if the unripe orange ripened in a split-second) did she make her way through the crossing and turn the corner. By the time they made it up one block, the whole Amsterdam Avenue opened itself in front of them like a long pasture, full of green lights.

Almost every native New Yorker must have appreciated the masterful manner with which she managed to drive around the block without having to stop even once.

But Gin's passenger just clicked his tongue angrily when she adjusted her speed to that of the lights on Amsterdam.

"Can't you go a bit faster, PLEASE? I'm in a hurry."

Gin began explaining that sure, she could, but then they'd have to stop with a thud at every block and wait for the green light anyway. So even when those twenty-two or so miles per hour seem awfully boring and slow, they're gonna get there just as fast.

But the gentleman wasn't interested.

"OK, OK, OK. Don't lecture me, all right? Shut up and step on it, will you?"

"Do you want to get out, by any chance?" Gin asked, turning the wheel toward the curb. She didn't like arguing with her customers. Even though this guy might be the last customer of today's night, she wouldn't shed any tears over the few bucks this call might bring her. On the other hand, if she lost her marbles over every customer who recommends that she shut up, she wouldn't even make the daily lease.

After 11 p.m. manners went downhill. She had to take a lot from drunks and Jersey kids out for the night. But this guy didn't look drunk. At least she couldn't smell spirits on his breath as he stuck his head through the partition, getting mad right behind her neck. And it was obvious he didn't feel like getting off. Presently he made himself more comfortable on the back seat and repeated with a touch of friendliness: "Just shut up and drive!"

"You haven't told me where you're going."

The meter clicked to $3.50. They were getting close to 106th and Gin didn't like it anymore.

"Go up!"

"You have to tell me where you're going. I need an address. There's a rule for that."

"Give me a break."

"The address, where you are going, has to be written right here, on the tripsheet. There's a rule for that. And besides, I have a right to know where I'm going."

"So you can choose the longest route around, right?"

"So I can choose the shortest route!"

"I'll show you where to go. Make a right here."

"On 110th?"

"Yeah, yeah, right here, shit. And quit turning to me all the time. Just go. I'm busy."

He jerked up angrily. Gin was watching him in the rear-view mirror. A thought flashed through her head: Perhaps he'd stuffed some coke up his nose recently. It would make sense, after all, if he was in one of those bars around 78th and Columbus. On the other hand, if she was to throw out of her cab everybody who'd stuffed coke up his nose before getting into her cab, she wouldn't even make enough money for gas.

"When you get to 8th Ave, you make a left. Shit, where you going?"

Her blond passenger jumped up so fast the whole cab shook. "Not a right, I said, a left, I said. I've gotten used to the fact that cabbies in this City don't speak English. I've gotten used to the fact that most of you drive the car like it was an ill-saddled camel, that, too. But you don't even know right and left!"

"There's a traffic circle. Look!" Gin explained, and she let the tone of her voice be permeated by exactly that kind of patience that made most people hopping mad. "I'll go to the right first, and then I'm allowed to make a left. It doesn't seem very logical, I know, but all you have to do is lift your eyes up toward the darkened sky. Look: NO LEFT TURN."

The sign with a crossed out arrow was hanging above the crossing, glistening with tiny raindrops and swinging menacingly.

"I know, I know, I know, I know! You're trying to make the meter click again. Another stupid fucking quarter. Out of MY pocket. That's what you cabbies are trying to do, aren't you? You're trying to rip me off. Sometimes I think, if I could, I'd shoot you all. Point blank. Right between the eyes. I'd make those chicken brains of yours splatter all over."

Gin lifted her gaze to the rear-view mirror again. Her customer's nostrils got flared, forming a vicious-looking snout. Gin had often noticed this facial expression on black guys, that is, American black guys. She never saw one of her husbands do it. But this guy was white, even though, judging by the fashion he was wearing, one could conclude he was trying whatever he could to become black. Some people call guys like him wigger, well, that's a racist term, too, she reproached herself silently, I shouldn't use it, no. But the truth is that some white guys really did manage to look like some black guys. It wasn't just the fashion – it was their walk, their motions, their accent, even their voice timbre. Nevertheless, Gin couldn't understand how it's possible that a guy with SO white-guy a kind of face can flare his nostrils exactly the same way some black guys do. Especially those who hate all white people. Gin had had her experience with guys like those. A trip in her taxicab to the middle of nowhere (where they didn't pay) was their idea of revenge on the white race for three hundred years of slavery.

"Do you know who the nicest, politest, most amiable customers are, Gin?" her colleague Geoffrey used to say. "They are the ones who are getting ready to stiff you for money. So they're sweet to you 'cause then you don't pay attention. Can you believe what happened to me once, Gin? Once I'm driving four guys to Brooklyn, it wasn't deep Brooklyn, not very far, but they were supposed to pay seven fifty, if I remember right. They were four of them, and that doesn't make it easy to run away, does it? One was sitting on the front seat, even, right within the boxer's reach of my steel-enforced fists. We get to their destination, and one of them in the back starts counting out money. We gotta give you a good tip, he says, since you drove us all the way to Brooklyn. How much is it? Seven, he says, eight, nine, ten. And as soon as he said ten, all three doors flew open and all four of them got away. Seven, eight, nine, ten. If it wasn't for the goddamn seven fifty, I'd be laughing at that one to this day. But you should know, Gin," Geoffrey continued, "that the absolute sweetest of all passengers are the ones who are already pushing the safety on their gun, getting ready to put it to your head. Whenever you meet somebody THIS sweet, your cabbie's radar should start bleating. 'Cause you should be seeing the barrel of their revolver through their sweetness."

If Gin could rely on this, she'd be perfectly calm. According to Geoffrey's theory somebody as rude as her current passenger would have to throw at least a five-buck tip on her and bow on his way out.

Gin's radar, the one she usually kept turned off, today refused to be turned off for some reason, though. It kept turning on inside her against her will, bleating like crazy.

She could swear her passenger was looking for a place to rob her. She'd heard some guys did it like that. Go over here – they take a look around – No, no, no, go somewhere else . . . No, no, not here, either – Just go a little farther and here . . .

"Where are you going?"

An angry snort could be heard from the back seat.

They have gotten pretty close to the place where Gin now lived. They were racing up 8th Avenue which was called Douglass Boulevard here, past a closed-up deli on the corner of 112th Street where several bullets got stuck into a wall in a neat arc. In the neighborhood people said the shots were meant for a certain drug dealer but they killed a fourteen-year-old boy who was standing there, licking a lollipop.

Gin's thoughts wandered off to the knife in her knapsack. It was sitting there, protected by a scratched leather sheath, surprisingly far away from her reach. ("When you're driving somebody who's the tiniest bit suspicious, and he wants to go somewhere you don't exactly feel like going, stick this knife into your sleeve. Like that," Kenny told her and gave her a demonstration. "A leather jacket, of course, would be ideal, but even a long-sleeved sweatshirt would do. Anything with cuffs. You arrange the handle against the cuff but the blade has to aim toward the elbow. Down here, you see? When you do it well then nothing, I mean nothing can be seen. Nobody can tell you got a knife there. You gotta practice this trick a lot, otherwise it don't work. Because if a situation develops, you can pull out the knife with a single motion of your right hand. And at the same time—" Kenny made a wide gesture, gripping an invisible knife, "with the very same, uninterrupted motion, your elbow turned just a bit to the side, just like I told you, you plant it in between his ribs. It's just like planting rice or something. Like this, Gin, look!")

Gin took a sideways glance at her knapsack that held the knife. It was right next to her and awfully far at the same time. Obviously she hadn't practiced how to pull that knife out from her sleeve. She hadn't even practiced how to put it there. She didn't have a leather jacket on. Not even a sweatshirt or a sweater with something like rubber bands in the cuffs. The not exactly long sleeves of a T-shirt were hugging her elbows tight.

"Goddamn it!" she cursed quietly.

But she grabbed her bag, anyway, and put it on her lap.

The guy on the back seat was watching her, his nostrils flared in disgust.

"Go to . . . 125th and Lenox!" he ordered suddenly.

Gin began to rummage through her knapsack. She fished out a paper tissue and blew her nose.

"Are you going to Sylvia's? Why didn't you tell me?"

Sylvia's was probably the best-known restaurant in Harlem,

famous for its southern cooking. Whenever some white guy wanted to go to Harlem, it was usually to 126th and Lenox.

"125th and Lenox," the passenger said. "One two five and Lenox, dammit." And then he added: "Go to Lenox and 145th."

"To the projects?"

Gin was driving with her left hand and with her right she was desperately rummaging though her knapsack. A wallet. A notebook, the leather on its cover soft with overuse, just like the knife's sheath. The surface structure of things surrounded her. Gin found a lipstick and absent-mindedly took it out. She gawked at it for a second and after an unfinished attempt to stick it in her sleeve she pulled herself together, adjusted the rear-view mirror and swiped the red color across her lips.

"Who are you putting your makeup on for? For me? Or for these niggers around? Make a left. I said: Go up Lenox, dammit. Don't you speak English?"

Gin threw the lipstick back into her knapsack, and with the very same motion, as Kenny might say, she discovered that knife.

Not that she knew how to protect herself with this knife, she shouldn't be kidding herself. But it's not bad to have that stolen little slice of a sky right here, near your elbow. She was trying to undo the snap on the sheath with one hand. The naked knife slid into her palm, stroking it with its coolness. It became the pivotal point of her cool-bloodedness. She snatched a look in the rear-view mirror, and as that dude in the back was presently inspecting his crotch, she entrusted the wheel to her knees for a second and stuffed the naked knife under the tight sleeve of her T-shirt.

If I keep my left hand on my lap, she thought, nothing can be seen. Nothing. She scratched herself with the knife a bit, and although the cut hadn't had time to start stinging, she could feel the moisture of the first few drops of blood as it seeped through her sleeve.

"Fuck!" she howled. But somewhat just inside.

She was holding her hand in her lap.

"Jee-zus Christ, why is it taking you so long? You're caught at a red light again? Step on it, goddammit, I don't have much time."

"You don't even know where you're going but you're in a hurry to get there," Gin mumbled cheekily.

Kenny's knife gave her an illusory feeling of power.

They got to Lenox and 145th.

Gin's passenger took a look around the dark brown buildings of the housing projects and clicked his tongue. "Make a left here!"

"Where are you going?"

For some time now Gin felt like a broken record. After all, the whole situation had begun to resemble one. Where are you going? A tongue-click. Shut up and keep driving!

She was sitting behind the wheel of her taxicab, her regular Yellow dream, her shiny Yellow stallion; from behind the wide-open partition (which wasn't bulletproof, anyway) a passenger who should have been divided from her by at least four yards of solid brick wall was barking at her, and the silhouettes of the housing projects on 145th and Lenox (as the word had it, one of the worst housing projects in a City that wasn't exactly famous for the luxuriousness of its housing projects) were standing sharp against the sickly pink sky in her rear-view mirror.

Harlem was, even now, around 2 a.m., surprisingly lively.

Some characters were loitering around the Jukebox, which wasn't even a store, just a segment of a sidewalk in front of the pulled-down shutter of a local deli. Still the Jukebox was said to be the world's capital when it came to the uncut cocaine market.

Various characters were bopping down the street, back and forth, and even though there were not too many streetlamps around, Harlem was breathing a much livelier air than Downtown Manhattan did at this hour on a Tuesday night.

Various characters were sitting, leaning or standing around on the curbs and on the stairs in front of houses, playing various types of music on their boomboxes. Rap, salsa, reggae, heavy metal, rock and jazz were weaving through one another in an almost deafening cacophony. Every kind of music formed a little island around itself, as big as the shooting range of the loudspeakers – islands with pretty tattered coasts; the musics were out-shouting one another, kicking each other away from their turfs, they were awfully thick, and they covered 145th Street with the most colorful quilt Gin ever knew: a quilt, sewn together out of materials that didn't get along at all, even though their combinations were in fashion in this City: leather, felt, lycra, denim, velour, cotton, spandex.

Among all those sounds – where would Gin's crying for help fit in?

Harlem was lively. But never before in her life did she feel more abandoned.

There exists a borderline beyond which people, even taxidrivers, begin to shake with terror. That borderline can't be seen and it can't be touched. Or, more precisely, it can't be touched the same way a soap bubble can't be touched: as soon as we feel it on our fingertips, we've already broken the surface membrane, and we have bored our way, almost without knowing it, into a completely different reality from which we can't find our way out. This borderline enters us through more than one sensory route, and when we can feel it in front of us we believe for a second that there is a way to avoid that flickering, indefinable trip wire – make a fast right turn; hit the brakes so suddenly that the action-reaction kicks us off the seat, throwing the driver against the wheel and the passenger against the partition; spin the wheel rapidly and, without much of an explanation, crash the car into the nearest lamppost – but no . . . At that moment that borderline has already exerted its power over us and we've suddenly become armless, like a car with a stalled out engine in which the power brakes and power steering don't work any more—

Gin hit that wall, that bubble of terror that paralyzes us,

somewhere around Bradhurst Avenue and 145th. Beyond it, there was only fear.

How many police cars does a cabdriver run into, every night, when he least needs it! They flutter like butterflies, lights blinking, to every major crash; they make their way through red lights, slowing down traffic; they block the cabbie's way while rushing through one-way streets in the wrong direction, blowing their horns; they prowl next to street crossings, hidden behind the corners of buildings or newsstands, giving out tickets; they alight on 14th Street at 3 a.m. like a flock of vultures to give out double-parking tickets to Yellow Cabs – often twenty of them at a time – who've been hopefully lining up, waiting for customers in front of the packed nightclub called Nell's!

Whenever you desperately needed them, there were no cops around.

Gin realized that her moody customer had circumvented the police station on 124th and Powell Boulevard; that they didn't go near any crossings where it was likely to meet the pigs.

That, perhaps, he wasn't even thinking of a place to rob her. He was just getting there via a detour that was pretty pernicious for Gin.

Of course it occurred to her, God knows how many blocks back, that if she managed to drive up to the side of some police trooper, then it's more than likely many a cop would, in response to a redheaded cabdriver's plea, remove that guy from her car. But where to look for cops at the moment? When you needed them the most, there were no cops around.

She heard the wail of a police siren somewhere in the distance. For a while it seemed to her it was getting closer but then it started getting farther and farther again. All Gin could do was listen morosely as its wail, made lame by distance so it sounded almost like the crowing of some night pigeon or other, disappeared behind the building blocks and came back up again, weaker and weaker . . .

Another siren could be heard, somewhere up north, but at

the same moment it became clear to her that this lovely, oh, so lovely flickering of the cherry lights was reaching her from the highway overpass that connects Saint Nicholas Avenue, right up the hill, with Macombs Dam Bridge that crosses the Harlem River, running into the South Bronx.

But at that moment they – Gin, her passenger and her cab – were already UNDER it, under that overpass over which the police trooper was presently speeding, and from the slope above them the underbrush of Jackie Robinson Park was stretching their vines toward them.

That night, Jackie Robinson Park, neglected for years, breathed out the moisture of late spring, mixed in with the rooty, mysterious smell of its thick, entangled underbrush. They were strong smells, quite overwhelming. Gin could feel her head spin in an upward spiral.

Her thoughts wandered off to the stately as well as repulsive arch of the bridge. The space they were sitting in was one of the strangest spaces Gin had ever seen in New York City. In fact, it was a dead-end street, a couple dozen yards long, at the very end of Bradhurst Avenue, at the spot where it ran into 155th Street. 155th Street ended with a long, slimy stone wall with several silverish graffiti on it; to the north of them the Polo Ground Houses Project was standing, and a staircase, at the bottom of which a shattered cast-metal lantern remained, led up toward Saint Nicholas Avenue. It was a steep stone staircase with cast-metal banisters. It was tall, its upper end disappearing in the darkness and a thin haze, and a gloomily abandoned twilight painted it with a thin bluish hue, similar to the color you can see at the outer reaches of the light of a gas lantern.

From the open partition of Gin's cab the barrel of a gun was aiming at her.

"Maybe it occurred to you I will choose this place, didn't it? Or do you, yourself, know a better one? Just name a single place in Harlem that would fit this occasion better. You can't name it 'cause a place like that doesn't exist. Just take a look around: nobody can spy on us, nobody! It's just like a cozy little hotel room, just for you and me. Not even those niggers can't eye you here. And now look up. Come on, lift up your head, I'm telling you!" He lifted her chin with the gun. "You see that space? That arch? You see this wall? Solid stone. This wall makes a great echo when you fire – and it'll vibrate in the ribs of this bridge long after you won't give a flying fuck. 'Cause you'll be dead, you see? You'll be dead."

Gin's passenger on the back seat lifted up half his butt and farted. "Sorry. But you're not the one and only I'm bringing here. Last time I finished a nigger here. A real one, from some African backwoods. I couldn't even have a talk with him, didn't speak English. He got out of his cab and ran, he thought he could run away from me! But I caught up with him and I gave it to him, and that echo, it vibrated under this bridge like a . . . like a thunderclap! Yeah, I'm a poet, right? Don't even tell me, 'cause I'm so spoiled when somebody tells me I'm Sappho, I get mad and I write a poem about his death even before it happens to him, see? How old are you?"

"— —"

"Oh? So you don't want to entrust that to me, hah? I can hear just some strange bubbling coming out of your throat. Me, I was born in August 1966. You know what that means?"

"That . . . that you're . . . born . . . under the sign of . . . Lion?"

"Oh, give me a break, I'm not interested in horoscopes. It means, girl, I'm a blackout baby. Heard about it? Total blackout in New York City and vicinity, from Bangor down to D.C. That's how I've entered this world. Wanna know my name? My name is Stanley – Staley, that was the brand name of the elevator my mother was stuck in for three days, no food, no water, not a single flicker of light, and the only connection with the outer world was the surface of that name, Staley, engraved in block letters on a copper plaque on the wall. My name is Stanley, the N made it in the name somehow, convention, I guess, or they call me PH, for penthouse, that's where the elevator was stuck for three whole days, but my friends call me

27. That's how you can call me now, OK, before I blow your balls off, pardon me, you're a lady, I meant to say brains. Yo, 27. Say it."

Gin made a serious attempt to do that but "Yo, 27" came out more like some bubbling sound. She simply wasn't used to people holding a gun barrel four inches away from her skull, demanding to be addressed by their most intimate nickname.

A lot of things were happening inside her at the same time. Her childhood memories. Her memories of Talibe. Little adventures, which had been shelved for a long time in the most remote corners of her subconscious, were emerging and parading in front of her inner eye. She got alarmed: they say exactly this happens to people who've fallen into a coma they're not gonna wake up from.

"27, that's my name. I was conceived in the elevator in the darkness, without a single flash of light. In total, absolute darkness. D'you dig how dismal it is?"

PH's eyelids fluttered, he was visibly sorry for himself.

"And that's why, girlfriend, that's why – What should I call you? I mean, intimately? No, no, you don't have to tell me. I'll call you Cunt. 'Cause only a cunt like yourself will be lured into coming all the way up here, under this bridge, into this perfect tomb, you see? Or a guy who is a cunt. D'you believe you're, by far, not the first Cunt-cabbie I've brought over here? Some of them, they got away. But the ones who got all the way here . . . I gotta collect 27 of them. Because 27 is my name, that's why, my dear Cunt, I was conceived in darkness in the elevator, and in the darkness I light up! Wanna see how I shine? Turn around!"

Gin moved her neck muscles. They were so stiff they screeched. Then she hit the barrel of the gun with her gaze; the gun invaded her nostrils with the smell of steel and something else, something that made it shine so much – linseed oil, perhaps. The gun aimed down for a second but immediately it straightened up again. Stanley, a.k.a. 27, rested his right wrist on the edge of the partition, rubbing it with his left palm.

"I talk too much, don't you think? We'll have to end it. You know what? My hand hurts! Have you ever held a gun in your hand, aiming it at some Cunt, five minutes, ten minutes, HALF AN HOUR? It's like holding a brick in your palm. We'll have to end this. But I like this space 'cause it has such a good echo. When you fire a gun like that, a simple .25, it echoes in it. It reverberates like a symphony. Would you believe it? I'm kind of sorry you can't hear that. By the way, before you die, wanna tell me something funny?"

"F . . . funny?"

"Yeah. Some joke, some pun, a little poem, a riddle, anything by which I can remember you. If I like it, I mean, REALLY like it, maybe I let you go . . . Or, if I DON'T let you go, at least I'll give you a chance to think up an epitaph they can put on your grave. But it should be funny. You see?"

"F . . . f . . . f . . . funny?"

"Come on, give it a try. Tell me something. I'm sure you've had some funny story, from the taxi. Just entertain me a bit."

Never before did it represent a problem for Gin to remember – or to make up – some funny story from the life of a cab lady. If people wanted to listen, she could pour a couple dozen of them from her sleeve at any time. But now . . . now her mind was a complete blank. Or, more precisely, it was occupied by a single thought that wasn't funny at all:

THIS MAN KILLED MY HUSBAND! In fact, he told me as much. In this place, he said, he shot – from a TWENTY-FIVE! – an African guy. Here, underneath this bridge. Less than a mile and a half from Harlem Hospital. It seemed like an impossible chance, that's right. But chances . . . chances WORKED in New York City! Once, Gin had the same customer in her car three times in the course of a single night. Gin would meet people in the streets who, she had been convinced, she would never, ever see again. Chances in this City worked in surprising and twisted ways . . . Chances, after all . . . that was that huge, variegated tree in whose branches a whole bunch of coincidences were swinging. THIS MAN KILLED MY HUSBAND!

The man behind her back snorted impatiently and said: "Yes? . . ."

"Well, I'm dri-ving one day," she started, her words dissolving in a hopeless stammer.

"Where are you driving, Cunt?"

"One day I'm driving with a taxi and I pick up a woman. She had a dog with her. I mean, a little, tiny dog, and she asks me—"

Gin interrupted herself in mid-sentence. It seemed to her for a second that the amulet, which was swinging between her breasts, got all red-hot at that moment. She shuddered and lifted her hand but a sudden motion of the gun barrel made her change her mind.

"Sit and don't move, Cunt. Continue. You're doing fine."

"She asks me, can she take the dog with her into the car. She says the dog is gonna sit on the floor. So I said yes and—"

(Yes: that's what happened. Everything fits together. Nobody ever found out where Talibe got shot. And how. And by whom. Talibe kept mum about it. Even when a detective arrived in the hospital, Talibe didn't tell him anything. Talibe had other things to take care of. The detective introduced himself with vigor, he rattled off his series of questions once in English and once in lousy Spanish, then he shrugged, said, "Very well!" and made his leave. Gin didn't even know whether he'd taken that hollow point bullet from Dr Whitehead as evidence. Less than ten days later Talibe . . . Talibe . . . Gin couldn't pronounce that word, "died," now, not even in her thoughts.)

"Who did you talk about before? Who did you . . . finish here?"

"Comeoncomeon, Cunt! You're not concentrating on your story at all! What happened next?"

"She put the dog on her lap but then she must have put him on the seat next to her, probably, I couldn't see nothing in the rear-view mirror, and . . . and the dog . . . the dog . . ." Gin got all queasy because, all of a sudden, she needed to use the bathroom real bad. She'd heard about this. It apparently has to do with common fear. "The dog . . . he pissed on the seat and the woman didn't tell me anything about it, she didn't say a word, only I was surprised that, when she got off on Park Avenue, she gave me two dollars for a tip, and I didn't even take her that far. And a couple blocks later on Park Avenue . . . this other . . . other passenger gets in the car . . . you know, one of these uptight rich old cows, she's all decked out in an evening gown, half a ton of makeup on her face, the doorman of her house opens the door pompously and stuff – and she lands right . . . right in the dog piss. First she thought it was water so she says, I wanted to give you a half-dollar tip but you won't even get a quarter. But then she starts sniffling, and soon as she finds out it's piss, she starts yelling, Police, police, put this taxidriver to prison, she has pee on the back seat, put her to jail!"

"And you think that's funny, Cunt? What if a dog was sitting on the seat before me? What if I sat in it?" PH emitted a self-pitying sigh.

A rat ran over the wet stones at the foot of the staircase. Its shadow got imprinted in Gin's consciousness while this guy was aiming a gun at her head, a gun she desperately wanted not to see but its shine was reflected on her thoughts even more than the wet stones around.

The arch of the bridge above them (that's right: that claustrophilic space she used to visit by the dozen during the era of Alex the God) seemed to be the most impossible of all imaginable graves.

"What African did you talk about? You said you shot him. I . . . I . . ."

"Come on, come on, my dear Cunt, what do you care? My dear girl, I'm not so picky. I didn't finish that nigger here 'cause he was a nigger. Or maybe I did. I finished that nigger 'cause he was a nigger. And in the same spot I'll finish you, 'cause you're not a nigger bitch. You're a Cunt from Europe. 'Cause you are . . . Czecoslavian . . . Yugoslovakian . . . what is it that you said? That's why I'll finish you. I'm the spawn of darkness, Cunt, the offspring of darkness, and that's one of the reasons I dress like a nigger. You believe in God?"

"No."

"I don't believe in God, either. I believe in darkness. I was born out of darkness, so I know there's no God, there's just light and there's darkness, and our life, that's the twilight zone, all our lives, so I send people to darkness, I borrow their light from them, you see, because the world OWES me the light, you see that, Cunt?" PH gave a sigh. He made himself comfortable, his elbow resting on the partition. "Have money on you?"

"Well . . . I have a bit of money on me," Gin confessed, half-choking. "The night wasn't very good but . . ."

"Money? You're offering me MONEY?? Money, that's for niggers. For niggers, you hear me? Sure, I could take all your money, but I don't feel like it, I throw shit on it. I could pick it out of your purse while you're already in darkness, but, my dear Cunt, have you ever seen the human brain splash out, mixed with blood . . . If you ever saw that, you'd understand that once it's . . . once it's . . . finished . . . I really won't feel like rummaging through that . . . mess."

PH lifted his hand with the gun in it, yelling: "I'll blow your motherfuckin' brains out! Gimme all your money!"

And that was the sentence. The sentence she'd heard dozens of times, pronounced by her colleagues, as well as Kenny, whenever they made their little educational lectures and demonstrations to her. It wasn't scary at all. Perhaps it was because Stanley a.k.a. PH a.k.a. 27 pronounced it with exactly the same stormy voice others liked to use for demonstrations. And then they gave her a fatherly wink and asked her: "And what do you do, Gin? When someone yells something like that at you? What do you do?" – "I'll give it to him?"

Gin lifted her right hand from the steering wheel. She'd held it there, rather absent-mindedly, during the whole length of 27's monologue because we all have learned from the movies that if somebody is aiming a gun at our head, it's usually better not to fidget too much. She made for her knapsack on the seat, when she heard a snort behind her back and the gun at her ear gave a metallic click. Shit! a thought flicked through Gin's brain (the brain that still hadn't splashed all over her taxi) –

he'd been aiming at my head with a gun with the safety on! Jee-zus! I AM an amateur! Unintentionally, she gave a little laugh.

"Put that hand up! You whore! I know what you're trying to do."

But Gin's laughter had the time to pierce through that paralyzing bubble of terror.

She turned toward him, sneering in his face. "I just thought you wanted your money right now, before they get covered with my brains." Laughter was bubbling out of her in little rivulets, choking her like breadcrumbs.

"You have the nerve to be sassy with me, Cunt? Really, I thought you'd shit in your panties. Put your left foot on the wheel!"

"Foot??"

"Yeah, your foot, Cunt. Put your left foot on the wheel. And now, Cunt, take off your shoe and pull off your sock – yeah, right, I knew you'd have a few Jacksons there, I just knew it!"

Gin's naked foot shone white in the semidarkness.

At that moment Gin, thanks to some mysterious function of her brain, shook off her fear completely. Perhaps it was that laughter just a while back. Perhaps it was the hot touch of the good-luck charm. Or perhaps that trail of blood, seeping through her sleeve, gave her power. And hope.

"And now, Cunt, you hand me these two Jacksons!"

PH rested his tired right hand with the gun on the edge of the partition. He panted with exertion. Gin was slowly lifting her left hand with two rumpled 20-dollar notes.

"Bring them right here! Into my hand! That's right!"

Gin was handing him the notes with her left hand. She stretched her right hand behind her shoulder.

And before PH had the time to realize what was happening he was already screaming with pain, trying to pull back, as the partition hit his wrist. He yelled: "Shit, I'm gonna make you pay for that!" – but at that moment his gun had fallen on the front seat – and the car was divided into two bubbles. In the rear one PH was yelling like they were vivisecting him, rubbing his damaged wrist. In the front one, next to Gin, the gun was lying. It was unbelievably tiny. Its grip was inlaid with mother-of-pearl and alongside the barrel (which, in this position, didn't look deadly at all) a notice, engraved in the metal, read:

Beretta USA Corp. ACCK.MD
– READ MANUAL BEFORE USE –

This notice seemed irresistibly funny to Gin. Or, at least, it confused her. Well, perhaps I could do him in with his own weapon, she thought, but that manual, well, I'm sure I don't have the time to read it right now. PH was already opening the door, sliding out and reaching for the handle on Gin's door. The door was locked. But it didn't occur to Gin that she could just drive away. When you have a naked foot up on the steering wheel, the thought doesn't occur to you just like that. She made her way out through the passenger door, forgetting the Beretta on the front seat, but something made her push the lock button before she slammed the door behind her. PH lost a few critical seconds jerking the door handle. In the cabin, in plain view, as if it was exhibited in a glass museum case, the Beretta .25 was lying.

Then PH decided he could handle her no matter what.

"I'll get you, you fuckin' whore! Just like I got that nigger!"

Under her left foot she felt the cold moist soil and asphalt and mud and glass shards and shattered crack vials with their colorful caps scattered all over, and then she could feel the wet cold of the staircase on the side of the bridge, that bluish staircase that led up to heaven, or, at least, to safety, up to Saint Nicholas Avenue. Away from here.

I should have done some exercising, she scolded herself, I should have gone jogging every day, doing at least three miles or so; had I been exercising just a little bit I could escape him quite easily now. But that asshole is running, in those oversized sneakers of his, like a motherfucker. Never mind they're untied.

"Just you wait, I'll get you like I got that nigger!" PH, a step behind Gin, was howling, reaching for her calves.

Apparently he had forgotten he didn't have his piece on him. When he made it just a few steps behind her, he reached out, hooking his elbow on her calf. He yanked at her feet. And Gin was presently falling. But in that split second, right before he knocked her off balance, she put her hand into her sleeve. The blade of a weapon called a "survival knife" flew through the air.

"I'll kill you, just like I killed that nigger!"

The blade of Gin's knife made an arc in the air, an unfinished circle, a circle reminiscent of the huge hoops in whores' ears, the same arc that made some desperate folks, Gin included, spend their unfinished nights in hourly hotels, the same arc with which the bridge above was slicing through the sky, connecting Gin with – what? Hope? The world? God?

"I'll kill you, just like I killed that nigger!"

And that sentence got imprinted into the creases of Gin's brain, raping her thoughts; it opened a cavern inside her, it turned on her reptile brain. That sentence got printed for her in the sky. She could actually see a shard of the sky now, all hazy. She screamed: "You know what? YOU are a nigger!"

Then she shuddered. The vulgarity of that word, that word, considered by some the nastiest word in the English language, paralyzed her tongue. This was the first time in her life she pronounced this word aloud. How could she do that? Gin didn't want to believe her own ears, but her ears were bringing the echo of this word back, reflected from the shiny-wet stone of the wall next to her. How can she be so vulgar?

And then she started to excuse herself to herself. After all, I didn't start all that, did I? I just answered this guy here, who's a white guy, after all, even though he dresses like a homeboy, with the same expression he used all the time and without remorse. After all, she, Gin, didn't ever say anything like that aloud. No. That word, that came out of HIS mouth, simply reflected off of her tongue, and, after all – after all it's not so bad – is it? – using this word on a white guy. She felt a little better.

Of course, the problem of what to do with the body still remained.

Yeah, with a body, she realized instantly. Even though she'd never before stabbed anybody through the heart.

What am I supposed to do now? she thought demurely. What the hell am I supposed to do now? Should I load him on the back seat and rush him to the hospital? While it's obvious that as soon as I get there the first doctor won't tell me more than that he's a goner? Should I wrap him up in plastic, stick him in the trunk and bury him under the Brooklyn Bridge?

Bullshit! she reproached herself almost aloud. He's quite a big guy. I can't even lift him up. I'll have considerable difficulties rolling him off this here staircase into the bushes, Gin thought, yanking on the knife in PH's chest. The knife had cut through the tricolor hooded jacket with a neat slit, and not a single drop of blood seeped out around it. Had she spent years and years practicing, she couldn't possibly have killed him better. And at the same time she wasn't even sure whether she'd really stabbed at him, or whether she just, as she was falling, had leaned on his chest with the knife the same way a skier might try to save himself from a tumble by using his pole. The knife slid into the heart and the heart had sucked it in; no matter how hard Gin was jerking at the handle, the dead heart of 27 refused to give it back.

Finally, that aphorism 27 wanted to hear from her popped up in her mind.

You see, she told him, you were conceived in an elevator, and you died on the stairs.

Then she carefully wiped any fingerprints off the knife handle, and, with a lot of huffing and puffing, she rolled 27 down to the roots and vines of Jackie Robinson Park. Into the darkness made fragrant with the smell of roots. Into the darkness that already stank like a tomb.

Her need to go to the bathroom became overwhelming. No, no, you gotta control yourself, she thought, first you gotta get out of here.

Her taxi was parked nearby, looking lonely but with its

headlights still on. In their glow, glass shards and shattered crack vials were glimmering, as well as scattered nails and squashed beer cans. Gin cursed. Now she'll have to make her way across that mess, with only one foot shod. She stepped on an earthworm with her left foot, squashing it. Her stomach raised up to her throat. No, no, no, I must not puke now, no – I must leave as little of myself here as I can.

Her Yellow, like an improbable sun, was purring softly; its engine was on. Gin was wading toward it like a shipwrecked sailor. And the way a shipwrecked sailor might reach for a loose beam rocking on the waves, Gin reached for the door handle.

The door was locked.

Yeah, obviously, she realized. I had locked it. While 27 was coming after me, it was the only smart thing to do.

And now the locked Yellow was laughing at Gin. And as the key was still stuck in the starter, it purred contentedly.

Gin found a rock. She took aim. She banged at the window with it. The window showed no reaction. She moved a couple of steps back, lifted her arm way up and tried again. On the window of her cab a cobweb spread out. It hung there for a second, glimmering in the reflected light like the white down on angels' wings. Then it collapsed at her feet.

Under the dramatically abandoned arch of a bridge that bang finally resounded.

It vibrated there, bouncing off the ribs, metal beams and concrete; it ran back and forth, hiding behind huge metal screws, freeing scraps of paint from the bridge so they started showering down in huge flakes. On one side they were misty blue, and on the other, where the base coat was, orange like a newt's spots.

Another sound then was the screech of tires. Gin was making at least sixty as she rushed toward 145th Street.

The main thing now is not to lose my head, she thought, brushing sharp shards of glass off her seat with a blood-covered palm. The main thing is to sweep all tracks behind me, that's the main thing. And she smeared her own blood all over her face as she was trying to wipe the sweat off it. 'Cause I'm not gonna go report this to the cops. No, sir, I'm not that dumb. How could I prove I REALLY killed him in self-defense – and by mistake? And how would I explain that knife to them? When a taxidriver must not have a weapon on him? How about those four notches on the handle – after all, wouldn't they pull Kenny into all this, too? And then: Doesn't 27, I mean, his dead body, possess some special American-style rights I've never heard about but that could get me fried? And even if they don't fry me then . . . then they'll definitely drag me through all the TV channels as a cabdriver-murderess . . . No, I'm not going to the cops.

So the main thing is not to attract any attention to myself, she thought, hitting a streetlamp with the right door, the bang reverberating through the whole neighborhood. I gotta drive really carefully, she repeated to herself, and by mistake she made a left turn on red down Amsterdam Avenue, which resulted in the screech of brakes and the endless horn-blowing of some asshole who she almost crashed into.

She got all sweaty. I gotta be TERRIBLY careful, I must not drive like a jerk – and she took the bumper and brake lights off a parked Toyota Corolla.

As soon as I get some place a bit farther Downtown, some place AWAY FROM HERE, I'll stop and use the bathroom in some restaurant, and then I'll sit at a table for a moment and I'll pull myself together and—

On 113th and Amsterdam Avenue her eyes turned the wrong way, all inside her head, and she came to only when a voice reached her from the back seat: "Ya hear me? Whass wrong with ya? 112th and St Nick. Ya hear me? Hello!"

That voice was penetrating the still-closed partition. It was sing-songy, a little throaty and indubitably Harlemity. On the back seat of Gin's stallion two guys in tricolor hooded jackets were sitting, and in between them a girl in whose ears humongous earrings were hanging, as big as basketball hoops.

Shit! Gin cursed inwardly. I forgot to lock the back doors.

"You wanna go to 112th?"

"Ya got a problem with that? We pay ya—"

"No, no, no problem, I just . . . This is 111th, isn't it?"

And she spun the wheel to the left. She drove up on the sidewalk and a gilded statue with some angels and saints reproachfully blocked her way. "Oh. Not this way. I see . . . this is not a street, this is a park. I forgot."

"Man, where did ya get that shit?" the guy to the left asked congenially. "That shit you put up your nose? Can't ya spare some, man? My leg be hurtin' like motherfuckin' hell."

"I . . . I just wanted to take the shortest route," Gin mumbled like a lunatic. "But here, there is the park. Morningside Park, I know. So I'll have to go down to 110th—"

"Goddamn it, what a day!" the guy to the right complained. He was sitting, all pent-up, on the seat, talking to her through the hole in that funny-looking thing into which the passenger, when the partition is closed, should stick money for the driver. "First I nearly get arrested 'cause of some bullshit crap, and then a taxidriver try to make her way through the wall with me. What a day."

"Ya shut up, will ya?" the girl reproached him with regal airs. "If ya wasn't so abrupt—"

Meanwhile, Gin remedied everything. She backed up off the sidewalk and then she was on 110th and Amsterdam, obediently waiting for a green arrow. If there's any danger anywhere then it certainly doesn't emanate from these three. She pulled the plexiglass on the partition open and turned around. "It was a long shift today. Sorry."

"Are ya really so goddamn high, or ya have a body in the trunk?"

(I don't have a body in the trunk, no. He was too heavy.) And she said: "I mean, I . . ."

"Ya wouldn't believe what happen to me!" the girl in hoops entered the conversation. "Today I—"

"Today ya! Today ya was whoring around with—"

"Gimme a break! What d'ya mean, I was whoring around!" the girl struck the shoulder of that impertinent guy to the right. "I give a leetle kiss to here Josh, man, I ain't seen him for days, and—"

"And yer boo-boo stab my leg!" Joshua screamed. "I can't believe—"

"So you, I mean—" Gin said.

Gin was just driving, from St Luke's Hospital, a rather unusual trio. Two guys fought over a girl, one of them ended up with a switchblade in his thigh, then all three went to the hospital to have him sewn up.

While they were telling her all that, one on top of the other, behind her back, the blue light of a police siren appeared in back of her car.

Jee-zus Christ! They got me already! Well, that was quite a fast investigation, I gotta give them that much. But I – I won't confess a thing, she promised to herself, hiding her bloody elbow from view, stepping on the gas without even knowing. I'll get away from them. No, no, I won't. I . . . I won't confess a thing. No! I'll say I was just on my way to report the robbery, I'm going to the police station. Which one??? No! I'll get away from them. No, I won't.

"Seems them piggies is after ya," the cut-up guy commented drily. "Ya should either step on it or pull over. One or the other."

That's what I've been telling myself, Gin thought, putting on the right-turn signal. In this City, and in this taxi, and with these people on the back seat I just can't not stop. She half-passed out with fear.

A face appeared in Gin's broken window. It didn't look menacing. Actually, it gave Gin a sweet little smile as soon as it saw it had something to do with a lady. On the lapel of his uniform the cop had a neat name plate: OSARODION.

"Routine check," the face said. "These three guys here, Miss . . . driver—" Mr Osarodion aimed his flashlight at the faces of her passengers, making them blink and cover their eyes. "Did these passengers give you any problem, Miss . . . driver?"

"No, none at all."

"Where are you taking them?"

"I'm taking them to . . . to . . . shit . . ."

At that moment Gin, without thinking, looked down at the front seat. Right next to her, a Beretta .25 was lying, giving off a mother-of-pearl shine.

Gin lost her voice completely. "Ah–ah–ah–I . . ." She turned to her passengers. "Wh–where am I driving you?"

"112th and Saint Nick," the guy on the back seat said, grinning at the cop. "Just make it snappy, OK? We don't have all day."

The cop sent another bright beam in his eyes. "Do you want them to pay you up front, Miss? I'll make them. Here in Harlem—"

"No, it's OK. I—"

"All right, you may continue."

The blue lights behind them went off.

"Goddamn nigger!" the cut-up guy spat out.

"That's just because we black, ya see?" the girl chirped in. "But we pay ya. Don't ya worry, Miss."

"He a cop in Harlem an I bet he live in Westchester. He don't know shit 'bout what it's like to live in here and he dissin' us. Goddamn stupid motherfucker!"

Gin covered the Beretta with her black knapsack, as inconspicuously as she could muster.

"Gee, look what our lady cabbie got right here! – Dead presidents lyin' all over!" the guy to the right exclaimed, handing her two twenty-dollar bills through the partition.

The girl in hoops gave him the look.

"Why shouldn't I give her the money back? It was lyin' on the floor. Some motherfucker must've dropped it. And she all right. Ain't she?"

On Saint Nicholas Avenue they got off, paid, wished her a good night and a swift recovery from all that shit she'd put up her nose, and waved their goodbye. Gratefulness and relief shot through Gin like she was an electric wire. If she could, she'd get out of the car and hug them all. At once.

But at that instant she realized that there were still the gooey remnants of an earthworm on the sole of her left foot.

*

Tripsheet. Tripsheet is a piece of heavy paper with lines printed on it. On each of them – according to the rules – the driver must put down where and at what time he picked up how many passengers, where they wanted to go, what time they got there and how much the trip cost.

While taxidrivers in New York still worked on commission – cabbies giving 50–60 percent to their garage – the tripsheets served as a checking device. The owner of the garage looked at them, and he usually could tell whether his driver was kidding him or not.

Today, tripsheets are good for only one thing: to make it easier for the cops – or the Taxi and Limousine Commission inspectors – to bug the cabdriver.

From this point of view, the tripsheet is surprisingly well-designed.

If you put everything down right on the spot, during your shift, as it comes, hour by hour, then it's an easy task, rather primitive in fact, easily mastered by everybody, including people whose own alphabet is written from right to left and whose handwriting, even in English, resembles spilled tea leaves. But faking a tripsheet isn't easy at all. The miles showing on the meter must correspond with the distances (allegedly) driven. You must put in just the right amount of time, not too little and not too much, and while doing it, you have to keep traffic in mind, as it changes hour by hour. In addition to that, if you drive slower than some ten miles per hour, then every seventy-five seconds another quarter appears on the meter. This fact must correspond with distances and the number of red lights encountered and—

(Gin was nervously chewing a white-and-blue ballpoint of the Bic brand.)

—And all that must correspond with the little numbers that the meter shows and that you had to put down on the tripsheet at the very beginning of your shift. And those numbers are not talking of dollars like the tripsheet does, no, they talk about "total" miles and "live" miles, and about the mysterious "units" which are basically the number of quarters that the meter shows, but minus the first dollar-fifty for the first one-fifth of a mile. Or something like that.

And then the fake tripsheet, the brand new sheet of heavy paper with the address of the garage and your boss's autograph on it, must be submerged a bit, but not too much, in the little puddle of spilled coffee that's presently drying out on the salmon-colored table at the Munson Diner, it must be rumpled up a little bit, but not too much, and your handwriting on it has to be almost calligraphic at the beginning and then uglier and uglier as the night rolls by.

All that needs to be kept in mind, and at the same time you must look inconspicuous, not too concentrated, not too beaten . . . You must not chew that Bic pen to pulp. And you must not hide your work every time the waiter Kasif passes by the table, throwing little loving smiles at you.

And you must—

I mean, the tripsheet must look beautiful, it must look absolutely gorgeous, that is, it must look exactly the same like any other tripsheet from any other day . . . it must not be any different from the stack of those Gin has been rather absent-mindedly collecting in a plastic milk crate . . . And then you must get rid of today's tripsheet – that is, the real one – (the best would be to rip it to tiny little shreds and throw them all over the City) and – Jee-zus Christ, the knife sheath! – OK, I'll carefully wipe all fingerprints off it and throw it into a sewer. Somewhere. Somewhere really far away from 155th Street and Bradhurst.

"Oh God, oh my God, what happened to you?" Kasif, the cook, the waiter and the busboy in one, was staring at Gin's face. She'd concentrated on her work so much that she'd rested her chin on the palm of her hand and her whole jaw was covered with blood. "What HAPPENED?" Kasif was screaming, handing her a wet paper towel. Gin obediently wiped her face on it.

"O-oh, it's nothing. Just on my hand. I cut it when – when some asshole broke my window with a stone."

Kasif nodded his head. He dragged Gin into the kitchen

and poured sizzling peroxide on her palm. "People make terrible things to taxidrivers, you know. Wait, don't move now . . . Hold your hand like this . . . People make terrible things to taxidrivers. It was a nigger, am I right?"

If only I could, she wished a little later, sticking the beautiful, scratched and polished-with-wear sheath of a certain knife through the bars on a sewer cover in the most abandoned slum she knew: Red Hook right next to the Brooklyn shipyard, the port cranes' silhouettes standing tall against the sky that wasn't dark anymore – if only I could rip today's whole night into pieces, just like I've ripped to pieces the real tripsheet of today's night – and scatter its shards around the City, under the curbs and among the used condoms dry-rotting on street corners . . . If only it was possible to rip this whole night to pieces, dismantle it to basic elements and then throw these into the sewer with the same splash with which the Beretta .25 said goodbye to me! If only it was possible to slit this whole day into thin threads and bury it in the murky waters of the East River some place on the Brooklyn side of the Williamsburgh Bridge, in the same spot where, as they say, the empty carcasses of stolen cars tend to end up. If only it was possible to undo, unlive this whole day, make it not have happened, throw it away so professionally nobody can ever, ever find it, or – if a couple pieces of it did get caught behind some detective's fingernails, then at least make sure that no one, no one can ever glue out of them the mosaic of Gin's night that had just passed.

Gin turned the key in the fourth lock and the door of apartment #5C flew open. "I'm washing!" she yelled in place of a hello. She threw her knapsack into the corner, kicked her sneakers off in the direction of a wastebasket, and was presently pulling down her socks from which, when she shook them, a few sweaty banknotes of a promisingly greenish hue fluttered down.

"I'm washing!" she bellowed, lifting up her left palm from which a few coagulating red drops were leaking. But she didn't even have to do that. Ouagadougou, a mixture of tragedy and sleep on his face, was already pulling his sheet off the bed and moving to the living room floor, getting ready to sleep there. He didn't as much as mumble something to the effect that she had been washing less than two weeks ago. His wife's menstrual cycle represented a mystery one wasn't allowed to mention.

Anyway, Ouag will leave her alone for a couple days at least. She lay down on the bed – it was surprisingly comfortable now, when the whole thing belonged just to her – and immediately sank into sleep as deep as the waters of the River Styx.

Chapter 39

Moments

Gin was sitting on a bed at the Liberty Inn on 14th Street, the hotel that rented rooms by the hour, and waited for pleasure to shoot through her body like blue lightning, like the blade of a knife; she waited for pleasure to cut her into slices the same way the prickly lights of police sirens cut through thick white fog; she waited for pleasure to slash through her, just for a little moment, for a few seconds that then get imprinted in her body like it was sensitive magnetic tape.

Life consisted of moments.

Of unfinished circles down which she was entering hourly hotels; and in them pleasure was waiting, and orgasm, even love, maybe.

Life consisted of rhythmic moments.

The City throbbed thanks to its traffic lights: red green yellow—

—and every glance, every experience, every emotion, every love had to fit in between those flashes.

Life got turned on like a lamp, pulsating, all chopped up into segments each of which made perfect sense but all of them, taken together, did not . . .

"You still have that knife?" Kenny asked her.

"I forgot it," Gin groaned, "I forgot that knife of yours . . ."

"Where d'you forget it?"

In a certain motherfucker's heart. Actually, I didn't. His heart stole it from me.

But she didn't say that aloud. All she did was sink deeper into the throbbing. She bit his shoulder, the fragrance of gas and sweat. She sank her teeth hard so she didn't have to answer. So this moment would get imprinted into Kenny's shoulder, staying with him until the bruise fades out.

Life is a throbbing, the City has a heart . . .

Today they didn't manage to close the whole circle, it was just an arc, a spiral that led somewhere, to the heavens, perhaps, and Gin rested her head on the metal box, painted khaki, one of the metal boxes that directed the traffic on street corners, the flickering of red green yellow – and she listened to the heart of that City; she was teaching her own heart to beat the same way, she was teaching her thoughts to fit into it . . .

She chopped her whole life into segments defined by the heartbeat of that City.

That City in which she had, with her own hand, stopped the heartbeat of somebody. The heartbeat of a certain white nigger.

Chapter 40

Must Not Make a Mistake

I should have watched more gangster movies, Gin scolded herself now. I should have read police annals and tabloid newspapers. I should have studied how the investigation is usually led when the cops find, on 155th Street, a relatively fresh body from whose heart a survival knife with four notches on its handle is sticking.

I should have studied how the New York Police investigate a murder.

Because as soon as they find him there, it will be clear to everybody that that motherfucker didn't stick that knife into his heart unassisted. (On the other hand, who knows. She'd heard that some ten years ago a certain guy, a rather unpopular Democrat from Queens, committed suicide by stabbing himself through the heart TWICE.)

I should have known much more about killing before I killed that jerk.

Or, maybe, it's just the other way around . . . maybe it's my very lack of knowledge that has protected me so far. Just like the fact that I'm anything but dexterous when it comes to blade handling helped me to hit his very heart.

Maybe the unbelievable luck of rookie gamblers (that luck Balzac writes about) was on my side there. They are those people who make a fortune in the casino, on their first day, but only because they've never before seen a roulette wheel.

Maybe this first and only thrust with a survival knife helped me survive precisely because it was the first and only.

Every day now, Gin bought all the tabloids available in New York City, but the headlines on the front page of *The New York Post* didn't say "NO SURVIVING SURVIVAL KNIFE"; *New York Newsday* didn't run a little brief titled "NARY A DROP OF BLOOD" and not even *The Daily News* speculated about a killer on the loose roaming through Harlem, killing folks with a single, professionally executed thrust of a knife. Even *The Amsterdam News*, the Harlem street daily, didn't yell and scream that when somebody finds a croaked white man in Harlem, the media are on it right off, while not as much as a dog gives a bark over a murdered black man.

As far as Gin knew, over this nixed white man a dog didn't as much as lift up his leg.

Is it possible that nobody found him yet? Or was he not even worth a mention in the paper?

Or . . . or are the cops waiting for the murderer to return to the scene of his crime?

Every day Gin had to fight a sharp, painful desire to go there again and look. To park exactly on the same spot where the guy who's a body today was holding a Beretta .25 (READ MANUAL BEFORE USE) next to her head. To make sure that HE is still lying there, among the vines and roots, that the footprints of her bare left foot didn't stay there, under the highway bridge. As well as the imprint of her right shoe, with its sole made uneven by stepping on the gas and brake pedal, which made it obvious to anyone with half a brain that she was a driver for a living.

Or would she find the whole zone surrounded by yellow

tape that says CRIMESCENECRIMESCENECRIME-SCENECRIMESCENE and rattles in the wind?

She'd heard somewhere that every killer (with the exception of hit men, perhaps) always returns to the place where he had killed, within three weeks. It's just like that.

Gin's wheel, on every possible and impossible occasion, would now automatically turn toward the north – and she, with all her might, held it back, down, away. Whenever a customer dragged her above 96th Street, then Gin, as soon as she dropped him off, would brake next to a curb and, her head resting on the wheel, try to convince herself that the magically claustrophilic space under a bridge on 155th Street ISN'T a magnetic mountain, that her oars are stronger.

And every day, just before dawn, when she was falling asleep by Ouagadougou's side (with Talibe's good-luck charm, which she wasn't hiding anymore, resting on a chest of drawers, far away from either metal or any text), she would listen to the sounds that came here from the north – the wail of police sirens, and music, and lonely shrieks. She was listening to the flapping noise of pigeons' wings and to the quiet humming of New York City palm trees as they were slitting, along the seams, the flat of concrete that otherwise almost completely covered the whole Manhattan Island. Ouagadougou, all exhausted, breathed regularly, cuddling lovingly next to her, and none, NONE of the sounds that penetrated inside their apartment had anything to do with the fact that several days ago on 155th Street Gin had iced somebody.

She made a trip to the Public Library on 42nd Street, and typed WOUNDS, STABBING on a computer keyboard in the Main Reference Room. A bunch of medical books fell off it, and that is how she discovered she must've hit PH's heart just at the moment it began to contract, going from diastole into systole. At that moment the heart is sucking in blood with such a might that it sucks in the blade as well, closing the wound – and that's how it dies, embracing that blade. In rare circumstances it's possible to survive a wound like that if it's operated on right away. At least there have been known cases . . . But usually death is pretty instantaneous.

And as the knife that pierced the heart serves as a bottle cork, it's likely, or at least possible, that from the chest of the stabbed person, and often from his mouth as well, not a single drop of blood escapes.

So the whole thing does make sense, after all, Gin thought. If only I could have a discussion about it with Dr Whitehead!

Chapter 41

Love

The taxi parking lot at La Guardia Airport was a study in yellow. On Friday at 5:45 p.m. everybody was escaping from New York and not so many people were coming back. But hopeful cabbies were still flocking to the parking lot that was full to overflowing. On one end of it, the glistening yellow was coming in little rivulets and on the other it rolled, painfully slowly, toward the main terminal, like lazy drops of quicksilver. Gin landed gracefully with her Pegasus behind the last car in row number eight. She turned the engine off, leaned back on her seat and made herself comfortable with her feet on the dashboard. It was perfect: to know that it doesn't matter one bit whether or not she'll lose two or three hours of the best-business time of the day, stuck at the airport. Ever since she'd become doubly – no, triply – illegal, Gin didn't have the slightest problem making money. Unless an oil check or some repairs were necessary, all she had to do was show up at the garage on 47th Street once a week on Monday afternoon, give Alex a chance to paw her butt and then, in the company of the green parrots, give the money to his wife. Gana always smiled at Gin whenever she handed her a neatly folded weekly mobster roll, but from her eyes lightning bolts were shooting. Alex had set a truly humane price for Gin: 230 bucks a week. And Gana probably judged Alex's relations to a certain driver based on the weekly lease he paid. $230 a week made her certain that there was, after all, something going on between Alex and Gin. In less deviant garages a cabbie would pay for a weekly lease of a car and medallion – for twenty-four seven, as they called it – something between eight and nine hundred. Even though, on the other hand, this Yellow was a funny car.

Alex had arrived at the concept of funny cars only a short while ago, some time after he'd discovered the best way of stealing police cars.

"Jee-zus fuckin' Christ, Alex, you STOLE A POLICE CAR?"

"CARS, *krasavitsa*. Not only just one. What you think? And not stole. I'm stealing! As we talk here, maybe some Blue with cherry lights changing owners. Right now! And new owner is me! What do you think you drive your beautiful butt in, Gin? All my Yellows, like you see, all of them are stolen Blues! And you like driving in them, no?" Alex made an all-encompassing gesture with which he indicated that the whole street, as well as a couple of adjoining blocks, now belonged to him. "But it is not REALLY stealing, my dear Gin. Because who has to pay, so cops have their cars? So they don't walk on foot in a old, patched uniform? Who pay? YOU and ME, taxpayers. So it's NOT stealing, to take what we own. What you say, Gin?"

"I say you haven't become much of an American," Gin sighed. "You sound like real socialism. But here we are in America. Make sure they put you in some jail that's not too far away. I'll come and visit you every even Wednesday of every odd month."

"In a stolen Blue, Gin?" Alex chortled, fluffing up the remains of his hair that had gotten plastered to his skull with sweat and pomade. "Don't be stupid. It is not dangerous. It is very simple. Only thing you need for it is tow truck."

"I still can't believe that—"

"You drive tow truck in front of police station any time night or day, you look for a nice Blue, you hook it up – and off you go. The cops are looking at you from the window, they drink coffee from cup what say I LOVE NEW YORK, and EVERYTHING can be stolen from them, not only police car."

(Gin nervously shifted her weight from one leg to another. All of a sudden, that butt on which she was, so far, sitting so comfortably in stolen police cars, started to ache.)

"You know what stolen cars never go reported, Gin? You don't? Stolen police cars, that's it! Once in couple years cops count their cars, and if seems to them they not have enough, they ask the City for new cars. You know, is weird, do you not think, if cop lets somebody steal his car, and it's also most probable that their colleagues cops stole it from them. And cop can't do this to cop, to report stolen car to cops. Cop can't report cop, or can cop—" Alex kind of stumbled over all those cops. He stopped short, then continued. "I'm trying to explain to you, my dear Gin: If you ever want become criminal, you start with stealing police cars. It is like training for the beginners. You even can do something like that, I swear."

In the tiny warehouse behind the garage there rested peacefully – in among screws, bolts, reflective glass, windows, doors, hoods and bizarrely twisted multiple sculptures of exhaust pipes – at least twenty sirens, removed from the roofs of police cars.

The droplets of yellow paint in the moustache of a guy from Guatemala – who was now living here in place of Ramon, communicating with the other mechanics thanks to a strange mixture of Spanish and some unheard-of Central American mountain Indian dialect – took on a completely new meaning.

From the maze of brand new dreams that invaded Gin's sleep one was sticking out – a mysteriously unsettling one at that. Behind the closed shutter of Alex's garage the illegal alien from Guatemala is standing, armed with a spray gun, and ten thousand butterflies are fluttering around his head. The butterflies are obligingly positioning their translucently blue wings – and the Guatemalan guy is covering them with a thick layer of yellow.

It didn't take long before Gin started wondering how it was possible that the Yellows around Alex's garage got to be so numerous all of a sudden. After all, Alex owned only some seven or eight medallions, and now it was hard to find a parking spot on the whole block in front of his garage. Alex strutted around his Yellows, patting their hoods lovingly and calling them "my Yellow sheeps."

"And I will have more and more, my dear Gin. I will not more lose money with this my garage. I will have more and more Yellows, Alex will be a millionaire, you believe it or not. And all you who were faithful to me, I will make sure you will drive your ass in most beautiful and most CHEAP Yellows that this City have them. What you think, have a car for twenty-four seven for weekly money, I say, two hundred fifty?"

"Well, I'd like that," Gin replied. "Listen, Alex, have you gone mad or what?"

Alex pushed her behind one of his "sheeps," leaned closer to her and said: "Look around yourself, Gin. Find me 5H58. That right. We standing next to it. And now you look on the other sidewalk. Can you believe your eyes, my dear Gin? 5H58, is it right? And now you tell me which of them is right one."

And that's how Gin got to know what a funny car is.

Actually, everything was the City's fault.

Some time around 1935 the City of New York decided to "freeze" the number of taxis in Manhattan. It sold 11,787 official numbers known as medallions. Private cabdrivers could buy one for 100 dollars, taxi garages who bought bulk could get them for as little as 10 apiece. The number of Yellows, the only taxis entitled to pick up people off the street in the Manhattan Business District below 96th Street, hasn't been upped ever since. So the value of medallions has been progressing steadily; right now it was in the vicinity of 200,000 bucks. Just about the same price as a small family house somewhere in Westchester County.

Anyhow, the number that shines on the little dandelion on the roof of a Yellow Cab costs about eight times more than a beautiful new car. Even if that car hasn't been stolen. And so Alex's concept of funny cars made a lot of sense.

"It is very simple, Gin!" he was now boasting. "Only thing you must do is DOUBLE this medallion. You take new car, you put this little thing with number on the roof, you spray-paint the same number on the door, just like you're supposed to do it, then you pay somebody to make two new license plate with same number – it is no problem, Gin, if you know right people – you fake sticker you must stick on windshield, and the card with medallion number on it that you have on dashboard. You be surprised, you know what cost you more than everything? This registration plastic, something like that they call it, and then you bolt it to the hood. This piece of plastic has on it the same number, also. Only when you start making funny cars, Gin, you find out every Yellow has many, many numbers hanging on it, like Christmas tree. They not make it easy, fucking motherfuckers!" Alex sighed, leading her to the other 5H58. "Now you look at this two cars. Tell me which one is right one."

Gin walked around both 5H58s. Everything was in place. The license plates. The windshield stickers. The card hanging on the dashboard. Even that funny-looking piece of plastic with a medallion number branded in it, bolted to the hood of both Yellows.

This little piece of plastic changed every year. One year it was a yellow skyscraper. Another year a red apple. Then it was a green car. Right now it was a purple oval.

"They not make it easy for us, Gin," Alex sighed mournfully, yanking at the piece of plastic. "You know how much this piece of shit cost making? $57, Gin. They make for me in factory in Jersey City. OK, you can tell which one is which one?"

"No, I can't," Gin admitted.

"But Alex, I . . . I . . ." Gin stammered a few moments later. "I'm not saying it wouldn't be nice if . . . if I could have a cheap car like that. But what if anything happens? If they caught me, I'd . . . I suppose I'd go to jail . . ."

"Jee-zus fuckin' Christ, Gin! You worry too much! If they catch you, you're dumb. You just came to new garage. You work for me since it was yesterday. And everything, just not you worry, everything is my fault. But then I will be in Florida. But main thing is, they not catch you. That is I want to not have all these Yellows here all the time. Here they are like on exhibition. I just give all them to you and you will show up in my garage one time in a week, so you can give me the money. If you not in love with driver who drives the twin of your car, nobody will ever find out I'm multiplying all this Yellows, very, very pornography, you know?"

At the beginning it seemed strange to Gin, to be driving around in a stolen police car on which – to make things worse – the doubled-up medallion (or, for all she knew, perhaps tripled-up medallion) was hanging. If they caught me, she thought, I'd go to jail!

(To jail, Gin? You're driving a stolen car and you thinking jail? You already KILLED, remember?)

"OK, Alex," she agreed. "But what if I paid you just two hundred a week, not two fifty?"

Gin, her legs stretched and resting on the dashboard, was lazily watching the hustle and bustle at the airport. In her funny car she was her own mistress. And especially since Kenny – out of old friendship – attached a 20-percent pixie under her hood, her stacks of greenbacks kept growing and growing. Sometimes she felt weird, knowing she was stealing like that. And whenever some passenger took a deep and searching look at her meter, whenever he wondered mildly how is it possible that a trip that usually costs nine or so, today came up to eleven or eleven fifty, Gin felt a bit awkward. Jee-zus, how embarrassing it would be if they caught me!

And then she started laughing. Get real, Gin, come on, pull yourself together! You've already KILLED!

No matter what, her stacks of greenbacks kept growing higher. Her milk crates in the living room (right! even those milk crates were illegal!) got to be a regular burying ground of green President Jacksons, green President Grants, and green President Franklins, even. In a while Gin will drown in all this money like it was the greenish waters of a sea.

That translucent underwater feeling, actually, flushed all over her. Like she was a manta ray that lies on the bottom of the ocean. Whales were swimming above her, lifting off the runway with a roar, and as a mild southern wind was blowing, they passed right above her head while gaining height, they turned their silver bellies toward her as if begging to be petted. Gin was soundlessly floating in some fluid – a viscous oil of sorts – that made every motion, thoughts included, really difficult. Reality for her was all out of focus.

If she got truly concentrated on something – on talking to a customer, on the route she had to take, on making change, on the streets rushing by and on the colors of traffic lights – everything was more or less all right. But every thought was kind of tattered on the edges, her thoughts now had to squeeze through a narrow tunnel of sorts, and the rough walls of that tunnel were skinning her alive, baring her meat.

She was trying to emerge from her private ocean, to rise above herself along with all these planes, and project in front of her eyes the over-filled Yellow parking lot, either as an abstract painting, or as a children's game with yellow pegs. She tried her best to stash her thoughts someplace else – any place, in fact, as long as they didn't chafe her soul.

Because every look on the sky, joyfully blue and sporting tiny white clouds, revealed the missing slice of it in the shape of a certain blade.

Then someone knocked on her window.

"Yo," a high voice with an improbably bulletproof South Bronx accent recited, "cain't ya 'forda spaire sump'n, mees, foe a pooh ole cwack-head mah-fah?"

And on the seat next to her Geoffrey Bitten Off Nose was

making himself comfortable, hospitably putting a cup of hot coffee on the dashboard, right next to the soles of her sneakers.

"You really should lock the front doors, Gin," he said didactically. "You never know who—"

"I absolutely agree with you, I certainly should have," Gin repented. "But now, as it seems, it's too late!"

Geoffrey guffawed, threw his head back, and banged the metal studs on his helmet on the partition with a loud thud.

"You look like an astronaut!"

Geoffrey was dressed in leather and metal studs from head to foot: metal studs on his leather helmet, metal studs on his leather jacket, boxing bracelets with metal studs on his wrists, and on his neck three or four metal chains in place of the usual one or two. Even his boots were metal-tipped. As the days went by, Geoffrey was getting better and better protected for his entry into the atmosphere of the deadly planet called the Streets of New York City.

"Now I could tell you by your 3Y50, Gin." Geoffrey presently found an opening in his space suit and touched his coffee cup to his chapped lips. "Not just by your flying hair the color of a rabid foxtail. But I'd swear 3Y50 used to be a real heap of junk, as far as I remember. Did that mobster asshole you work for finally get a bunch of better wrecks?"

"Yeah," said Gin who hadn't completely emerged from her private ocean depths, "I guess he did."

Geoffrey lighted up. "Are you fucking him?" he asked, reaching for the doorhandle, so he could run fast, should Gin's reaction be of the physical kind. But Gin merely lifted her gaze up, blew into her coffee cup and hid her face behind a waft of vapor.

"So this 3Y50 is now just yours, Gin? Or who else is driving it? 'Cause I'd swear that I met with a 3Y50 less than an hour ago, as it was driving toward Manhattan across the Triborough. It was driving all empty, and out of its window one of Alex's Igors was stickin', you know what I mean: that classical bashful Russian mobster type – nose reaching down to his shins, a swollen gut, his head all bald, you know, simply your basic cabdriver of the transport-export-import-pimport kind. If you know what I'm saying, Gin."

"Hmm."

"So I yell at him across three lanes: Why are you taking Triborough when you're empty, it costs three bucks. And he says he just started his shift and he has no intention to spend the whole evening on that godforsaken Queensborough Bridge. And now YOU ARE HERE. Isn't it strange? – How long d'you think we'll be stuck here for?" Geoffrey continued, unruffled, when no answer came. "There's great business in the City now, you know?"

Gin mumbled something not fit to repeat and shrugged. Another couple dozen Yellows for whom there was no place left in the parking lot were swarming around the lot entrance like yellow jackets, blocking the road and blowing horns like Judgement Day came. The drivers must have hoped that the deafening cacophony would attract the silver superbirds, and with them a whole lot of business.

They were completely stuck in the parking lot, hopelessly blocked by hundreds of cabs of all the hues yellow color can possibly have. The only way of escaping would be to lift straight off the ground. Gin tried to do exactly that in her thoughts, but Geoffrey's voice reached her immediately.

"You're truly gregarious today, Gin! Who did what to you? Or maybe they did NOTHING? It won't go up, no matter what?"

Gin repeated her gesture with her eyes embedded in her car's roof and the vapor rising from the coffee cup.

Geoffrey impudently patted her thigh and commented that, if worse comes to worse, he'd sacrifice himself as long as it would improve Gin's spirits. His wife isn't the model of fidelity herself, how could she be when he's roaming around night after night, but then the Amazons on this continent would be on him like white on rice – "if I dared to harass you or whatever, don't you agree? But it seems to me, Gin, that YOUR brain hasn't gone all soft as yet, how long have you been here? Two, three years? European girls, if they're any good, often take five or even six years to go completely stupid. But they all go stupid, you can mark my words. From the soil over here some vapor or whatever is wafting, and it makes a cow out of every woman. Every single one. Trouble is, American girls tend to be cows in first grade already but women who come here from Europe, or Asia, they have some five or six years left before going stupid. Then, of course, it comes with a vengeance. Just look at Ch—I mean, Miss Chang—"

"Well, if women are so awful, then there are young boys left for you," Gin said lazily. "All nice and sexy. An earring in their ear—"

"Man! Don't ever do that to me again!" Geoffrey screamed with theatrical horror. "Are you sitting on both your brain cells or what? Me a faggot! How could you—"

And he slammed the car door behind him.

It occurred to Gin that if he really was so touchy, then any time she wants she can—

"And you know they're after me all the time, Gin?" Her thought was interrupted by Geoffrey, who, less than three minutes later, was sitting next to her again, in a no less homey position. He was finishing a plastic sandwich, filled with a mass called hamandcheese. The grub made him so happy he didn't even mind that his tongue got hopelessly glued to his palate.

"Once I'm driving one," he muttered with a lot of effort, trying to unstick his jaws, "he was going to Greenwich Village, and he didn't look like a local, so I took a bit of a detour, right, and when I tell him on Perry and Bleecker, That's 8.50, he kind of wiggles his butt and says, Ushually it'sh jusht four. And why do I go from Tensh Avenue to Wasshington Shtreet via Broadway? So I get scared and I start rattling something about a lot of traffic and I'm as new as this year's snow and shit, I've only been behind the wheel for less than a week, this kind of bullshit, but he focuses on my hack license number and he says, he's absolutely right: You've been working in thish field for almosht sheven yearsh. DO YOU WANNA FUCK ME? – OK, Gin, I'll tell you right away: I got covered in cold sweat. But that's the trouble with English, you see, it's such a language that even if you were born here five times over, you still don't know what people are telling you. I was convinced he was complaining, right, 'cause I tried to rip him off, and I can already see a summons to the Taxi and Limousine Commission, a customer's complaint, a four-hundred dollar fine and never-ending bullshit, but then he touches his finger on the back of my neck and he repeats in this voice, sweet like honey: Do you wanna fuck me? We're gonna go have a drink somewhere, then we can go to my place, and I'll be undressing you, bit by bit, from that knight's armor of yours . . ."

Geoffrey rattled his spiky bracelets with the expression of an incensed porcupine. "Me, Gin, I was beside myself with rage. Do I look like a faggot to you, you fuckin' idiot? I scream at him and I show him my boxing ring – See, if I hit your muzzle with this, asshole, then you'll have only your butt left to seduce your lovers with, but then again your butt will be as red as a baboon's before I'm through with you—and—and—GET OUT!" Geoffrey screamed suddenly, making Gin jump up. "G-GET OUT of my car, I yell at him, you-you-you—"

Geoffrey got so engrossed in his story that he spat the remains of his sandwich on the windshield, which they were now decorating, "—and I'm getting ready to pull him out by his hind leg so I can throw him on the sewer, where he belongs, but he's already climbing out at a record pace, he's throwing a fifty on me and as he's running for his life, he's yelling on the whole Perry Street: I'll fantashishe about your manlinesh and I'll mashturbate! – Just imagine, Gin: I'll fantasize about you and I'll masturbate? Wouldn't you shit your pants?"

Gin, about whom a whole bunch of customers had already fantasized and masturbated right on the back seat (and some of them were so well-practiced at it that they could hold conversations on various social topics during the process, their faces – with just the slightest touch of pink – pressed into the partition, all the while so professional that only the final "Ooof!" gave them away), didn't say anything. Ever since – that – happened, she wasn't exactly talkative. The extrapolation of each story was hanging dangerously close to that hole in the shape of a knife that was killing the sky over Gin's head.

("Geoffrey, you haven't killed!" she felt like saying right now. "And that's exactly why you keep bitching about it all the time . . . am I right? And remember Sengane? You think it was true, what he said about how he killed that guy . . .? I don't think so. I sort of can tell these things now. Because, you see, this thing happened to me . . . D'you think that every taxidriver should kill somebody, Geoffrey? D'you think it's a . . . rites of passage of sorts?")

But she must keep this question to herself. Lock it inside her with seven keys. Even if it hurt her A LOT.

That's because she . . . has gone through the rites of passage. Because she – has killed.

She felt closer to her victim now, that guy who wanted to do her in, than to anyone else on Earth. Perhaps that was because he also had killed. Gin felt now that she could see that mark of Cain in people. Whenever possible, she curled up in Kenny's arms, because Kenny had killed, too. With the very same instrument, in fact. And even though she couldn't tell Kenny anything, either, she had a feeling that . . . that perhaps he'd understood that much. Gin now couldn't function alongside people who hadn't killed. If there was a Murderers Club in New York, she'd become its member today.

For a long time she hadn't desired so painfully to find a true love. Not the open circles of hourly hotels with their surprisingly clean bedding out of which they kick you in two hours, unless you pay some more. Not the indentured Ouagadougou who she learned to lead by her own unremoved clitoris, the same way a strong bull can be led by a metal ring in his nose. She doesn't even want . . . understanding. Sympathy, friendship. No. She needs LOVE. Affection that will take this hex off her. Passion that will coil up in her belly like a colorful poisonous snake.

Something similar to what – for a single flickering moment – Clyde had meant for her.

*

That day her hunt for a customer only became successful around eight in the evening. And the game in question was a balding white guy a bit over forty, decked out in a suit of a brand so grand that not even the thirteen-hour journey from Anchorage, Alaska, managed to ruin the perfect creases of his pants. Over his shoulder a leather pouch was hanging and behind his heels a leather trunk on wheels was running like a well-trained dog.

"OK, where is it?" Gin sneered at him.

"Manhattan, Hotel Pierre," the customer replied mildly after having put his luggage in the trunk himself, resting it right next to a nondescript spare. "But, would you mind taking a little detour over Brooklyn?"

"Over Brooklyn? And you're going to 60th Street? Did you go mad?" Gin asked him over her shoulder, getting her wheels off the asphalt with a swooshing sound and turning the meter on. With a 20-percent pixie a trip like that should come up to . . . well, at least up to sixty.

"Yes, over Brooklyn, as long as you don't mind too much. I just would like to look at something." He had a cultured accent of an intellectual and a guilty look on his face.

Gin agreed grudgingly. "But if you're planning to go buy drugs in some back alley of Brooklyn, I'd—"

"Oh, no, it wouldn't ever occur to me!" The guy was taken aback. "I am just completely beside myself at being in this City again after several years. In fact, I just would like to get—"

"Intoxicated by the skyline of Manhattan?" Gin asked sarcastically.

"That's right, how did you guess?" The guy seemed pleased like a seven-year-old who was just offered an ice-cream cone. "I love the skyline of this island. Even though," he added with a mysterious air, "even though I didn't manage to change it."

The traffic on Grand Central Parkway, going toward the City, was pretty thick. Gin was forcefully making her way – over dead bodies and car wrecks – into the middle lane which seemed to be going the fastest. "If Grand Central looks like this," she grumbled, "then the Brooklyn-Queens Expressway will be one huge parking lot. Goddamn!"

And in the spirit of well-adjusted veteran taxidrivers she spat out of the window. The gob landed on the windshield of a red Pontiac to the left of them. "See how dense the traffic is?" she said demonstratively, while behind the tinted side window of the Pontiac a closed fist appeared. The driver was screaming something that they couldn't hear and waving his raised middle finger. Gin reached to the seat next to her and stuck a sign I LOVE YOU, TOO out of the window. The driver of the Pontiac was soundlessly fuming.

"That's really nice," Gin's passenger commented, "to come to New York for a little visit after all these years and right on one's trip from the airport to run into a taxidriver who dares to be a lady."

"See what this job is doing to me?" Gin said, a little embarrassed. "As recently as a year ago it was pretty hard for me to get as much as 'fuckin' shit' across my lips."

"No, no, I like that. You're as fine a woman as they come. That hair color, forgive me for asking, is it your own? It reminds me of aurora borealis on certain rare windy autumn nights."

"It should've dawned on me right away!" Gin turned to him. "You live in Alaska. A woman and a half per five square miles, something like that?"

"If only that many!" the neat-looking intellectual sighed. "And they're usually married and faithful on top of things. I'm a bachelor."

"Well, that explains a lot."

And she frowned at the slice of her face that fitted into the rear-view mirror. She was feeling incredibly ugly today. She didn't have as much as a milligram of makeup on, she felt colorless and tired like a ten-year-old pair of underwear, her eyes were puffy, her eyebrows bushy and – oh yes! from her chin a long, thick witch's hair was growing. She made an attempt to pluck it out, but it slipped through her fingers – and at that moment she caught her passenger's servile look in the rear-view mirror. He'd just opened his briefcase and he was handing Gin a pair of tweezers.

Gin shuddered and got a little sweaty. The way he was stretching his arm toward her through the partition reminded her of another night when – it happened to her quite often now, in fact. Whenever customers were paying. Whenever they were showing her which way to go. Whenever they leaned on the partition in a familiar manner, sharing their secrets with her.

"Thanks!" she screamed, yanking the tweezers out of his hand. "No need to bother."

"See how I'm taking care of additional enhancement of the beauty of female cabdrivers in New York?" the passenger was cajoling her. And he added: "I'm Stan."

"Stanley??"

"Well, yes, Stanley. But everybody calls me Stan."

On Gin's sky – yes, exactly at that spot where the traffic jam of colorful little cars ended, at the spot where the asphalt touched the sky – a shiny survival knife appeared.

"Stanley, Jee-zus Christ!"

"What's wrong with that?"

"No, nothing, I just—"

Within a split second a whole array of disgusting possibilities rushed through her brain, including the reincarnation of 27 into this businessman, or the unlikely chance that the detectives put this guy into her car at La Guardia in order to try some evil psychological trick on Gin.

She pulled herself together.

"Me . . . I . . . I used to know a Stanley . . ."

"OK, I should have guessed it would be about love," Stan visibly calmed down. "What did that no good guy do to you?"

Gin spat out of her window again, this time without success. She took a quick glance to the right and then made a leap, across three lanes of heavy traffic, to the ramp that leads you, through a concrete tunnel, toward the Brooklyn-Queens Expressway. She held onto the wheel with her left hand, devoting her whole concentration to plucking out that hair from her chin with her right. "Thanks," she said when the hair fluttered down on her knees. Then she threw the tweezers back at Stanley.

Immediately afterwards, she made an attempt to kiss the concrete wall of that twisted tunnel with her right front fender. "I told you the BQE would be a parking lot. See? Here we go!"

Gin had just tried to create, at least morally, since physically it was downright impossible, another traffic lane, right on the side. That's how she managed to make it a couple dozen yards forward and then she made a quick leap right in front of an Oldsmobile. It was a miracle she didn't get stuck there, on a wedge of asphalt that narrowed down like a slice of a cake, squeezed by the concrete of the wall from one side and the metal of rival cars from the other.

The guy on her back seat clicked his tongue approvingly. "You're a great driver. And – see how beautiful you look? You drive, if you excuse me, rather daringly, and nobody blows their horn at you."

"Hm. Maybe it's because there's a bumper sticker on my car that says HONK IF YOU HAVE A SMALL DICK."

Gin's customer gave a grateful laugh.

Yeah, that's right, exactly! Gin thought. You have to spit out of the window, frown all the time, be a little nasty and drive like a fuckin' asshole in a stolen police car with a fake medallion and a fast meter. Then they all will start loving you.

If you're driving southbound on the Brooklyn-Queens Expressway, you'll encounter a kind of curve. The second you pass it, the skyline of Manhattan jumps suddenly out, hitting you right in between your eyes. There are not many places in New York where this happens so suddenly. Manhattan hatches out from behind the grayish asphalt and concrete (which is what limits a driver's horizon in the northern part of the BQE) and it just hangs there like it was a phosphorescent postcard, backlit by the sunset.

Gin's passenger gave a deep sigh. "Isn't it beautiful? For more than seven years I saw this skyline only in my dreams."

"I've been seeing it in my nightmares for three years," Gin grumbled. Even she, however, was taken by it. Sometimes it seemed to her that this skyline was the only thing that kept her – and quite a few others – in New York for years. The skyline of Manhattan. From the east. From the west. From the south. From Triborough Bridge and from the Brooklyn Bridge. From that part of the Long Island Expressway that carries you to the sky for a second, before it dumps you headfirst into the Queens-Midtown Tunnel. Gin was convinced that many people spend years and years in New York just for the sole purpose of solving the puzzle of how it's possible that this rough City possesses such an unbelievably fragile-looking skyline.

Gin's customer sighed with bliss. "I'm just sorry that – I mean, I should explain to you why we're taking this way . . ."

"Yeah, I'd be really interested."

"I . . . I am an architect," Stan blurted out. "And I have . . . Have you ever been to Alaska?"

"Not even in my worst dreams."

"OK, in Alaska . . . a three-story building is a skyscraper there."

"Hm . . . I didn't know that an igloo can be so tall."

Stan gave a sad half-smile. "In Alaska a three-story house is truly tall and—and I had wanted, just once in my life, to build a REAL skyscraper, you see. At least fifty, eighty floors. I wanted to . . . to leave a mark, you see."

"With those eighty inches . . . I mean floors . . ." Gin, who had always felt somewhat suspicious of overtly tall buildings, commented.

But not even that made Stan mad. "Sure, I've heard about all this sexual symbolism, associated with skyscrapers. But . . . it's not always so that us architects compete whose is the biggest . . . Even though . . . do you know that new building on West 56th Street?"

"Oh, the Trump Dick Building, you mean?"

“Yeah, it does belong to Trump. And there’s a lovely little cupola on top, one can’t help thinking—”

“—that it can’t be an accident. But you wanted to leave a mark,” she reminded him.

“And I entered a competition. For a certain building on Third Avenue. Now, you must understand: a competition like that, it’s not just exactly fun. Just imagine: Administrative problems. Financial problems. Endless trips to this City. Endless discussions with myself as well as with my colleagues. Endless wanderings around those few blocks on which your building is supposed to be standing, so you can get the hang of the place, so your proposal will fit perfectly with its atmosphere, so you can imagine in detail how the neighboring buildings will be reflected in the glass on the walls of your skyscraper; you gotta know exactly what the final effect is going to be. Then endless sketching. Tons and tons of paper. Paper models. Gypsum models. Computer images of what this City with your skyscraper incorporated into it will look like from the west, from the east, from a helicopter . . . I mean, once you waste so many thoughts and so much time and so much money and . . . and love on a single project . . . you simply can’t not fall in love with it. It’s like writing a novel. Like composing a symphony. Like designing a whole MOUNTAIN! And then, after you’ve designed the most gorgeous skyscraper you’ve ever seen in your life, I mean you’ve NEVER seen in your life because it’s one of a kind and absolutely unique! Colorful! Thick at the base but made optically slender with black stripes. Dressed up as if it was shopping at Prada! With a beautiful skyline! Well – once you’ve finished a project like that—” Stan spread his arms wide, waving them in the air like he was getting ready to fly up to the sky and complain to God about so much injustice, “—when you finish a project like that, someone up and says it seems more PRACTICAL to him to build an awful, ugly, indescribably un-unique building your competitor had designed – IT’S RIGHT THERE!” Stan howled and pointed, behind Gin’s back, to a cluster of buildings on the horizon somewhere around 40th or 50th Street. “This is the first time in my life I'm seeing that terrible thing with my own eyes! It took me seven years to get ready and come here to look at it. And now I recognize it at a glance. Because it's standing there like a . . . like a . . ." Then he added bashfully: "LIKE A DICK!"

"They all do. Haven't we talked about it?"

"You see, you just can't imagine what it means, losing such a POWERFUL hope! Once you design a skyscraper it becomes so . . . so unbearably real for you – you see it in your dreams, on the sketches, on computer screens, on models – and then they decide not to build it. It feels like it died!"

"OK, OK, quit blubbering!" Gin advised him gently.

At that moment they were crossing the Kosciusko Bridge whose curvy arch ran over the canal known as Newton Creek that divided Brooklyn from Queens. The bridge took them up to the sky, making Gin feel, just as it had done so many times before, like she was walking on stilts. The surface of the bridge consists of some kind of metal mesh that rattles under your wheels. You could swear that the landscape under you shines through the holes in the metal mesh; you feel like you're suspended in the air on a ski-lift, especially since you first have to go up on a hill and then you go down from it on the other side, sliding on that funny surface made of metal bars and studs. The bridge curves a bit to make things worse, and you're divided from the roofs of houses and factories and warehouses under you by nothing more than a dinky little railing made of rusty corrugated iron.

Gin always got a little sweaty whenever she was driving across the Kosciusko Bridge.

"You see, Gin, I've discovered a way of bringing them down!" Stan exclaimed in a great big voice, made just a little slurred by alcohol. He pulled his glasses up on top of his bald spot and looked into her eyes. His irises were light green with a yellowish-brown rim.

"Bringing down what?"

"Skyscrapers! I mean to say – that skyscraper that's standing there in place of my own!"

They were sitting in the over-lit Junior's Bar on the corner of Flatbush and Fulton Street. Gin was on her third screwdriver, Stan on his fourth Manhattan. The Yellow was illegally parked right in front and Gin peeked out of the window every now and then, making sure no cop with a ticket book was approaching it. Stan had promised to pay for the trip, and for the time she would lose, and, of course, for all these drinks. He didn't want to spend his first evening in this City all alone.

"I'll tell you how to bring down skyscrapers, Gin!" He took a deep breath and gulped nervously. "You can bring a skyscraper down with vibrations. All you have to do is swing it with force and—No, don't worry. Wind can't do that. Today skyscrapers are built so sturdily they can survive an earthquake, even. At least, at least that's what the public wants to hear. But do you know what skyscrapers definitely can't take?" Stan took a deep breath again. "They can't take LOVE! The vibrations that love can cause!"

Stan brought his cocktail glass to his lips and gulped. He gave a little cultured hiccup, said, "Excuse me," and touched a tiny handkerchief to his lips. "You can bring skyscrapers down using the vibrations of love. The only thing you have to do – now listen to me – is to move the weight of PEOPLE inside it from one side to the other. Just imagine that in the building next to it two people move a . . . what do I know . . . a desk right next to the windows so they are in plain view and then they . . . forgive me for talking about it like that – get undressed slowly, as if they had no idea how many people are watching them and then they—"

"Fuck?"

"Make love on that desk. So all the people in the neighboring skyscraper run over to one side, and mind you, we're not talking dozens or hundreds but THOUSANDS of people! And just imagine the weight of all those business folks and secretaries and receptionists and executives and big shots and . . .

what do I know who else works there. What happens? The building is going to tilt."

Over his glass of brownish liquor Stan was eyeing Gin with a victorious glare. His eyes, the same color as the drink called Manhattan, widened with a lion's hunting passion. He said:

"And if you make sure that at the other side of that building another couple will . . . forgive me . . . have sex, too, but at a different time interval, then . . . then THOUSANDS of people will start running from one side of the skyscraper to the other, at a time interval that you can pre-program for them. If you orchestrate all that well they'll start acting like puppets on strings. What will inevitably happen? The skyscraper will start swinging. And it will swing more and more, only nobody will notice. And then, all of a sudden, there will be this terrible din and crash and the skyscraper you hate will topple down and— Will you have another drink?"

"Sure, why not?" Gin said.

She was sitting with a glass of yellowish ice in her hand, sucking the little remnants of alcohol-flavored water with her straw. Stan's tale reminded her of – well, she wasn't sure what exactly. Perhaps the legends of Greek heroes who'd climbed up Mount Olympus and died, hit by Zeus's lightning. Perhaps the legend of the Tower of Babel that was supposed to reach all the way to the sky. The skyline of Manhattan, even though it was built by human hand and human technology, acquired, after a time, the same never-changing forbearance of mountain ridges, huge canyons and endless deserts . . . Gin would swear that very specific kinds of gods got born on the tops of New York skyscrapers, and mortals should not disturb them. Stan's theories sounded very much like heresy to her.

Not even now, after spending years in the City, could Gin believe all the changes the Manhattan skyline went through during the two hours they'd spent at the bar. New York now was nothing like the user-friendly City that had pierced the peach-colored horizon not so long ago.

New York was a dark crenelated battlement, covered by a

grayish-black blanket of fog. Wind tore off tattered shards of the fog from the sky, and they were descending on the City with an almost theatrical dignity . . . They circled the World Trade Center, hiding its tips from view. The City's skyline vibrated with the will-of-the-wisps twilight of colorful neons . . . Lights twinkled as little hazy clouds were periodically covering and uncovering them again. Shards of fog and rain were now taking New York far away from Gin and Stan but once in a while offered a little detail of the City to them seen through fast-changing peepholes. Gin was driving fast.

From the fleecy blanket over their heads, microscopic droplets of fog were raining down, covering the road with a thin, sleek slick that made it look as if wrapped in glistening plastic.

That's the worst driving weather you can hope for, Gin thought. This thin coat of water acts like an oil slick, it won't allow the tires to get connected to the road . . . it lengthens the skid track tremendously . . . Actually, it's probably even a bit more dangerous than a real, honest downpour that floods the road completely, turning the streets into stormy lakes and your car into a hapless sailboat.

The traffic on the Brooklyn-Queens Expressway wasn't heavy anymore, and the naked highway, covered just by that sleek water slick, was sucking Gin into it. Ahead. Faster and faster. Gin was a little tipsy but it didn't matter one bit. The familiar surface of the road took care of everything. Gin herself probably didn't even need to be here. Her Yellow's wheel gripped the road and the road led her forward. It cut the corners of curves for her. It avoided potholes. It was flooring the gas pedal.

Gin gawked at the skyline of Manhattan, and at Stan, who, a touchingly childish expression on his face, was dozing off on the front seat. Or maybe he just pretended he was asleep. Gin was telling him about the tribes of deities who make their residence at the tips of skyscrapers and who had better not be disturbed with audacious theories about how to bring down mountains using love. And about the blades of knives – that's what she was telling him, too, at least some knives, those that, when you unsheathe them, cut shards in the shape of themselves out of the sky. She told him a lot of things. Then they reached the Kosciusko Bridge.

The elegant arc of the bridge brought them, without Gin having anything to do with it, a bit closer to the skies. That funny bridge surface rattled under her wheels. Those metal bars and studs through the holes in which – at least that's how it seemed to Gin – the landscape under them could be glimpsed. It seemed to her that the wheels of her taxi were tasting the whole column of air under them, that they were getting intoxicated by its taste just like Gin had gotten intoxicated with six screwdrivers; that the landscape underneath them was stretching esoteric tentacles toward them . . . that if they happened to fall off that bridge, boring through that thin railing, then her Yellow would turn into a Pegasus, in an instant it would sprout bright yellow canary wings – and it would fly up to say hello to the aerial gods of Manhattan.

Jee-zus Christ! By sheer accident, Gin's eyesight dropped down to the speedometer. A blue 80 was shining on it, at the moment flicking to 82.

They had made their way over the highest point of the bridge. (84 . . . 85 . . .) The bridge was angled down like a slalom slope . . . and the left-hand curve below was coming at them at 85 . . . no . . . 87 miles per hour. Gin held her breath. The bubble of terror sucked her in, she couldn't make a motion – but, somehow, she took her sole off the gas pedal and slammed it on the brake.

Instantly, they lost the ground under their wheels. On a road consisting of metal grills that was covered by a slick of condensed water vapor, her car got into a perfect skid, and it was presently zigzagging, at 68 miles per hour, across all four highway lanes.

"JEE-ZUS FUCKING CHRIST GODDAMN IT!" Gin screamed.

From the seat next to her the quiet, serene, somehow huge

voice of the failed architect from Alaska could be heard: "Don't curse! Pray!" he told her. "We'll meet with Him in no time."

Gin leaned on her horn, hoping that the other cars will manage to get out of her way; that she won't kill anybody else anymore; that she won't take anyone else with her into that realm of darkness the other Stanley had talked about – and which was already shining through the holes that the rust and time had made in the dinky corrugated-iron railing.

They were rushing straight for that railing right now. At an incredible speed but for an endless amount of time. Time was already losing direction for Gin.

"You killed me," Stan informed her quietly.

"Sorry but you're not the first one," Gin assured him.

. . . How . . . How will that flight be? Where are they gonna land? Will her cab blow up? Will the street kids of Queens, who should have long ago been in bed at this hour, anyway, watch this spectacle, their eyes widened with disbelief? Will that flight of theirs be worth a mention in one of the tabloids? And . . . how do they bury female cabdrivers in New York, after all? Do they dig a round grave for them with white letters

LANE
FIRE

on top and will they let a beautiful, variegated Tree grow out of them in the middle lane of Third Avenue?

Gin passionately hugged her wheel, waiting for the terrible crash that would start their flight. Her thoughts got all thickened, the film reel of her experiences was doing the fast-forward in front of her, getting projected on the silver screen behind her retina. The whole life, the whole New York was replaying itself in Gin now – every street corner, every day, two thousand traffic lights. All the apartments she's ever lived in in New York. All her loves. All the . . . art. And the trails of reversed arrows that pigeons' toes had left in concrete sidewalks navigated her thoughts all the way to hope.

She was waiting for that crash.

Chapter 42

There are More New Yorks Than Just This One

— But no. There was no crash. The taxicab quiveringly stopped all by itself, it was now standing by the side of the bridge, purring contentedly. It had only touched the railing with its right side, leaving a few molecules of yellow paint on it.

On the same night, just before dawn, when the City was reflected in puddles, the traffic lights stretching long, flickering stems of joyfully meadowlike hues toward Gin's taxi – on that same night just before dawn, on chance number 526, the Tree was standing. Gin's heart stopped. The Tree's hair (that was winter branches and raven's wings at the same time) sucked into it all the lights of the street so that the Tree himself was a black gap, outlined by the lights and the glistening. He was standing timidly on the curb, holding a guitar under his left arm and stretching his right one toward the road like half a cross.

Gin was stuck at the lights on 7th Avenue; the Tree was behind the crossing. And from 55th Street, from the cross direction, a competitor with a lit-up dandelion on his roof emerged, rushing right for the Tree. The driver turned on his signal light, began to slow down – but Gin leaned on her horn and that shriek made way for her while she jumped the red light, scaring the competing Yellow off. He was already angrily disappearing southward.

And so the door of Gin's cab opened and that Tree was climbing in. "Thanks," he told her in a surprised voice. "I can tell you that beautiful lady cabbies in New York City usually don't exactly fight over guys like me."

No, it wasn't Clyde. But he ABSOLUTELY looked like him. He leaned toward the hole in the partition and in Gin's rear-view mirror whole fireworks of jet-black branches erupted. A few of them fell down to the seat next to her – and they smelled there. Like a forest. No . . . like a sea. Like a forestsea.

Gin turned toward him and looked into his eyes: "Listen, can I ask you a question? Did you ever kill anybody?"

"Jee-zus Christ, don't you feel it? You really don't feel it?" The Tree was getting mad all over 116th Street, as he was loading the seventh holey plastic milk crate into the trunk of a yellow Chevrolet. "You don't FEEL that whole continent that's stretching in front of you, you don't FEEL how it's pulling you into itself? You don't? I just don't get it, I don't get it how you could stay in New York SO LONG! New York, that's – excuse me – a vertical hell; how could you not see the Great Plains; how could you not see the DESERT in the southwest; how could you not see the ROCKY MOUNTAINS! How could you never watch the waves of the Pacific get covered with silver and gold and the seals are sticking their noses through it! How is it POSSIBLE that you're stuck on this continent for THREE YEARS – and you've never ever left this concrete jungle for a single day?"

It somehow happened that they decided to get frozen together in that bliss that had descended upon them unexpectedly . . . Yes, this was LOVE, no doubt about that. They decided to stay together in that bliss – maybe for a few moments, maybe for thirty years. They didn't know. All they knew was that their private paradise must be somewhere west of here.

It wasn't exactly a tearful parting. Gin picked up her seven boxes, then she threw the whole bunch of apartment keys, wrapped up in a "Dear Ouag" letter, in the mailbox, and then she transported her seven illegal crates across the sidewalk (all polka-dotted thanks to the colorful chewing gum wads) into her Yellow that – let's face it – wasn't exactly legal itself.

Less than an hour later they were swallowed by the Holland Tunnel on their way to Jersey.

The tunnel was long, rimmed with yellow halogen lights. She knew it well from those nights when she drove, at the very end of her shift, whores like Sunshine with an ugly scar on her face into little hotels in Jersey. Only this time the tunnel was exceptional. It became a concrete birth canal through which Gin was coming into the world. The world that was the whole American continent.

And when they emerged from the tunnel, then the gray highway I5/I9 was carrying them farther and farther west like a friendly conveyor belt – and in Gin's rear-view mirror the skyscrapers started collapsing soundlessly. They crumpled down, turning into rubbish: a surplus of love had made them rock.

The Tree put his head into her lap. She leaned over, burying her face, for a second, in the smell and the structure of his branches. Silver-and-gold happiness washed over her like the Pacific Ocean she'd never seen.

Suddenly she started crying: "I . . ." she sobbed, "I've never been anywhere else but here. NEVER! ANYWHERE!" she yelled. "I . . . I know that it might be better not to show my face around New York very much, I've explained that to you. But now I don't know if I'll know how to live without New York."

The Tree looked into her eyes. In his pupils, the City was reflected, too. A tiny little one, its horizon all curved. Only, in his eyes the skyline of Manhattan was whole.

"I'll be your New York!" he promised to her. "You know

New York, and I know it. We'll carry it with us everywhere. Now picture the corner of 79th and 3rd Avenue. As precisely as you can."

Gin wavered in her lane, trying to picture that corner behind her closed lids.

"You see it?"

"Yeah, I see it!"

"OK, so you see!" the Tree said. "And then – d'you really think that there's only one New York? Don't you believe that! There's Paris in Texas, Manhattan in Kansas, Moscow in Idaho, Rome and Athens in Georgia, Venice in California, Berlin in Wisconsin . . . If we drive far enough, we're bound to find a New York!"

A really nice private car with the blue New Jersey license plates was entering Pennsylvania. Its color was inconspicuously beige but it was sprayed over rather sloppily in places. A sharp observer may have noticed that there were holes in the roof, in those places where that little dandelion blossom with a medallion number had originally been, or that the front seat still carried the imprint of a plastic partition. When will Alex post up the xerox copy of the hack license of a certain female cabbie named JINDRISKA FOFANA, scribbling underneath it with a blue marker: STOLE A CAR . . . ?

But that thought didn't worry her for very long. The deep green of the American continent banged her between the eyes with its fists. It was as if in front of her, in the westward direction, ten million traffic lights started shining, inviting her to GO. All around them trees were growing. But that one Tree, the one she loved, was sitting next to her, playing his guitar, touching her once in a while. He was making sure she was real.

Every touch shot through them like neon lightning.

Fireflies were passing by them, carrying their little lanterns like they were baskets of strawberries or, maybe, the way some girls carry their breasts: like something truly valuable that also weighs you down. Some of them died on the windshield.

They built a tent in the woods. The Tree was hugging her with all his branches, discovering her with his palms, he was looking for openings, for skin folds through which he can look inside her. He circled her navel with his index finger as if he wanted to get tied to the umbilical cord of her past. He was touching that old appendectomy scar which the doctors back in Czechoslovakia had lousily sewn up with seven stitches. Those seven stitches were seven bridges he wanted to cross on foot to get closer to her.

"I'd like to have a baby with you!"

Gin shuddered. That sentence reminded her of both her husbands. Even though . . . today . . . it was somewhat different. "Only," she told the Tree, "only if he has exactly the same dreads like you as he's emerging out of my belly."

And so for the whole rest of the night the Tree was weaving little baby dreads on his children's heads in her belly.

And when they woke up, the whole inside of the tent was washed over with golden light. The late-morning sun was penetrating its orange canvas, tickling their faces. Gin buried her head into the color on the Tree's shoulder to make her night last. And in the structure of his skin, in those little dots, spots and splotches she could see a whole long novel that she'll be able to try to make sense of for years. Sentence by sentence.

She allowed herself to be surrounded by the Tree, she pushed closer to him. The touches sparkled. It wasn't important at all – where they're gonna go together, after all. Gin will follow the Tree. Because the Tree will attract her with the unbeatable power of gravity that very few things tend to have over us; usually only big cities.